Murder and Suspicion on a Third World Island Called Caribe

Caribe is a gripping thriller of deception and violence that is at once both political and intensely personal. It takes us from the mean streets of New York to the even more savage back alleys of rebel hideouts in Mexico City and the brutalizing torture rooms of a Caribbean prison. With unforgettable characters and a plot that twists and turns with breathtaking surprises, *Caribe* will entertain and astonish even the most jaded readers of fast-paced suspense.

"The narrative has the sheen of quicksilver, and it manages to blend brutal scenes of New York City drug wars, hints of the supernatural reminiscent of a South American fable, and political intrigue worthy of John le Carré. . . . The complex plot offers interlocking instances of an eternal struggle between good and evil: in each case, the reader finds himself cunningly misled. Sprechman's theme, hinted rather than hammered at, is that life is a moral conundrum in which people are forced to make choices long before they can grasp the consequences."

—*Time* magazine

J.R. SPRECHMAN

CARIBE

A Novel

McGRAW-HILL BOOK COMPANY
New York   St. Louis   San Francisco   Bogotá
Hamburg   Madrid   Mexico   Milan   Montreal
Panama   Paris   São Paulo   Tokyo   Toronto

Reprinted by arrangement with Dutton

First McGraw-Hill Paperback edition, 1988
1 2 3 4 5 6 7 8 9 AG AG 8 9 2 1 0 9 8

ISBN 0-07-060345-6

LIBRARY OF CONGRESS CATALOGING-IN-PUBLICATION DATA

Sprechman, J.R.
  Caribe.

  I. Title.
[PS3569.P675C3 1987]   813'.54   87-3464
ISBN 0-07-060345-6 (pbk.)

To my wife,
my children, and
the spirit within

I

THE DESCENT

The dwarf, it was told, had been condemned centuries ago with an unspeakable curse for an unknowable cause.

In Port-au-Grasse, that turbulent port in the Caribbean, Latour was known as *le gnome*.

A dwarf of unknown origin, Latour was distinguished from others of his kind by a bulbous nose and a potbelly of sorts. He had a grayish, crinkly skin and outsized ears. His ears, he liked to think, indicated great keenness of mind—a correlation, he was grieved to admit, that had escaped the notice of researchers into such matters.

In the afternoons, on time off from his duties at the palace, the dwarf would tend his garden inside the massive walls surrounding the Fortress. Wearing white culottes and a floppy straw hat for shade, he cultivated a variety of exotic weeds and poisonous mushrooms. Passersby kept a wary distance from the garden and from Latour, who was *valet extraordinaire* to Barras, dictator of Caribe and deputy of its morbid nerve center, Port-au-Grasse.

The dwarf's stomach was still churning from the excitement of the morning.

At 11:05 Barras had received word that a company of regulars, ambushed in the hills by a rebel force, had been chewed up by mortars and automatic rifles.

In a fury the dictator summoned his General Staff which had delayed informing him of the disaster in the hills. Assembled in the War Room were generals and colonels with maps and excuses. The ranking officers—blacks, with some mulattoes among them—wore splendid uniforms that were vestiges of French *gloire*, of a colonial presence long since gone. A few whites were present, advisers in civilian dress.

In the center of the room was an oval table of handworked ebony. It was here, as everyone knew, that Barras five years ago celebrated his accession to absolute power by toasting the annihilation of his enemies with champagne from an iced bucket that contained the sorely dismayed head of the former chief of staff.

Standing before the General Staff, Barras erupted with anger. His powerful body, in its white tunic, dominated the officers. Before he was done he had sacked a lieutenant general and demoted a full colonel to the ranks. Concerning the commander of the ambushed troops, Barras cried out, "If he's alive, hang him. If he's dead let him rot on the gate, so no one will forget this day."

An hour later the hapless commander was hanged without ceremony from a gallows outside the Fortress. His body hung there all day; and it was commanded that it hang for a week, as a reminder, for all to see.

* * *

THE DESCENT

Later that night, the dwarf shuffled to his room. His shoulders drooped and tiredness seeped from his pores. The dwarf's room was a garret in the upper reaches of the presidential palace. It was a room that by custom had been assigned to valets since the days of that emperor later known by the prefix *Mad*.

On the ceiling of the dwarf's room was an old stain, remnant of a tropical storm that had swept the island years before. The table and bed and everything else in the room were out of proportion to the dwarf's size. In truth, he was a small being, existing in a world where all the shelves were out of reach.

The dwarf dreaded his room. At night, in his room, tremors of remembered violence would stir in his mind. In his time he had witnessed much cruelty. It was his lot in life to serve men and witness their madness. It was his curse that he had to relive each night what he had witnessed—remembrances like a vomit in his soul.

Of all the violence the dwarf had known, none stood out in his mind as vividly as did the execution of Damiens in the year of our Lord 1757, or the year 4323 using the calendar of gypsy dwarfs which began in the Year of the Immaculate Egg.

The dwarf's recollections, to be sure, went back even further, back to obscure times that could be remembered only in dream states.

Once, it happened, the dwarf had been put into a sanatorium for some unaccountable disorder. It was in Vienna, he recollected, seven decades ago more or less. At the sanatorium he had startled his examiners by his recall of events centuries past. As a result he was passed on from one doctor to another as a freakish curiosity, an indignity he had to endure until he fled one day with the morning garbage. But he could not put his indignation to rest until he had collected from outlying farms a cartful of ripe compost and returned to dump it all, as a final comment, on the newly mopped steps of an unwary sanatorium.

5

He was a stranger. You could peel him to the bone but even the bones were strange.

Manhattan

I t was almost noon and still raining, not hard but steadily. Dempsey was cruising in an unmarked car, listening to calls. He felt he had to move, as if movement itself were an end.

His face was bony, a rough face with not an easy line on it. His black worsted jacket hung loosely over his service revolver in its holster.

Robert Dempsey, lieutenant detective, NYPD.

Hair: black. Eyes: dark. Five-eleven; one-eighty. Single. Vietnam veteran. Rank: major. Twice wounded in action. Age: thirty-six.

He thought of it. He was thirty-six, with nothing to show for it except old scars and older violence—the debris of years.

He stopped off at Roosevelt Hospital and went upstairs and down the hall to Maggie's room.

The attending nurse looked up when he came in. She caught the slight nod of his head indicating he wanted to be alone with Maggie. The nurse hesitated a moment; then, without a word, left the room. The authority in Dempsey's expression was one that few questioned and fewer still tested.

He was alone now with Maggie and she smiled up at him, with a wan smile and broken teeth.

Her arm was in a cast. She had a cast too on her left leg that was now covered with a sheet. Her face had been badly beaten. The medical report he had seen was a litany of massive bruises, bone breakage and a ruptured spleen. The doctors hadn't yet told her about the spleen.

"Hi," she said weakly, feeling her way with him.

He looked around, taking in the room, as by habit; there was little he missed.

"Tell me what happened," he said in a dry, official tone.

She shrugged, only one shoulder moving. "Had too much to drink," she said.

"And?"

"Fell down the stairs, I guess."

It was a lie and they both knew it, but it was her way of saying nothing. She was fearful of Scapa and she wasn't looking for more trouble.

In his mind Dempsey could reconstruct Scapa drinking and in a rage. It didn't matter the reason. Scapa had a short fuse and it didn't take much to rouse him to anger. As it turned out, Maggie had ended up two nights ago in a battered heap at the bottom of a hotel stairway.

Dempsey remembered how Maggie used to be. She had the

7

kind of looks you remembered, an innocent expression, a few freckles and a friendly smile.

Dempsey had met her once at a coffee shop; afterward she began to call him late at night. She was a young kid, maybe seventeen at the time. She was tempting, full of fun, a little kooky, but too young to take seriously.

After a week or so she understood and stopped calling, and the next he heard she was seeing Scapa. Afterward Dempsey ran into her now and then, and he could see the change in her. The smile was gone: she had become Scapa's woman and her look of innocence was gone too. The few months with Scapa had already eroded her.

Later Dempsey had a basket of flowers sent up to Maggie's room. He sent it without a card, not wanting it to be personal.

He thought about Maggie. Her bones would heal; in time her bruises would disappear; her ruptured spleen, though, was a more serious matter.

It was still raining as he drove from the hospital. A grayness hung over the city. He was aware of the rhythmic sweep of the windshield wiper. Scapa was on his mind, and he knew what he had to do.

Dempsey waited for Torino in the back section at Joly's, a café on Bleecker Street. As he sat there he read a newspaper, not really reading, glancing up now and then, taking in the café with its old gnarled chairs, its potbellied stove and paneled walls.

Once as he looked up he became aware of a young woman sitting toward the front near the edge of a wall which partially divided the café. She seemed cool and unemotional as if that were all that was expected of her. She had ordered iced tea and was smoking a cigarette.

She wore a blue sheath dress and had flowing blond hair. She was probably in her early twenties, he guessed.

Presently Torino came in; he had a lean, creased face. He was soft-spoken, a bit gray, and he spoke for the family; he had that authority.

Torino passed Dempsey without a look of recognition and sat down at the next table in the corner, his back toward Dempsey. By prearrangement the tables around them were empty.

Torino presently unfolded a newspaper and began to read the financial section.

Dempsey heard a low, resonant voice, Torino speaking into his newspaper. "Dow's up again," he heard.

Dempsey was impatient. "Where's Scapa?" he asked directly. There was no answer.

Just then Albert, an old stick of a waiter, came around to Torino's table.

"The usual?"—Albert inquired with respect.

"Yes, the usual," said Torino with equal respect.

Albert left and Dempsey kept waiting for Torino's reply. As he waited he observed the young woman sipping tea. Her table was partly cut off by the protruding wall. At first it had seemed she was alone but he began to see that she was speaking to someone who was obscured from view by the wall.

Once he saw her frown and once he saw a man's hand on the table, a strong supple hand without a hair on it. Later he caught a glimpse, a bare glimpse of horn-rimmed glasses.

Torino's voice again. "Why Scapa?"

"There's a girl in the hospital."

"I heard about it."

"She's a friend," Dempsey said, and Torino understood.

Albert came around again, serving Torino, then inquiring of Dempsey, by look only, whether he wished more coffee. Dempsey shook his head.

Albert withdrew and Dempsey said, "I'll find Scapa. I may upset a few things along the way but I'll find him."

"The girl will be taken care of," Torino said.

"Not enough," Dempsey said. "I want Scapa. The old man owes me that."

Torino was silent.

Dempsey was now watching the young woman as she got up from her table. Her eyes were turned in his direction and she could see him looking at her. She had a stunning body. She kept looking at him, then suddenly turned away and began to walk toward the door. Dempsey caught a glimpse of her escort. A thin man, medium in height, a young thirty or so, with a bookish look. His face, the profile, was cold. A deadly cold.

Again Torino's voice.

"You're asking a lot," he commented.

"Remind the old man of his son, Vicenzo."

"He needs no reminder."

"Remind him of the Mekong."

"He remembers."

"Vicenzo was half dead. I carried him—"

"It's not forgotten."

"Tell the old man I don't give or ask favors but this is something else. He'll understand."

Again, silence.

Then, crisply, "I'll let you know," Torino said.

"Give my best to Vicenzo."

"Of course."

Dempsey heard Torino fold his newspaper, push back his chair and get up. Presently he saw Torino pass by on his way to the front; Torino, the image of an investment banker on his way to the Street.

A few moments later Dempsey beckoned to Albert, who came over.

He said to Albert, "That woman who sat there—" a gesture with his head.

"Yes?"

"Seen her before?"

"Now and then, yes."

"She live nearby?"

A shrug. "Her name is Catherine," said Albert in a low tone of confidence.

"What else?"

"You might find her at the Masque," Albert suggested.

Later, taking his time, Dempsey left Joly's and walked to the Masque, a small nearby theater in an old brick building.

There were several handmade announcements outside—*The Theban Woman*, by a Welsh playwright, was opening in two days.

Dempsey went inside and took a seat in back of the auditorium. On the lighted stage were cutaway pieces of a temple and three actors in Greek costumes and wigs.

In a while Dempsey was able to make out scattered groups near the stage. Among them, a figure addressing unseen ears—"Mike, the spots came in late. And Cathy, pace yourself. Too much emphasis is no emphasis. When you come down the steps, first the gesture, then the words. Remember, you can only reveal, not change."

The figure sat down.

"Now try it once more."

The chorus of elders came in, a timeless background to the agon, recounting the curse of an outcast woman, a tale of transgression and of doom. Out of the temple moved a pale figure. Her words were like a cry, and when the words were said there was silence, a last commentary. Even the elders were silent in the face of the doom and purge.

There was a break now and Dempsey went outside. At the corner he saw Catherine standing alone at the side stage entrance, smoking a cigarette. She wore a coat over her costume. He approached her.

"It's quiet here," he said, feeling he was intruding on her thoughts.

She looked up at him, recognizing him.

"I saw you inside," he said.

She acknowledged that with a slight nod.

"Where's your friend?" he asked.

She paused, then—"He is *not* my friend," she said with an emphasis.

He saw her observing the hard cut of his face.

It was late afternoon and windy.

She said to him now, "We're opening in two days."

Two days. She had set the timetable.

She let her cigarette drop and she ground it with her sandal. "I have to go in now," she said and turned to go back into the theater, giving him a nod as she left, no more.

The door closed behind her.

In a while he walked to the corner.

The next move was his, he thought. She was cold and she'd be trouble, he felt, but he knew he'd see her again.

A momentum was stirring in him; it had been in him for some time now and had to burn itself out.

Dempsey later went to the gym as he usually did three nights a week. Changing into a sweatsuit he began to move into a rhythm of sweat and exercise—jogging in place to loosen up; on the mat, bending, pushing, twisting, stretching; on the parallel bars, lithe and purposeful. Later he worked out on the punching bag for fifteen minutes, no more, no less, speaking to no one, mindful of no one, alone, nothing breaking his rhythm. Twenty laps in the pool without pause. A sauna, five minutes. A cold stinging shower, three minutes almost to the second, internally timed. And dressing, moving with an easy flow.

On his way out to the lobby he saw Turner, his new partner, who had been waiting for him. Turner was young, an eager kid, anxious to please, but inexperienced.

Turner's face was showing disappointment.

"Came up dry," he said to Dempsey.

Turner was referring to Scapa. He'd done a lot of legwork trying to track down Scapa but had come up with nothing.

Dempsey kept walking without pause, going out the front door into the dark, windblown street. His jacket hung open.

He walked toward the avenue, with Turner alongside him still trying to explain. Dempsey hardly listened. He knew that one way or another he'd find Scapa, and for him the will was the act. His reason for tracking Scapa was beginning to fade; Maggie, in fact, was far from his mind now. A case for him, like an action in combat, had its own being, existing only in itself. After a time, the whys didn't matter.

On the avenue Dempsey paused for the light. He nodded to Turner. "See you tomorrow," he said abruptly without meaning to be abrupt. The only essential on his mind now was Scapa.

When the signal changed he moved ahead, leaving Turner behind. It wasn't that he didn't like the kid; it was simply that Turner did not count for much within the framework of Dempsey's job. It had been the same with his other partners; he had worked with them but essentially he worked alone.

Dempsey had had three partners before Turner.

Bruckner. Terminated, permanently disabled; gunshot wounds.

Sully, dead.

Wesco, dead.

It was said that with Dempsey you were either quick or dead. Maybe so, Dempsey thought. Maybe he took more chances than most and it rubbed off on his partners.

But it wasn't that simple an equation either. In one way or another each of his partners had made mistakes or didn't have it. A miscalculation, a fraction off, and it was over for them. Bruckner had gotten overweight and Wesco had missed a first shot. Christ, *missed!* It was a matter of reflexes out of tune, of hesitation, of doubt or fear. When you went in, gun against gun, you couldn't hesitate. You had to go in, prepared to die, and that was your edge, sometimes your only edge.

Later, after supper, Dempsey went back to his apartment to wait for a call from Torino. It would be either yes or no, he knew, and without explanation. It wasn't an easy decision for the old man, to turn Scapa over to a cop. An impossible demand, really. Yet a favor was owed.

In his room Dempsey stood a while at the window looking out toward the riverfront, and waited. Behind him, the room, lit by a table lamp, was at a quiet pitch. It was a large room with a high ceiling and a baroque fireplace that he never used. The room had a few pieces of unpainted furniture and not much else. Some books on a shelf, a Cinzano ashtray, a Japanese print.

One of the books was a translation of the life of a seventeenth-century Samurai, master of the long sword. Another, a book about a holy order and its rule of life that was embodied in words that hung halfway between meaning and unreason—*to suffer and die.*

At eleven he got the call from Torino. A few words, dryly spoken, like a matter of business. An address in Brooklyn.

Dempsey hung up without words of thanks. In the circumstances that would have been graceless, and it wasn't expected.

Dempsey thought about it a few moments. The old man probably had given in for reasons other than returning a favor. Dempsey guessed that Scapa had become unmanageable and had lost his usefulness for the old man. At any rate Dempsey had what he wanted and didn't question it further.

Afterward he felt a vast restlessness. He was thinking of Catherine now, and wondering about the man she'd been with at Joly's. He recalled the man's cold, icy expression. It was the sort of face that meant trouble; but for Dempsey, the smell of trouble, like the smell of a woman, was evocative and almost irresistible.

* * *

Later he went to an all-night café to see Carla, a waitress there. She had dark, joyful eyes; and as always when he came around, she greeted him with a smile that had few secrets.

As he sat there having coffee, she came by his booth now and then, pausing with a few words and whispers that were like soft undercurrents. She was waiting, as he was, for her shift to end, waiting to go with him to her apartment nearby——

——but through it all, through the coming and going, the nuances and the whispers, the image of Catherine kept intruding on him. The image of her so persisted in him that in time it was Carla who began to seem like an intruder into his thoughts.

Somewhat later then, before the shift ended, he abruptly excused himself, saying he had to leave. Carla took her disappointment with a rueful shrug.

"Some other time," he told her as he got up to go, leaving her an unusually large tip, and feeling as awkward about it as she did. And by her expression he could tell that she knew—knew what he himself had only vaguely felt until now, that he was really saying good-bye to her.

When he left the café he began to walk in the wind-bleak streets, feeling at odds with himself. He had thoughts of going back to Carla, and intermittently he felt aroused, foolish, awkward, quixotic, stupid and naive, but he kept going, moving against the night and the winter wind.

In the beginning was the promise.

The next day Dempsey stopped off at the hospital and spoke to the woman in charge of accounts. As she looked through her files he said to her, "Send me the bills."

The woman, scanning Maggie's record, looked up at him now. "It's been taken care of," she said. "A Mr. Torino—" She saw his look— "Is there a problem?"

"No." A pause. "No, not at all."

Shortly then he went upstairs to Maggie's room. It was mid-morning. Maggie was asleep under sedation. She was curled up a bit, like a child asleep, one hand on her Snoopy with its long black ears.

He came closer, reaching out to brush her hair from her eyes, and saying to her, "It'll be all right," saying it but not feeling it. His words, he knew, could not take the pain or hurt from her; and he was remembering then the time when he could have reached out with a healing hand. It had been a time then of magic and of promise, a time when all things were possible.

He remembered himself as he once was, a small boy on an isolated farm in Maine. Remembered his father, Matt Dempsey, a lonely friendless man who raised potatoes and worked at night shaping iron at a rundown forge. His father had been to sea once; now he was a man with a solitary silence who took nothing and gave nothing. At his forge at night he would hurl his hammer down with hard, fierce strokes as if an awful secret lay between hammer and anvil.

For the boy, his father at the forge was an awesome figure, and the boy's first image of God was fused in his mind with the gaunt shape of his father; and he, the boy, was the *son*.

The boy first learned of God from his mother, who was devout and read from the Scriptures even before breakfast, while water boiled on the stove and her mouth was still sour in the morning. At four he began to read from the Scriptures. At six he had memorized it all, from Genesis to the Book of Revelation.

The small boy lived in a world of innocence and magic, a world of signs and mysteries where all things were possible. He carried in him God's promise. In him was the knowing and certitude of God's covenant that had been laid upon him. It was a secret he could share with no one, and he held it within himself.

The wonders he could do! He could wither a leaf by the touch of his hand but he had to touch many to wither a few. When someone in the village was ill he had but to make a sign and recite certain prayers and a healing would occur. It had to be done exactly, with nothing left to chance. It occurred to him once to end his supplications with the entreaty, "If Ye be willing, O Lord!" In so doing, he let the matter pass into God's hands. In the process, whatever the outcome, the boy's magic became infallible.

The boy was five when he had his first experience. He had been in the woods, feeling light and marvelous. It was autumn and almost evening when he saw a covey of birds flying in faultless formation across the motionless sky. The sight entranced him and he felt a joy rising high. His body seemed to float and he was lifted upward with an incredible rapture.

When he regained himself he was in his bed. The doctor was there and his mother stood by him, anxious and disturbed. The boy wondered how he had gotten into bed. He felt peaceful and could not understand why his mother cried. He had been found cold and rigid on the ground. On his hands and feet were observed the marks of the stigmata.

The doctor gave the boy an elixir and later the pastor came and said prayers with a stern face. Afterward the mother smothered her son with care and anxiety.

Together Dempsey and Turner got into the car. With Dempsey at the wheel driving hard in and out of traffic, they headed east into the Midtown Tunnel, then on to Brooklyn, to Sheepshead Bay where Scapa was staying.

On the way Dempsey kept thinking of his father—over and over, remembrances, like unburied flesh turning to rot.

He remembered his father sitting in the stable by a kerosene lamp, tracing exquisite designs of ironwork. It was always surprising that out of those rough hands could come such beauty. Later he would see his father pound and shape metals into the forms of the drawings. Out of the fires and erupting steam would come delicate ironwork which was put away to rust; for the villagers had no use for him or his work.

The shapes of ironwork were like fragments of his father's years at sea. A gate of a brothel in Shanghai, a balcony in the French Quarter, a lamp in Bombay or somewhere along the Great Trunk Road, somewhere beyond Capricorn and the trade winds. Remnants of a past that told something but never quite revealed. The drawings faded in his father's rolltop desk and the ironwork rusted in the stable. You could almost cry when you saw it.

The boy's mother was concerned as she watched him growing up in the image of his father. Sometimes as she sat with a waxlike expression, reading or knitting, her needle going in and out like quick thoughts, the boy would see her stare at him in a way that made him uneasy. His father had once been in an asylum for the insane; and that thought, unspoken, was the fear in his mother's eyes.

The boy felt the uneasiness that lay upon the house, and the troubled silence between his father and mother. Often he would escape from it into the woods near the lake, to his secret world of magic and promise, where he knew what he was and what he was meant to be.

Always afterward he remembered that time when he was seven and the woods ran with the russet and gold of autumn, and expectation was caught in the throat like a cry. In retrospect, there were hints, but nothing more, to foreshadow the violence and horror that was to come.

There had been no warning.

The first intimation the boy had was the sight of the overturned pot on the kitchen floor. A few moments later he saw his father coming out of the bedroom. His father's eyes were glazed; his clothes were blotched. In his fist, clenched downward at his side, was a bloody carving knife.

The boy moved fearfully toward the bedroom. He could see his mother lying partially on the bed, her knees on the floor, almost in a praying position. Her back was toward him; her hair was in a neat bun. She was naked, not moving, with dreadful wounds in her back, blood still oozing from them.

The boy could utter no sound. Time seemed not to move. He wanted to approach his mother, but she was naked.

Later again he saw his father, who had gone out and had come back. His father was crying now, "I'm sorry, I'm sorry," saying it over and over, but the words had no meaning for the boy. His father reached out his hand toward him.

He heard his father saying, "Forgive me—God, forgive me!" The boy drew back from the bloody, outstretched hand and ran from the house into the woods.

Later, in his hiding place, he heard the blast of a shotgun from the direction of the stable, but it was some time before he could bring himself to go there.

Afterward as he came near the stable he could see his father lying in the doorway, half in and half out. He saw the shotgun on the ground. His father was dead, his jaw blasted away, an obscene mass of bone and flesh, a grotesque ugliness.

Later he remembered his father as he had been, his hand outstretched, begging forgiveness, but the boy could not forgive him, not then or ever.

At the funeral the pastor said words that were without meaning for the boy. The limestone earth was turned over, leaves drifting over the churned earth. When that was done the boy went home alone, taking comfort from no one.

He shut himself in his room. He felt unclean—his pores, flesh, mouth and breath, corrupted. Whatever he touched, or whatever touched him, was foul. There was dust everywhere, and dust on dust. When night came it hung like black rust.

He wanted to say something. Something had to be said, but what? The room was cold and he shivered uncontrollably.

Later his anger erupted and he could not contain himself

now. Looking upward he cried out, "Damn you, damn you, damn you!"

He could not stop. "Damn you, damn you!" he cried out at the image in his mind, which was of God and of his father, one within one.

Until then he hadn't cried but now tears began to pour out of him, out of his eyes and mouth and out of his depths.

In the morning when he woke he was empty. He did not cry again, not ever; only the bitterness and anger remained.

Later a woman from outside the village came to take him away to a home. No one from the village came to see him off. They shunned him as they did the house, for there was a curse upon the house and upon the boy and they could not look upon him nor speak of him. Later someone burnt the house to the ground and the charred hulk was dismembered and covered over.

When they got to Sheepshead Bay Dempsey parked a block from the address Torino had given him. He and Turner got out. Turner was nervous; he'd heard of Scapa's reputation.

A sharp wind was blowing in from the Bay, and Turner buttoned his overcoat. Dempsey wore no coat; his worsted jacket hung loosely open. The stinging wind stimulated him. He wanted to move, to act, but he paused first to relax, to chew some gum, and to point out to Turner a single leaf clinging to a branch on a barren tree, saying, "It's a fighter, that one."

Now he was ready and they began to approach the house; it was a modest, two-story dwelling.

"Go round the other end," he said to Turner. "See if anyone's downstairs." Turner was quick to respond, and in a while he was back. There was no one in the rooms downstairs, he reported.

Dempsey nodded. That meant Scapa was upstairs, either in bed, alone or with someone, or he could have gone out.

"Wait here," he said to Turner. "In two minutes go round the back and wait for me in the yard. Keep out of sight," he emphasized, wanting to keep the kid out of the way.

Dempsey moved now to the front entrance, leaving Turner where he was. Turner was puzzled but he knew enough not to ask questions. It didn't make sense, he thought, going up alone against someone like Scapa.

Quietly, Dempsey managed to open the front door. In the living room he heard the sound of a television set in one of the rooms upstairs.

Quietly he ascended the steps. Upstairs, he paused on the landing. The sounds of television were coming from an open bedroom door.

A momentum was building up in him.

He drew his service revolver and approached the open door. A moment more and he was within the frame of the doorway, with a full view of the bedroom.

He saw Scapa, a huge hulk, sitting on the edge of the bed, absorbed in a Bugs Bunny cartoon on television. Scapa had on black pants, a white shirt and a blue cardigan. In bed, partially covered with sheet and blanket, was a woman, about thirty, a redhead with delicious breasts; she was reading *Cosmopolitan*.

Neither of them saw him for a while. Suddenly the woman turned and saw him. She cried out in fright.

Scapa quickly jumped up, turned and saw Dempsey's gun. Scapa froze.

Dempsey said to the woman, "Dress and get out of here."

She was immobilized with fear.

"Get out," he said again.

Scapa was asking, "You a cop?"

"That's right," Dempsey said.

Hearing that, the redhead became relaxed.

"Move," Dempsey said to her.

She smiled and got out of bed, naked. She had a luxurious

body. On the way to the bathroom she picked up some clothes.

Scapa was relaxed now too; he was almost smiling. "Gonna read me my rights?" he asked with sarcasm.

"Hands on your head," Dempsey said in a hard way.

Scapa obeyed with a slow, careless tempo.

"Over to the wall."

"Sure. Why not?" said Scapa. He'd been through this before. A piece of cake. He stood with his hands against the wall, at shoulder level, cool and easy.

"What's the beef?" he asked.

Dempsey did not answer him. He was watching the redhead. She had not bothered to shut the bathroom door. She was taking her time, still naked, looking at him with her whole body. He nodded toward her, to hurry her up.

She began to dress now, slowly, each movement a nuance of enticement.

When she was dressed she came into the bedroom, put on a coat, winked at Dempsey and said to Scapa, "See you tonight, huh?"

"Sure, sure," said Scapa, looking around. "This won't take long. Just some misunderstanding."

Then she was gone and Dempsey was alone with Scapa.

"What's the beef?" Scapa asked again.

Dempsey frisked him.

"Face me," Dempsey said.

Scapa turned and Dempsey sized him up at close range, taking his measure. Scapa was a full 225 pounds of hard muscle. He'd been a stevedore once. He was tough, not as tough as he used to be, but tough enough.

Dempsey put his revolver back in its holster, and Scapa took his cue from that, as Dempsey knew he would.

"What'll it cost?" Scapa asked knowingly.

"Nothing."

"Come on," said Scapa with a man-of-the-world expression. "How much?"

"I'm taking you in, Scapa."

"For what?"

"Maggie. Remember her?"

"That little whore? Aw, come on—"

"You put her in the hospital and—"

"—just slapped her around a little."

"Down a flight of steps."

"So what's the sweat?"

"She's hurt—hurt bad. She may not come out of it."

Scapa's expression changed.

"It was an accident—" he began to explain.

"I'm taking you in," Dempsey said, and he could see Scapa glancing toward the chair where his jacket was and calculating his chances.

Dempsey came closer until he was not more than a foot from Scapa.

"Turn to the wall," he said, reaching for handcuffs; and it was then that Scapa made his move, lunging out, swinging from the side.

Dempsey had anticipated the move and he deflected Scapa's blow. He countered with three punches that were almost programmed, two quick jabs and a powerful thrust upward into the rib cage; it was like a rock exploding into Scapa, hurting him badly. At that moment the fight was over. Anyone else but a Scapa would have fallen in a heap or given up.

He let Scapa recover his balance. Scapa's cockiness was gone but he came in again because he was a scrapper and angry. He was hurt but he came in with a bellow of rage.

Dempsey responded with ferocity. He moved in, absorbing Scapa's blows. He bore in with savage chops to Scapa's midsection and head. Scapa began to buckle, and as he was sinking, Dempsey rocked him back, hammering him with blows. Scapa's head was

soggy and blood began to ooze from his mouth, and he sank unconscious to the floor.

Dempsey stood over him; his breathing began to ease. The fury
was out of him and he had no more feeling about Scapa. It was a
police matter now.

He bent to examine Scapa. The damage didn't seem too serious.
Bad enough, though—the jaw was broken and hung slack.

Later he called Turner. The kid came in and began to look
around. His blond boyish hair was ruffled from the wind. He was
astonished by the havoc he saw in Scapa's battered head; but, as
usual, he asked no questions.

"Resisted arrest," said Dempsey dryly and let it go at that.

Turner looked at him, curious.

"Call an ambulance," Dempsey said, and he began to wait,
becoming aware now of the television set still going. Popeye.
Popeye and Olive.

Later two attendants came and took Scapa away. From what
they said, Dempsey knew the damage was more severe than he had
guessed; and he knew he'd have some explaining to do. He shrugged
it off.

As he walked away he paused to look at a Bugs Bunny episode.
When it was over he turned off the set and nodded to Turner who
was still uneasy.

"Relax, kid," he said. "Save yourself for the hard days."

Turner grinned somewhat, not knowing how to take it. Dempsey's manner was casual, as if nothing had happened, and maybe
that was the way to roll with it.

On the way downstairs Turner asked, "What should I say
later?"

"Say what you have to say—the truth. Don't shave it, don't
bend it, and don't ever ask me that again—*ever.*"

* * *

In the War Room, when Barras was done excoriating the General Staff for the disaster in the hills, he dismissed them all except for Colonel Dufar of M-5, his chief of intelligence.

Barras's tunic was spotted with the sweat of anger; his formidable head, completely shaven, glistened with wrath.

"Idiots," Barras commented to Dufar as he sat down. "In one morning, half a company—wiped out by a shitful of ragpickers."

Colonel Dufar, a mulatto, almost white, was a thin man, thin in a way that suggested a straight-edged razor. He stood at attention, waiting for the next outburst, nevertheless pleased that he alone had been asked to remain behind.

Just then the dwarf came in and began to pour cognac for Barras. As the dwarf was about to leave, Barras said, "Latour, stay. Sit there," he pointed.

The dwarf shuffled to the end of the oval table where he squiggled into a huge chair as noiselessly as possible. His crinkly grayish face barely showed above the table. In keeping with the tone of the meeting the dwarf removed the wad of gum he had been chewing and affixed it under the table. His stomach was uneasy.

For his part, Colonel Dufar ignored the dwarf, resenting his intrusion into the privacy of the occasion.

Barras came to the point. "Dufar—tell me about the mortars."

"Yes. Yes, of course," he said. "It's clearly treachery," he added. His French was impeccable, graduate as he was of the Jesuit College St. Michel.

"Treachery? Whose?"

"Sorge. Sorge, of course."

"That is *not* possible."

"Each man has his price," Dufar suggested.

Barras shook his head.

"My ministers and generals have their price," he said. "Even you, Dufar, in the end would betray me, but not Sorge."

"You have no cause—" Dufar began to protest.

Barras cut him short. "Tell me about Sorge."

Dufar composed himself.

"To begin with," he said, picking his words carefully, "we must remember, Sorge is not one of us." He meant, of course, that Sorge, an American mercenary, was white; as such, Sorge was an alien element on the island.

"You forget Valmy," Barras reminded his chief of intelligence.

Valmy.

Five years earlier Barras had found himself pitted against the army high command. At Valmy, an artillery base, the high command had gathered one night against Barras. That same night, in one hour of unremitting terror, Barras retaliated and broke the spine of the officer corps. Sorge himself had a key role in gutting an entire generation of the officer elite. Sorge alone put to death thirteen of the officers, working with a precision that had been unnerving to witness.

Only a few officers escaped that bath of blood. One of them was the former supreme commander, Fouché, now an exile in Mexico City. Fouché, code name Bluebird.

"But Valmy was five years ago," Dufar persisted. "Times and loyalties change."

The colonel stood erect, his uniform crisp as it always was, even in the inquisitorial chambers of the Fortress where torture was still a procedural instrument of intelligence.

Barras settled back in his massive chair that emphasized his fierce power even in repose.

Dufar said, "I have reason to believe—"

"I am not interested in *beliefs.*"

"It's more than that," Dufar maintained. He was tenacious; he never let go. "Here are the facts," he said. "A shipment of sixty-millimeter mortars and automatic weapons of Czech manufacture, left Huerta—"

"Huerta?"

27

"A small island in the Gulf of Mexico," Dufar reminded him, "twenty-eight point six kilometers—"

"Yes, yes, go on"—impatiently.

"On the sixth of November at seventeen forty-three hours, to be exact, the shipment left Huerta. The freighter never arrived here; it was later found in the Gulf without crew and without cargo. By coincidence, almost a month later, that rabble from the hills, with mortars and automatic weapons, cut to pieces—"

"I know what happened!" Barras cut in explosively.

Calmly, Dufar continued. "We can assume," he said, "that the mortars were the same as those shipped from Huerta. Someone in authority diverted that shipment to the rebels. That someone had to be Sorge."

"Why not the shipper?"

"Krone? I've questioned him closely," said Dufar. "What had Krone to gain? On the contrary, the shipment was uninsured; it was Krone who bore the loss."

"And the captain?"

"It was not the captain. At least, not alone."

"Why not?"

"The captain was assigned to the ship only six hours before it left Huerta. No, it couldn't have been him alone."

"Who hired the captain?"

"Sorge, of course, as you know."

"Where is the captain now?"

"We have reason to believe that a charred corpse we came across—"

Barras interrupted impatiently. "What else do you have?"

"We discussed this before," said Dufar. "There are only three possibilities. We can rule out the shipper, Krone. The captain, acting alone, is an impossible conclusion. It has to be Sorge and the captain together. The captain is dead, but Sorge remains. The situation, as I see it," Dufar concluded, "has its own internal logic."

"No, no," said Barras. "It's too simple, Dufar."

"Perhaps Sorge counted on that. Counted on our reasoning he's not fool enough to risk a situation where he's the only likely suspect."

"No. No, it has to be someone else."

"But who?"

"You tell me," Barras said almost with contempt. "You have your network of mice in every corner."

"If you would allow me . . ." Dufar suggested.

"Allow you what?" Barras asked guardedly.

"Permission to recall Sorge for questioning and . . ."

"And what?"

"A free hand with Sorge."

Barras shook his head. "I told you before, Dufar, and I tell you again—*no*. Leave Sorge where he is. He'll know how to deal with this. Give him time."

"He's already had enough—"

"The matter," said Barras, "is closed." His fists on the table added a gesture of finality.

The dwarf, listening closely, could understand the dictator's reluctance to consider Sorge a traitor. It was Sorge at Valmy who had stood with him against the high command; and if Sorge were capable of betrayal, who then was there left to trust?

As Dufar, a dossier under his arm, was preparing to leave, Barras turned to the dwarf. "Latour," he asked, "what do *you* think?"

At the far end of the table, his head barely showing, the dwarf remained in thought.

"What does your nose say?" Barras persisted.

"My nose tells me Sorge . . ." the dwarf paused to savor Dufar's expectant look. With a glint the dwarf concluded, saying, "I'm sure Sorge is *not* a traitor."

Barras smiled. "You have a good nose, Latour."

Dufar took the rebuff without expression. Saluting sharply he left the War Room without a further word, leaving behind an impression of thin lips and a stiff spine that had been unreasonably affronted.

Shortly Barras dismissed the dwarf and Latour rose to leave, but not before he had retrieved his wad of gum from under the oval table. As he left he kept thinking of Sorge. It was true, of course; Sorge *was* an outsider, mistrusted by Dufar and others around Barras. The dwarf had to wonder: Was there a conspiracy at work against Sorge and ultimately against Barras?

The dwarf kept thinking about the matter. If Sorge didn't come up with an answer, or couldn't, how long would Barras continue to deny Dufar's request to bring Sorge back for questioning? And if Sorge were brought back it would be, all in all, a deadly encounter. Dufar, the Inquisitor, face to face in the interrogation chambers with Sorge, that perfect instrument of death.

> *". . . he knows that in the very depths of his being he has broken all ties with society, both in word and in deed. He breaks all ties with the civilized world, its laws, its customs, its morality . . . and if he has intercourse with the world, it is only for the purpose of destroying it."*

—*A Catechism*

NECHAYEV BAKHUNIN

A gale was moving in from the East River. The window shook as Smithy observed the brownstone across the street. In the dark he glanced at the luminous dial of his wristwatch.

Presently he went to the bathroom to shave, moving with quiet fluidity. He was thin, almost wiry; his eyes were a cold blue.

He began to shave, working with a straight-edged razor. His hands, devoid of hair, were like supple, precise instruments. He was over thirty but seemed younger. His eyes reflected nothing; as always they were without emotion.

Later, at the window again, he observed Krone and his bodyguard arrive at the brownstone at 2312 hours. Krone, the shipper, as Smithy thought of him. Krone, dealer in munitions, dealer in anything bought or sold.

Krone came to the brownstone once a week for a liaison with a woman who lived there. Krone's time of arrival varied, Smithy had noted, but the variances were within acceptable limits.

In a while Smithy left his room. He carried nothing with him that could identify him. His passport and other papers, which he occasionally used, were in a locker. The passport and papers all bore the name of a man long since dead—one more name among the many that Smithy had used over the years. In Port-au-Grasse he was known as Sorge—Maximillian Sorge—a name like the others that had been dredged from graveyard registers.

Later, as he walked in the cold on the avenue, he began to think of Cathy. Yesterday, when he had been with her at Joly's, she had been cold and wary. He knew he had to reckon with her coldness, and that was a factor in his plans.

He stopped to call her at a booth on the next block. He wanted to hear her voice again.

There was no answer. He hung up and called again, and later once more. He felt a deadness inside. Without her he lived in an abyss of nothingness.

Dempsey did not go to the opening of the play but did go later to Joly's where the company had arranged to wait out the first-night reviews.

Somewhat after eleven the group came in, Catherine among them. She sat quietly at one of the tables. She had an air about her that beautiful women sometimes had, an air that seemed to indicate that mere presence was enough. The rest you could never have.

Next to her was Max Caine, the director, a lean-faced man. At her left, an empty chair. An antique potbellied stove stood in the back section where Dempsey had met with Torino two days ago.

Dempsey rose from his table now and approached Catherine. He bent down toward her, saying quietly, "How are you?"

She turned as he sat down, and he could see her studying his unquiet face. Her eyes were a soft blue with a slight tension in them.

She lit a cigarette and let the smoke drift softly toward him, like a bit of intimacy, something of hers touching him.

"Did you like the play?" she asked.

"Didn't see it," he said.

"Oh?" A hint of disappointment.

He was looking at the way the skin creased at her neck, and the way her hair flowed as she spoke. She was pale, a winter pale.

"Why'd you come then?" she asked.

Her breath was close and sweet, and he was aware of her breasts without looking at them now.

He did not respond at once; her question had wanted, but did not need, a reply.

Finally he said, "You know why."

She shrugged with a slight smile.

"I hardly know you," she said.

"I'm what you see."

"Is it that simple?"

"My name's Dempsey. Robert Dempsey. Lieutenant detective."

She stared at him; she hadn't expected that.

"Homicide," he added.

There was a pause, a slight withdrawal. She exhaled a puff of smoke but not toward him.

At that moment, Max, the director, said something to Catherine and she seemed grateful for the diversion. She turned from Dempsey, engaging Max in close conversation, with Dempsey outside of it.

Later when she turned again she saw that Dempsey was gone, on his way out. He didn't look back. She knew he wouldn't.

She wondered about him. Homicide? Had it something to do with Smithy?

The Theban Woman closed down in two weeks.

On the last night of the play Dempsey waited for Catherine across the street from the theater; he had not seen her since the opening.

It was cold and sharp, and at the stage entrance a single light cast an ascetic glow.

In a while he saw Max Caine, the director, leave the theater and take a cab. Presently Catherine and another woman came out. He watched the pantomime between them, Catherine indicating she had a headache—a gesture. In the end she began to walk alone down the street.

Dempsey crossed over and caught up with her at the next corner. She looked up at him but said nothing. They walked together, yet separately, without a word, Catherine absorbed in her own thoughts—perhaps depressed.

"How's the headache?" he asked.

She looked at him with surprise, then shrugged, as if reluctant to be caught with an unexpected emotion.

She kept walking; she seemed fragile next to him with silence enveloping her.

"A drink might help," he suggested.

"No. No, I've got to pack."

"Are you moving?"

"I have to move," she said.

"This time of night?"

"I don't have much," she said. "We could take it in a cab."

We. Said in a matter-of-fact way.

As they got near the corner she said, "Don't come up with me now. Call me in five minutes. I'll give you my number."

"I know it," he said.

"It's not listed."

"I know that."

"What else do you know?"

"Max can't move you tonight."

She looked up at him. "How do you know Max?"

"I don't know him at all."

She was piqued but let it go.

She said, "When you call, if someone answers . . ." she paused and left the rest unsaid.

He nodded. He understood; she was running out on a problem.

He watched her walk away. She looked back once with uncertainty.

Later, as he entered the darkened room of her apartment, the light from the hallway momentarily illumined a suitcase and a few odds and ends on the floor. Catherine was standing by the window, a drink in her hand. When he closed the door the room was dark again except for the reflection from a window which jutted at a right angle.

She asked, "You didn't run into anyone, did you?"

He shrugged. "No."

Suddenly the phone began to ring.

He saw her staring at the phone.

The ringing ceased and began again.

"Answer it," he said.

"I don't want any trouble."

"If it's there it's there," he said.

"It's always there," she said.

The ringing stopped. She didn't move; she seemed transfixed by the phone. When it began to ring once more, Dempsey picked up the phone set, tore it from its connection and cast it aside.

"Now we can go," he said.

"He'll call again," she said.

"The phone's dead," he told her. "Dead."

"He'll call again," she repeated. It didn't make sense but he knew what she meant.

Later, in his car, as he drove to the East Side Catherine sat beside him in silence. He wanted to touch her but the moment wasn't right. From time to time he caught her looking at him. Once she started to say something but stopped abruptly.

When they got to her furnished rooms just off Second Avenue near the UN, he found she had already moved most of her things there. It was obvious she hadn't needed him to help her move.

She lay her suitcase on the bed, and from it she took a bottle of scotch, half used up. "Pour yourself some," she said.

He poured a double scotch neat and drank it in a swallow. He drank merely to do something for the moment. There was never any nicety to his drinking; it was usually done hard and quick.

"You always drink that way?"

He shrugged, not bothering to answer.

In a while she went to the bathroom and came back in a black silk robe, a sharp contrast to her pale skin. He watched the movement of her body and the way her thighs shaped her robe. Her body evoked a sense of ripeness.

She poured herself a drink and went toward the window, standing at the side, looking down into the street through the slats of the blind.

He came behind her and said, "There's no one down there." He said it, not knowing it, merely to get a response.

"You wouldn't know," she said. "He could be there and you wouldn't know it."

He. An anonymous he.

Dempsey's jacket was open and he touched her shoulder.

She turned and saw his revolver in its holster.

He was aroused and she was aware of it; she'd been aware of it for some time.

She put on a smile. "Can't you say it?"

"Say what?"

"That you like me."

He did not respond.

She said, "Have you ever said it to anyone?"

He didn't answer her, but she knew.

She was holding the glass of scotch between them, holding him off, he felt.

She turned then, went to a stand near the bureau and put on a record. Jazz, soft jazz, twenties jazz. A distraction; something to do.

She looked back at him.

She asked, "Why did you wait two weeks?"

"That's how it was."

"Did you think of me?"

"Yes, I thought of you."

"Much?"

"Enough."

She lit a cigarette and sat down on the edge of the bed.

There was silence between them. Glances, wondering, waiting, expectation, a bit of awkwardness.

She said, "You don't talk much, do you?"

"I'm not much at talking."

"I know, but you say a lot," she remarked. "You just don't say the words."

"I want you," he said. He hadn't had to say that before, not to anyone, but he wanted to say it now.

"I'm here," she said.

"You haven't said yes."

"Is it necessary?"

"No, but . . ."

"But what? You'd like me to say I want you?"

He stood there.

She said, "I hardly know you."

"What does that mean?"

"It means you can have me, but if you want me to say yes, it will take time."

"I have time."

"Don't be angry."

"I'm not angry."

"You look angry," she said, glancing at his revolver. "Must you wear that gun?"

"No."

She smiled. "Did you intend making love with that gun on?"

He had to smile at that.

"You can smile, can't you?" she said.

They were smiling now and it was something they had together. Not much but enough for the moment.

He took off his holster.

She turned now and lay on the bed, and she looked up at him, saying, "Why don't we just relax a while? You could rub my back."

That's how she wanted it, slowly, easily, not hurrying; and he came to her, sitting down on the edge of the bed. He began to massage the tightness around her shoulders. She was tense, very tense, and she became relaxed as he worked his hands downward to her waist.

He was aroused with a stiff potency.

He drew her robe upward somewhat and began to massage her naked legs. Her robe fell enticingly between the crevice of her thighs. When he came to her juncture she suddenly became tense again.

She sat up now and he took her to him, kissing her deeply. Her breath was warm and he wanted to draw it into him.

She began to gently loosen his tie. Then she opened his shirt, slowly, button by button. She saw his massive chest and his scars, one of them across his ribs, each scar like a memory of violence.

"Your job?" she asked.

"The war," he said, remembering.

"Do you think about it much?"

"It's dead," he said.

"You sound angry again."

He hadn't been aware of it.

She touched his scars and it aroused him further.

He leaned over to kiss her, holding her face in his hands, his rough hands enfolding the fragility of her face. He undid her robe and saw the rich opulence of her nakedness, her lush breasts and loins and her nest of secrecy.

Later, when it was over and they lay together in a quiet pause, he felt disturbed. She had remained cold and untouched, he knew. For her it was something that had to be done and gotten out of the way. In the end, what he had had was his alone; she had been remote and outside of it.

He began to dress; she was still in bed.

"What's wrong?" she asked.

"It's time to go."

She sat up. "Stay a while. Please." She was holding on to him with words.

"You had a bad day," he said. "You needed someone—anyone. I'm not anyone."

"I wanted it to be good for you."

"I'm not looking for favors."

"I did have a bad day," she explained.

"Let it go," he said.

"I mean, what with the play closing. It's always that way when it's over." She paused, remembering, old thoughts in her eyes. "Please don't go yet."

He was putting on his tie, looking at her, reconsidering. He let the tie hang undone, as a gesture.

He poured another shot.

"The play mean so much?" he asked over his shoulder.

"It could have run for months."

"What happened?"

"Max got word yesterday to close down. Just like that. He was sorry, he said. That's how it always is—we're sorry but . . ."

"It happens."

"Smithy must have gotten to them," she said with an edge of anger. "It had to be him."

Smithy. He had that now. One more piece.

Smithy. Caucasian; average height, thin, medium blond, horn-rimmed glasses, cold face, beaky nose, hairless hands.

She was lighting a cigarette; she put on her robe and stood up.

"It's his way of getting back at me," she said with an old bitterness. "He's done it before."

"Done what?"

She didn't reply.

He asked, "How bad is it with Smithy?"

"Bad enough."

"What kind of trouble?"

"The kind you'd run out on."

"What does he want?"

"He wants me back."

"Tell me about him."

She hesitated. "No, it'd only make more trouble."

"That's what I deal in, trouble."

"It's not a police matter," she said.

"I can help you, but you have to ask."

"No. No, you're only passing by."

"It depends," he said.

"No. One day I'd wake up and you'd be gone," she said. "I'd have to face Smithy alone. I'd be here but where would *you* be?"

He had no answer for her, and she knew it.

They fell into a silence.

Then he said, "Call me if you need me."

She nodded, but he knew she wouldn't call.

He finished knotting his tie. He put on his holster, his jacket, all the while waiting for a word from her but the word never came. He would have stayed but the word never came. And he didn't ask; he had that pride of not asking.

He said good-bye, feeling awkward about it. And later as he walked in the winter streets he wanted to cut her from his mind but he couldn't.

It was clear she had wanted help of one kind or another but was afraid to ask for it. She had needed assurance that she could count on him to the end. It was something he could not give her.

Let it go, he thought. Let it go.

It was night and drizzling outside as Smithy stood at the window of his room, again observing the brownstone across the street.

He thought about the coded cable he had picked up this morning at his drop in lower Manhattan. The cable from Barras was brief—on the surface, merely a request for more information regarding the cargo; but there was more between the lines. Barras was becoming impatient. Smithy had counted on more time but he couldn't overlook the imperative of the dictator's cable.

The second phase of Operation Bluebird was now in being. The first phase had involved the diversion of mortars and Czech weapons to the rebels in Caribe. For his services Smithy had received fifty thousand U.S. dollars through Fouché, now in exile in Mexico City. In the second phase the risks were considerably higher but the stakes were higher too.

Smithy packed his remaining things in a waterproof packet inside his overcoat. Everything else had already been removed from the room to a motel outside Newark. A Xerox of a manifest and a transmittal advice to the Banque Suisse were in an envelope in a locker at Grand Central Station. Everything was in order.

At 2302 Krone arrived at the brownstone across the street. Burry, his bodyguard, accompanied him.

Ten minutes later Smithy checked his Walther P–38 and left the room for the last time. He left no traces. The manager and neighbors would remember only a mild-mannered tenant named Jones, who wore horn-rimmed glasses. Smithy would have no further use for the glasses.

Time was tight and he moved now within a cool center.

It was night, nearly eleven. Dempsey kept driving through the rain; he was off duty and restless. He was listening to calls, keeping on the move.

He had stopped twice to call Catherine. There was no answer; she wasn't in—either that or she wasn't answering.

He drove past where she lived. The windows of her apartment on the fifth floor were dark. Was she out? Or asleep? Was she with Smithy? A tremor of irritation passed through his mind.

Later, turning down Second Avenue, he drove south to Sixteenth Street, passing a brownstone where he saw Burry, Krone's bodyguard, standing in the rain. He knew Burry. Burry had a baggy nose and seemed to be neckless. All Burry had to recommend him was that he came cheaply. He carried a gun but the way he carried it you knew he'd be in trouble if he had to get at it fast. Standing in the rain, Burry had a dumb, passive look that reminded Dempsey of the times during the war he'd seen oxen standing gently in the rain. You saw them again later, or others like them, dead by the road, cut down by shrapnel or explosives. Later when the rain dried and the ground caked you saw them bloated and putrefying, sometimes lying with their feet in the air like a child's image of death.

When he circled the block again Dempsey saw that Burry was gone from view. Burry, he guessed, was probably inside in the hallway, out of the rain, on guard for Krone against God knows what.

Krone, of course, was with Carrie. Krone, almost like clockwork, came to her place once a week. Krone was forty going on fifty and always out of breath—asthma, you could guess. Knowing Krone, you could imagine him working up a sweat with Carrie, and later counting out his money twice in small bills to make it seem more. Before leaving her he'd probably take time to primp the carnation in his lapel, an expression on his face like a melon gone sour.

As he did each week, Malder had opened the door for Burry. A middle-aged man in a cardigan, Malder took care of the brownstone and had the downstairs apartment.

Burry had asked him, "The back door locked?"

"It's always locked," said Malder.

"What you got to drink?"

"Beer."

"What kind?"

"Same kind you always have."

Malder always had some beer laid away. Burry couldn't tell one beer from another. He liked to appear discriminating but instead came off looking like an attendant who cleaned cuspidors at the gym.

In a while Burry drank some beer out of the bottle, wiping his mouth with the sleeve of his coat.

He remarked, "Mister K doesn't like me to drink on the job."

Then he went into the hall, walking up and down to make himself look busy. Malder kept his door open.

Burry came to the door once; he was lonely.

"Whatdja say?" he asked.

"Nothing."

"Thought you said something."

Burry shrugged and began to walk again.

Malder heard Burry walk up and down the hall—up and down like a metronome.

From the window Malder became aware of a man wearing a hat walking west on the near side of the street. It was a brief glimpse, a stray image that hardly registered.

Later he became aware of another passerby walking west, another fragment. When the man had gone Malder had an uneasy feeling. Was it the same man he had seen before? He wasn't sure —the first glimpse had been too brief. Yet in retrospect each image superimposed itself on the other so that both images became one.

Malder called Burry. He said to him, "I saw someone out there —twice. It may have been the same man."

"Did he stop?"

"No, just passing by."

"It's raining too hard," Burry shrugged. "Nobody'd be out—" a pause— "maybe I ought to take a look."

At the window Malder watched Burry on the street, looking up and down in the rain. The street was empty.

Burry came back. "There's nothing," he said and took up his vigil in the hall. "Mister K likes me to keep moving," he told Malder.

Sometime later Malder saw Burry standing near the glass-paneled front door, peering out.

Malder now heard a sudden burst and a splintering of glass. He saw Burry crumple under a fusillade of bullets.

Burry was lying still now, face on the carpet, blood draining from his chest and throat. The glass panel was shattered, fragments glittering on the floor. The burst of gunfire had come from the other side of the front steps, out of view of Malder's window.

Malder knelt by the body. Burry's eyes were glazed with surprise, his hat askew, still on his head.

Malder now heard the sudden opening of the door across the

hall. He caught a glimpse of Krone in his trousers, some clothes in his arms, fleeing the room. Krone disappeared out the back way.

Malder heard the sound of a siren coming closer.

Presently a policeman thrust his hand inside the broken panel and turned the lock.

It was 2312 when Smithy had left the flat. It was still raining but not enough to matter.

He passed the brownstone twice but Burry was not visible from outside. That was the pattern from time to time and Smithy had allowed for that.

Somewhat later his opportunity came. Circling a third time, coming from the opposite direction, he saw Burry's outline against the glass panel door. He emptied his P–38 at the figure. One or two shots would have been enough but the random fusillade, he had reckoned, would better serve his purpose later.

He walked quickly a short distance to the near corner and down to the next street. Three blocks further he rid himself of the gun down a sewer. The gun was clean, he knew; it could not be traced.

Later he took a cab to midtown where he got out and began walking the rest of the way to the Edison Hotel where he had a room. On the way he discarded his hat which, like all his clothes, bore no label.

Everything so far was on target. His plans, he knew, had margin but not much. If he erred, the game would be over for him at once; but it was a game on such a superb scale that it stimulated him.

As he walked on the avenue amid the stream of people there was little that would distinguish him to the casual eye. He had an almost anonymous look except for the slight beak-like cut of his nose and the cold, carbolic wash of his eyes.

Smithy was thinking of Cathy. He'd not have much time to settle matters with her, a few days at most. Time was tight now with little slack.

* * *

Dempsey was a half mile away when he heard the call. Swerving, he sped toward Sixteenth.

When he got to the brownstone Malder was standing by. Two uniformed men were already there. One of them, a rookie, was kneeling by the body, unable to keep his eyes from it. It was probably the first time he'd seen a dead man. A man was dead but there was only curiosity. What you knew alive had little meaning dead.

The other cop, more seasoned, came toward Dempsey. "Say, do you know who this is?"

Dempsey nodded. He didn't seem to look around much but he had the whole scene fixed in his mind.

Burry, the poor bastard. Dead. Probably dead before he dropped. A spray of bullets, a butcher's job.

Dempsey nodded to Malder and they went inside Malder's room, shutting the door.

Dempsey said abruptly, "Tell me about it."

Malder, still excited, told what he remembered.

Dempsey asked, "Where's Krone?"

"Ran like hell—out the back way."

Dempsey had an image of Krone running. Krone, a chubby man with a deceptive quality in his face: the cheeks soft but the eyes raspy, like meanness encased in flab. Always had a big roll of bills, Krone. You didn't see his kind around much anymore with their big rolls for peeling and touching and fast cash deals that were kept in the head.

Dempsey asked, "Anything else?"

"I don't know," said Malder. "It may be something. I saw someone walking by—twice."

"Twice?"

"I think it was the same man. Couldn't be sure."

"What else?"

"Couldn't tell what he looked like. Had a hat on."

"That's a start. Man with a hat. What else?"

"About medium build, I'd say."

"Keep going."

"That's all I know."

"Overcoat? Raincoat?"

"Overcoat."

"How much you guess he weighed?"

"Maybe one-thirty—forty."

"Age?"

"How would I know?"

"Guess."

"Maybe thirty."

"How do you know?"

"You asked me to guess."

"But how do you know?"

"From the way he walked, I suppose."

"Which way was he going?"

"That way," Malder gestured.

"What was the interval?"

"Interval?"

"You say you saw him twice."

"Oh. Five minutes maybe."

"Enough for once around the block," Dempsey commented. "What kind of hat?"

"The usual kind."

"Mustache?"

"Couldn't tell."

"What do you think?"

"No mustache."

Dempsey nodded.

"We'll talk some more later," he said. "Finish your beer."

"Beer was his," said Malder, nodding toward the hall where Burry lay dead.

On his way out Dempsey saw Burry once more, ripped across the neck and chest. Who would have wanted to butcher a cipher like Burry? Hardly a case of mistaken identity. You had to be blind to mistake Burry for Krone.

Burry, the dumb bastard, dead. It wasn't right; it seldom was. Only once in a while could you balance things out.

He was remembering now. Muller.

Muller, psychopath, extortionist.

One day a casual arrest turned sour, with Muller pumping two bullets into him. Afterward, two operations; and pain—the kind you'd always remember. And later, a search from place to place without letup. Finally, in a hotel room, he caught up with Muller.

In the early hours of that morning they carried Muller away dead. He had given Muller the draw, and Muller had been crazy enough to take it. It had been close, very close. In its way it was a rough justice; but you had to give away the draw to get it. You had to put yourself on the line to balance it out for yourself.

There had been no witnesses, of course, and a bad taste of doubt remained. The newspapers caught up with it, and before it was over, he was subjected to the probings of an outraged press; one cartoonist seeing fit to grieve publicly over Muller's torn body. In the end, though, despite the outcry, the inquiry cleared him.

In time Muller was buried and given into the grace of God with a few cadenced words of mercy and of sparrows and of abiding faith. With a few amens, Muller was lowered into sanctified ground, while outside the sanctuary the stench of the garbage—the Mullers and the Scapas—kept rising to the heavens.

Technically, he had been judged innocent; yet he knew, as did others, that he was guilty as charged. But it was, nevertheless, an outrage that had to wait its turn. In time, of course, it would all be balanced out; for it was in the nature of heaven to balance things out.

And in time, like Muller, he too would have a decent burial

together with words of grace, while outside, the garbage kept piling up, the stench of it rising with a symmetry of balance—garbage for garbage, stench for stench, until the heavens reeked of it.

In the end, to be sure, would come the reckoning. It existed for him somewhere, at an unknown time and place where an uncertain road cuts short; and he knew it with a knowing that was in the very marrow of his being.

In his room in a garret of the palace, the dwarf lay down on his bed without undressing. He felt tired and wretched, and he took some herbs to help him pass the night. Near his head the guttering light of a candle gave off a scent of hallucinatory incense. The dwarf wanted to sleep, to sleep forever, but there would be little sleep for him, he knew. Tonight, as every night, he had to witness the cruelties and savagery he had seen in his years. At night, every night, he was compelled to recall these horrors until his soul was drenched and warped. The memories soaked in him and seeped from his pores like the sweat of sickness. And it was always thus, night after night, year on year, century upon century, unendingly without remission.

And yet, as he waited tonight for his ordeal to begin, a faint hope existed.

Of late he had had visions. In the flickering light of the candle he had seen the image of an unknown face. The shape was hazy but he could discern a rough, powerful face. Several times too he had heard a voice speaking to him in an old tongue. The words were unmistakable—salvation was near! A stranger with a rough face was to come and lift from him his curse of everlasting life. Someone unknown was to take his place.

Despite what he saw and heard, the dwarf did not believe in his visions. He was a rational being, was he not? It was truly beyond reason to believe that he was a dwarf centuries old, bearing a curse. It was an illusion indeed. He might be mad, he told himself, but he wasn't *mad*—not *mad* mad. And yet, rational or not, his hope persisted, and he hung on to it; for it was this tenuous hope that helped him face the horrors of night which had now begun to envelop him again.

Early in the morning Krone got a call from Sorge to arrange a meeting. Krone had no other means of seeing Sorge except this way, unexpectedly at the whim of a call. Sorge had an answering service but the listing, Krone had found out, led only to a blind address.

Krone met Sorge at a café in Long Island City. As always Krone had to come alone. This time he took the precaution of carrying a .22 in his coat pocket.

At a back table Krone put his coat across his lap; underneath the coat the .22 was aimed at Sorge's groin. Krone, settling his pudgy body, ordered eggs and toast with black coffee. Sorge had only water—"without ice," he insisted to the waitress. When the water came he wiped the lip of the glass with a napkin before he sipped.

"It's unfortunate what happened," Sorge began in a tone that was, as usual, dry and critical. Sorge was imperturbable; he never sweated. Even in summer he never sweated.

Krone felt his way. "What's unfortunate?"

"Your man, Burry."

"It has nothing to do with me," said Krone with a gesture, as if to push the matter away.

"It smells bad," Sorge commented.

Krone resented Sorge's intrusion into his affairs.

"My people are disturbed," Sorge said.

"It hasn't touched me," Krone insisted.

Sorge sat back. He seemed young, too young—Krone thought—for the authority he carried.

Sorge said, "There's a leak in your organization."

"There's no leak. I tell you, there's no leak."

"Yet someone," Sorge pointed out, "*someone* diverted one of your shipments into rebel hands."

"It was *my* cargo. *I* took the loss, not your people."

"It happens that a company of our men was chewed up by sixty-millimeter mortars—yours, Krone."

"I'm not responsible for the blunders of your commanders," Krone argued. "Our security here is tight. I've examined every possibility."

"And your conclusions?"

"It has to be the captain."

"That's not possible," Sorge said. "The captain, I'm told, is dead. Who is left? You? Me? Is it *me?*"

"Of course not," Krone said quickly.

"But you did cable Dufar, accusing me, did you not?"

Krone flushed. "I felt it my duty—"

"Of course."

Krone shifted uneasily.

Sorge said, "If it's not you, if it's not me, then who? Someone in your organization? *Who?*"

"There's no leak here," Krone insisted once more.

"Very well," said Sorge, "but until the leak is found you are to hold back all shipments. Nothing is to move. Nothing."

Krone reacted. "But I have a shipment in preparation. Explosives. You yourself gave the order."

"Nothing moves."

"I have money tied up in that shipment."

"That doesn't concern me."

Sorge was inflexible. When he took a position you couldn't sway him. And he couldn't be bought either, Krone knew.

"Tell me," said Sorge, "if I were to cancel your shipments for good, how much would you stand to lose?"

Krone did not respond; he was sweating.

"How much?" asked Sorge. "Enough to make a pig like you sweat?"

"You've no right—"

"There's only one right. Someone betrayed a trust. That account must be settled. If not, I must break off all contact. There'll be no going back for you."

"You don't have that right."

"I'll give you two days to find the leak."

"I'll go over your head," Krone threatened.

"I'm under instructions from Barras," Sorge said.

"What does that mean?"

"It means what I want it to mean. And one more thing. Next time you point a gun at me kill me. You won't have a second chance."

Krone averted his eyes, somewhat unnerved.

Krone knew there was no getting around Sorge. For the time being Sorge held all the power in his hands.

Presently, without a word more, Sorge left the café. Krone remained behind, in a sweat.

Smithy took the subway back to Manhattan and became part of a crowd, merging into its anonymity, leaving behind his identity as Sorge.

The meeting had gone well, he thought. Krone was in a fester, fearful of his losses should the shipments be terminated. It was a fear, Smithy knew, that would work in his favor. It wouldn't be long, he reckoned, before Burry's death, that indiscriminate killing, would have its effect. The bait was set.

At 0924 Smithy was back at his hotel.

Dempsey had gone over every corner of the apartment. The technicians had been through it earlier. The rooms were immaculate, not a stray scrap, not a print around, hardly a trace that anyone had lived here.

He paused by the window that had a direct view of the brownstone. Behind him was Turner, his young partner. Over his shoulder, Dempsey said, "You came up with a good one."

Turner glowed; it was the first time Dempsey had complimented him.

Turner said, "No one was in here, so I saw the manager, and he got the keys."

Dempsey kept looking at the brownstone across the street where Burry had been cut down last night.

He was saying, "We don't know much about our man except his name was Jones. Sam Jones. Could be any name. Caucasian, average-looking. Stayed here five weeks. Apparently moved out last night. No prints. Obviously a professional." Dempsey's tone was flat, reciting the meager facts, as if to the window.

There wasn't much of a description to go on. The manager's memory of his tenant was unclear. He had seen the killer only once, five weeks ago, when he had taken the apartment. His recollection of the killer was that he was an ordinary-looking man. Dempsey had prodded the manager several times but all he could get from him was that the killer was, well, *average.* Dempsey got even less from the tenants. None of them, not one, could recollect even seeing the killer.

The setup, as Dempsey noted, had the earmarks of a professional killer, a careful man, probably around thirty, not too fat, not too thin, not too much of anything except average—a man, obviously, who had the patience to sweat out five weeks to make a kill.

Dempsey stood at the window. The killer, he thought, must have stood here at this same window, observing the brownstone, patiently waiting his time—for what? A hack like Burry? It didn't make sense.

Turner was asking, "Get much out of Krone last night?"

Dempsey shook his head. "Nothing," he said. He had been to Krone's house, had questioned him, but had gotten nothing out of him—you could have predicted that.

Dempsey came away from the window.

"What's Krone mixed up in?" Turner asked.

"Imports, exports"—a flat tone.

"Exports?"

"War surplus—contraband," he said, leaving it at that.

Later, as they left the flat, Dempsey glanced at Turner. "You asked to be assigned to me. Why?"

"I'd heard about you."

"I've lost three partners, you know."

"I know."

Dempsey was walking quickly to the car.

"They say I'm bad luck."

"I've heard."

"I take risks," he said.

"I know."

"My risks become yours," said Dempsey. "You know that."

"My father was a cop," Turner said by way of explanation.

"Retired?"

"No, dead. Killed in action."

Dempsey nodded; he understood.

As they came near the car Turner said, "I won't disappoint you."

"You'll work out," said Dempsey, getting into the car behind the wheel. He always drove; he had to be at the wheel.

They drove north. Dempsey said, "I'll drop you off midtown. Stay with Krone. You know what I want."

When he dropped off Turner he saw the eagerness in the kid's eyes but he wondered later how the kid would react in a crunch.

Later he called Cathy; there was no answer. Then he drove to her apartment.

The manager had watched from his window as Dempsey and Turner left for their car. He was nervous, scared. He had given them skimpy information. He didn't want trouble, not from the killer. If he kept his mouth shut he'd be all right, he told himself.

THE DESCENT

* * *

On his way to headquarters Dempsey had an impulse to see Maggie at the hospital. Before he got there he stopped off at a flower shop. The place was busy and he had to wait. He felt a rising impatience, so that finally, when the florist was wrapping some chrysanthemums, Dempsey felt he had to leave the shop. He was half a block from the hospital and he hurried there as if seconds counted.

In the lobby he had to wait for an elevator; his impatience now was almost an anxiety. A crowd was gathering at the bank of elevators, which were backed up. He waited a few moments more, then decided to take the stairs. In the stairwell he ran up the steps; and when he got to Maggie's floor he moved quickly to her room.

Her door was shut—he opened it. The room, he saw, was empty; and he knew. He *knew* what he had already known.

Just then the nurse came in. He had seen her before; she was a thin woman; her face was tight.

"When did it happen?" he asked.

"About an hour ago."

He had an image in his mind now. Maggie, holding her Snoopy. Maggie, rising suddenly and falling back with a startled, hurt expression.

The room now seemed unnaturally quiet. The bed had already been stripped and remade. There was still a small bag on the night table. In it were Maggie's things, the few remnants of her life.

The nurse said, "Is there anything—?"

"No," he said. "No."

"If you wish to make some calls—"

"Thank you," he said, and the nurse left him to his own privacy.

He sat down on the bed now. He felt numb, unable to move, not wanting to. He was thinking of Maggie. Maggie, a statistic now.

He thought about it. Wherever he touched, there was hurt. You could grovel and eat dust; you could cry out in anger but there was no ear to hear, no remission.

Later he began to rummage through Maggie's things on the bedside table. Inside the bag was a comb, a pocketbook with some lipstick and mascara, an address book, bubblegum, a handkerchief; the small, unimportant fragments of a life cut short. And there was Snoopy, that fabric with long ears and wondering eyes, years old and somewhat shabby with wear. Around its neck was a colored kerchief. On its feet were worn black baby socks to keep it warm — "Now you can sleep nice and warm, Snoopy," he could imagine Maggie saying. He could hear her talking to Snoopy, in a kind of baby talk, and hugging it. Christ, she was just a kid, he thought, and he was crying now. He couldn't help it, he was crying.

Finally he rose and took Snoopy with him, putting the dog under his jacket.

Downstairs, in the street again, as he began to walk to his car, he took in deep breaths of cold air. His head cleared and he was together, on duty once more.

In his car he lay Snoopy down on the front seat, but that didn't seem right, so he sat Snoopy up facing the windshield. As he began to drive he said to Snoopy, "It'll be all right," and he caught himself. Damn it, he was talking to a dog, a stuffed dog, except it wasn't a dog, it was Snoopy, and it had been Maggie's and it wasn't going to end up as junk in a garbage can.

Earlier, Dempsey had gotten a call, more an order than a request, to report to Martin at headquarters.

Martin made him wait, and when he finally got to see Martin in his office he could detect little warmth in the inspector's eyes. Martin was a chunky man with a round head and cropped gray hair. His desk was piled with departmental paper.

The Scapa complaint, Dempsey saw, was on top of Martin's desk. Dempsey had already heard about it. Scapa had hesitated, had delayed, but had finally filed a complaint; and now a necessary piece of departmental business would have to take place.

"You're late," said Martin in a raspy voice; it was the kind of rasp heavy drinkers had, except Martin didn't drink. "Sit down," he said brusquely.

Dempsey remained standing.

Martin gestured toward the complaint. "It's coming to a boil," he commented.

"Scapa?"

"That's right. He's finally filed a complaint."

Dempsey did not respond.

"His lawyer's on us—the whole damn family," Martin said. "Even his brother was down here just an hour ago—"

"His brother—the judge?"

"Yes, the judge, goddammit."

Martin was looking down, leafing through the complaint. His cheeks were loose and puffy.

"There was severe damage—" he glanced down at the page.

"I know. I heard about it."

"—severe damage under the fifth left lumbar—"

"He was resisting arrest."

"That's not what the complaint says, and that's not *all* the damage."

"You have my report," said Dempsey.

"Yes, it's all quite factual except—"

"Except what?"

"You went up alone against a potentially armed man. Why?"

"I made that decision," said Dempsey.

"In Scapa's room you left yourself open, *why?*"

"He wasn't armed."

"You put your gun back in your holster, *why?*"

"I had him under control."

"With your fists, you mean." Martin paused. "Trouble is, with fists like yours—"

"He was coming at me—"

"—with fists like yours you could kill a man, you know that."

Dempsey shrugged. "I did what I had to do."

"I know, and maybe I would have done the same in my time, but it raises questions, Dempsey. Your name keeps coming up."

"Scapa's garbage."

"He was a suspect, period," said Martin in a hard way.

"Yes, I know what the book says."

Martin wasn't finished yet. "Tell me," he asked, "what was between you and the girl?"

"Nothing. I just knew her, that's all."

Martin looked at him for a time, eye-to-eye. "Okay," he said, "I believe you. Anything else?"

"You have my report."

Martin was turning pages again. "One more thing," he said, stopping at a page. "Scapa says you told him the girl was badly hurt, *very* badly hurt."

"I told him that, yes."

"So that's what got to Scapa," said Martin, mulling it over. "But from what I heard she was coming along just fine—"

"For Chrissake, he's an animal, Scapa."

"It makes no difference, and you know it."

"She was just a kid."

"She'd been around, you know."

"He tore her apart; he kicked her down the stairs—she was a kid, damn it."

"What are you telling me?"

"I just came from the hospital."

"Is that why you were late?"

"She's dead, Martin. Dead." Dempsey's voice was beginning to crack.

"What?"

"The kid, she's dead."

"When?"

"About the time the judge was here."

"Don't dump that on me," Martin reacted.

"You know what she left behind? A comb, some lipstick, some bubblegum. Christ, bubblegum!"

"That's not the point. Damn it, you know it. Your name keeps coming up. Questions keep being asked."

"If you can't answer the questions, ask for my badge. You can have it but you have to ask for it."

Martin shook his head. "It won't be me," he said. "It may come to that but it won't be me."

"Is that all?"

"I'm not your enemy, you know that."

"I know," said Dempsey, remembering the inquiry into the Muller matter, with Martin standing up for him.

Martin said, "Just be prepared for a lot of questions." He paused, then asked, "Did you see the kid's family?"

"Her family's dead. She left no family, except . . ."

"Except what?"

"A dog—a goddam stuffed dog."

Dempsey parked his car in a yellow zone in the middle of the block not far from Catherine's place. An earlier rain had stopped and the street glistened with reflected lights. Next to her building was a construction site with its muted boarding and posters.

Dempsey focused on the corner window of Catherine's apartment on the fifth floor. A filter of light came through the slats and curtain. She was probably home, he thought. Maybe. Maybe not.

"What do you think, Snoop?"

Snoopy, sitting up, was busy with his own thoughts.

"Cold, Snoop?"

Dempsey put on the heater and waited, listening to calls; he was not impatient but he wasn't at ease either.

Somewhat later he saw the light in the window go out. His expectations rose, and time now became sharp and focused.

He began to time her progress. She was locking the door now. She was going to the elevator; she was waiting for it. He timed its arrival. She got in; she was coming down. There was a stop on the third floor; it was a hunch. Descending again; now getting out with a couple from the third floor. She was walking to the entrance, glancing at herself in the hallway mirror; the man was opening the door.

At that moment he saw her coming out into the street. She had come out alone.

He was ruffled that he had guessed wrong about the third floor stop. She had, in fact, come out exactly as he had timed her, but his exactitude had been based on a miscalculation.

Just then he saw a couple emerge from the doorway. When he saw the couple he nudged Snoopy and said, "Right on the nose. Not bad."

The Snoop was staring ahead. The Snoop was hard to impress.

Dempsey observed Catherine hesitate, looking in one direction, then another. She wore a cloth coat and a raised fur hat of Russian style. She began to walk now, away from him down the street.

He started his car and began to follow her slowly, staying behind her.

He saw her cross midstreet; she did not look in his direction. He accelerated somewhat, and near the end of the street came ahead of her, turning right and stopping at the corner. As she came nearer he saw her recognize him. He reached to open the door, wondering what to say to her but that became unnecessary. When she came to the open door she got in without a word said, as if she'd been expecting him. She brought the door inward, not closing it but letting him shut it.

He began to drive off.

He glanced at her; she had an angry look.

"Have you been following me?" she said.

"I was nearby," he said defensively.

"How long have you been watching me?"

"I called earlier," he told her. "You weren't in."

"Or not answering."

"Which was it?"

"Both," she replied with a bit of testiness. He let it pass.

He turned and drove north on the East River Drive along the river, past the Queensboro bridge which was lit up and heavy with traffic.

In a while he glanced at Catherine; she was easing up. He heard her say, "Who's your friend?"

"He's an orphan," he said.

"Does he always drive with you?" Then suddenly, *"Must* we listen to those calls?" The anger was still not gone.

"What would you like?" he asked.

"Anything. Anything else."

He turned to some music.

She was still frowning.

"Do you have a headache?"

She shrugged.

"I'm just tired," she said, "and I hate being followed."

"I wanted to see you," he said. "You weren't in. Or in, and not answering. Or both." He smiled. "I'm sorry."

"You're not. You're only sorry I'm annoyed."

"I wanted to talk to you."

"Then tell me about your friend," she said, putting an affectionate hand on the Snoop's head; and he knew it was all right now, at least for the moment.

Momentarily he looked at her delicate face, the hat at a slight angle, everything just so. Christ, she was beautiful.

"His name's Snoopy," he told her.

"God, everybody knows that," she said with a soft smile. "How did you get him?"

"He belonged to a girl I knew," and that was all he said.

"You going to leave it at that?"

"She was just a friend."

"*Just* a friend?"

"She died this morning at the hospital."

"A police matter?"

He nodded.

"And she gave Snoopy to you?"

"No, he was left behind, so I picked him up," he began to explain to her.

"Did she mean much to you?"

"She was just a kid, hardly twenty; had freckles on her nose," he said, remembering the empty bed. "They had already taken her away, and I was sitting on her bed and . . ."

"And what?"

"It doesn't matter."

"Except that you came to see me."

"I came to see you, yes."

"To talk—about her?"

"About us."

"It's the same thing now, you know."

He began to tell her, "I was sitting there, thinking of her and I . . ."

"You what?"

He shrugged.

"You cried?"

He glanced at her with surprise.

"Are you ashamed to say it?" she said.

"I hardly knew her."

"Then why did you cry?"

"I don't know. Maybe because she had no one, no family, only that dog. She was just a kid and I couldn't help her."

"She was dead. What could you do?"

He shrugged.

"She remind you of someone?" she asked.

"What?"

"When was the last time you cried?"

He didn't respond. He kept driving, accelerating, the wheel encased in his hand. He was thinking, remembering his mother.

He remembered her as she was on that last day, kneeling against the bed in a praying position, her body hacked and bleeding; he remembered the helplessness he had felt. He had been unable to help her, unable even to go to her, to touch her. It was a moment frozen in time. It was later that his tears came; and with it, anger —an anger that wanted to strike back against the mindless outrage.

"Slow down," he heard her say gently. She had put her hand on his arm. "Slow down," she said, and he knew it was not his speed that she meant.

"I'm sorry," he said.

At a slower speed he turned onto the Expressway and came south on the Henry Hudson Parkway. There was a barge on the river. In the distance, lights from the rising apartments on the west shore reflected on the river like a watery city.

Later he heard her say, "He's good company, isn't he?"

"Snoopy?"

"Do you talk to him much?"

He glanced at her.

She smiled. "You do talk to him, don't you?"

He nodded, almost smiling.

He said to her suddenly, "I missed you. I thought of you all day. I had to see you."

"Had to?"

"I couldn't let the day go by without seeing you."

"Do you know what you're telling me?"

"I kept remembering the words we said, and the touch of you, the smell of you—"

She smiled. "Do you know what you're saying?"

"What am I saying?"

"That you're in love."

He glanced at her with a suddenness.

"I've never been in love," he said.

"Yes, I know. I can tell."

They were silent then, and he was waiting for her response.

"It doesn't last," he heard her say.

He waited.

"The magic goes," she said. "It doesn't last." And her words were like a remembrance, a lingering sadness.

He kept driving, waiting for the words he wanted to hear from her, but the words never came. At the moment he would have settled for a lie, but she didn't give him even that.

Later they went to a café near Bleecker Street. He had steak, plain; she had clams and linguini. She drank white wine poured from a carafe, and she was having too much.

Over espresso she said, "One day you'll wake up and you'll wonder what you ever saw in me."

"That day won't come," he said to her.

"You'll see," she said as she lit a cigarette, inhaling deeply, and studying him.

"You know," she remarked, "you're a lot like Smithy," speaking of him as someone they both knew.

He let her talk, not intruding.

"You're good at what you do, probably very good. But you're all work. I imagine you begrudge the time it takes to eat; it's time out of your day. And if I had to guess, you make do with five or six hours sleep a night."

"Five," he conceded. In truth it was four, sometimes less.

"Smithy does with four," she said, exhaling now, the smoke from her cigarette like thoughts evaporating.

She was saying, "I imagine without your work you'd feel empty."

"I never think of it that way."

"I imagine not," she said. "You'd never admit to any weakness, would you?"

"What else do you know about me?"

"You're a loner; you're all inside."

She was saying it to him but it was Smithy who was on her mind. He understood; it was Smithy she was talking about.

She kept drinking the white wine, and it was showing in her eyes.

"Tell me about the magic," he asked. "When was it?"

"During the war," she said, her eyes looking back in time. "Smithy was on leave, and when I first saw him he was like a god, wearing his uniform, his boots all shiny, looking invincible. You knew, you just knew, he could walk into the fires of hell and come out whole," she said with remembered pride.

He stored that away. Smithy, veteran, about thirty, a loner. Occupation: unspecified.

She was saying, "I was young, and being with him then was magic, pure, crazy magic."

He felt a ripple of envy; it was a feeling he'd never had before.

She sipped more wine.

She said, "And then it was over, the magic gone; and when it goes, nothing is the same again, you know. Things you once liked, or overlooked, become hateful. Smithy doesn't understand that. Doesn't want to, I suppose. I remember once in Mobile—" She stopped.

Mobile. Another piece of information.

"You caught that, didn't you?" she said. "It all goes into that file in your head, doesn't it?"

She mashed her cigarette.

She said, "I'll try to be more careful with you."

"Do you need to?"

"You'd make trouble, I know."

"Then why are you telling me about Smithy?"

"I don't want you to get used to me," she said. "One day I'll be gone."

"That's up to you."

"He wants me back, you know."

"You told me that."

"I don't want to go back," she said.

"But you will, won't you?"

"I can't say no to him. I never could."

"You can if you want to."

She shook her head. "It's easy for you, but for me, I haven't the strength for it. I never had. Maybe I never will."

He saw a fragile look in her eyes.

He reached over to touch her. Her hand was cold. Gradually, almost imperceptibly, she began to withdraw her hand from his.

"It's time to go," she said.

Abruptly then it was over, and she was alone in herself once more. Alone, she couldn't say no to Smithy. But perhaps it wasn't that simple either, he thought. Perhaps, at the core of her, she didn't truly want to say no to Smithy.

Dempsey was with her now but her mind was on Smithy, he knew. It was Smithy who was with her in the deepest recesses of her mind.

Dempsey rose and he had the feeling that the night would end badly.

Later, as she was opening the door to her apartment, she said to him, "Why don't you come in? It's still early."

He hadn't been certain she'd ask him in, and for his part he hadn't intended to press her. She had had too much to drink and was tired. He didn't expect much. Perhaps all she wanted was to talk; she had a need to talk, he knew.

He came in with her. He watched her take off her coat and hat and put on the record player.

"Have a drink," she said to him. "I'll be right out."

She went to the bathroom and he took off his coat. He moved about the room, taking in details. On the bureau was some unopened mail, a bracelet, an empty goblet. A table with no setting; two chairs, a couch, a few prints: Dufy, a Miró and a lithograph of a white unicorn. He was listening to the sounds of jazz.

When Catherine later came back into the room he saw she had put on a robe and was holding a glass of scotch and water.

"You've had too much," he said to her.

"It's never too much," she said, meaning what she meant, whatever it was, probably just something to say.

She sat down on the couch, folding her legs, and lifted her glass toward him.

"Here's to another noday," she said.

"A noday?"

"It's a day," she said, "a day of nothing happening, a day of just waiting." Her eyes had a haze of drink in them.

"What is it you're waiting for?"

She shrugged; she said, "Another play, I suppose. Another part. It's all I really know how to do, or want. It always seems so close, a breakthrough, sometimes so close I can almost taste it. But it's always another day, another month, and the years go by."

There was a sadness in her voice, and he wanted to go to her, to hold her, but it didn't seem right at the moment. She merely wanted to talk and not be alone.

She was saying, "Even as a kid I had dreams of the stage."

"What were you like as a kid?" he asked in a questioning mode that was a habit of his work.

"How was I? Oh, God. Ugly, skinny, awful!" she emphasized,

making a face. Even her grimace, like everything she did, had its charm. She would move her hand, or gesture, or hold a glass as now, and it all became graceful in the doing and being.

She was saying, "I used to read plays in my room. It was all that preserved me. I never had a room of my own, you know. I always lived with strangers, always in foster homes, always wearing hand-me-downs."

"Where were you born? Kansas? Iowa?"

She was surprised.

"It's still in your voice," he told her.

"I thought I'd gotten rid of *that.*"

"Kansas?"

"Close enough," she said.

"You just changed your pitch," he told her.

"You *are* observant."

"It's what I do."

"It's part of your job, I suppose."

She was studying him, sipping now, and suddenly smiling, saying, "Am I a suspect?"

"Yes."

"What do you suspect me of?" she asked with playful anticipation.

"Of being sad," he said. "Of drinking too much, of being afraid and . . ."

"And what?"

"Of being beautiful."

"And what else?" she was coaxing. "Tell me only the nice—" She stopped suddenly, and he saw her looking past him.

"What's wrong?"

"The goblet—it's been moved!"

He turned to the bureau.

"Did you move it?" she asked him.

"No, why?"

"When I left here earlier it was at the other end of the bureau."

"Are you sure?"

She rose and came closer to the bureau.

"It's been moved," she said, her voice rising. "It has to be Smithy. He's been here. He moved it. While we were out he moved it."

"The door was locked," he said. He remembered, she had used the key when she came in.

"That wouldn't matter," she said. "Not to *him*." Her hand was tightening. "He must have followed us here when we moved my things. He must have seen us meet tonight."

"Why would he move the goblet?"

"He wants me to know he's around. It's the way he is. He's letting me know he knows about *us.*"

"Has he done it before?"

"He knows how I hate being followed."

Dempsey was moving now to the side of the window, and as she spoke he was observing through the slats, down into the street below; it was beginning to rain. He saw no one in the street. He scanned the doorways across the way. He could discern nothing, no movement.

He heard her say, "He's down there, isn't he?"

"It's hard to tell."

"He's there, I know."

She was approaching the window.

He came to her, saying, "Forget it. There's no one there."

"You think I had too much to drink, don't you?"

"I'm saying there's no one there," he told her. "Forget it. Forget Smithy."

"He's there, isn't he?" she said, and he could see she was distraught. He came nearer and reached out to hold her, to soothe her. She came to him, into his arms, and he could feel her hold on to him fiercely. She was like a child now, wanting to be held.

"Hold me," she said, her voice reaching out to him.

He was embracing her, and as he held her he saw her looking toward the window. Suddenly, out of the child's eyes came a woman's look. Her hands tightened into him, and he felt her body stirring against his—the woman in her feeling and wanting. He could feel her intensity and his own merging; and he wanted her, her breath and body; he wanted the warm feel of her—but suddenly she broke off from him. "Please, no. *Please.*"

She saw the look in his eyes.

"I'm sorry," she said, calming herself.

"What's wrong?"

"I don't know what happened. I didn't mean to—I guess I had too much to drink."

"Is that how *Smithy* makes you feel?"

"Please, don't—"

"Is this how it ends?"

"Please don't go away angry."

He began to get his coat.

"I'm sorry," she said.

"You said that before."

"Yes, we keep saying it."

He was putting on his coat.

She wanted to say something but didn't know how.

He was at the door now.

She came toward him, reaching out her hand.

He was opening the door.

"Robert. Robert—"

But he was already on his way out, and he didn't look back.

After he left Catherine he drove around the city for a time, in and out of streets, watching the night people, letting his feelings drain off. When he got back to his place he put the Snoop to bed, took off his holster, and for a time stood in the darkness by his window, observing the night murmurs of a city asleep. He was unsettled about Catherine; he had reacted to her badly; and for a time he wanted to call her, to tell her—

Just then the phone rang; he picked it up quickly.

It was Catherine.

"I've been calling you—" she was saying.

"I just got in."

"Did you put Snoopy to bed?"

He smiled. "Yes, he's asleep. In a drawer."

"You didn't shut it, did you?"

"No, it's open," he assured her.

"It's cold, you know."

"I covered him."

"Did you say goodnight to him?"

"Yes, I said goodnight." He had to smile. He was feeling at ease now. Time without her was dead time—Christ, he loved her!

"I had to call you," she was saying.

"I'm sorry about tonight," he said to her.

"I've been lying here in bed, thinking of you, missing you."

He could hear the slur in her voice and its tiredness.

"I don't know what happened tonight," she was saying. "I wanted you so badly. It's been such a long time since I've felt that way. I was afraid."

"Afraid of what?"

"I don't know," she said. "I don't know."

She was silent for a time, then:

"Robert."

"Yes?"

"I just wanted to hear your voice." She was fading.

There was silence.

"Robert."

"Yes?"

Suddenly the phone fell dead and she was asleep, he knew.

71

He began to imagine he was with her, sitting by her. She was in bed, uncovered, and he drew the blanket up to cover her nakedness, and he kissed her quietly in his thoughts.

Later, in the quiet of his room, he kept thinking of her; and he wondered if later she would remember what she had said to him. She had been drunk and drowsy with tiredness. Had she meant what she said, or had she been playing out some role with him that had its meaning in Smithy?

Smithy. The name began to gnaw at him.

Jitney drivers from Port-au-Grasse would point with a wink to the Villa of Pleasure, which was situated high on the cleavage of a lush, soft hill.

The villa, it was noted, was run by Mama Sere, who wore rings of precious stones on each finger, save one. That one naked finger, some said, was Mama Sere's gesture to the austerity edicts of the dictator Barras.

Some malicious tongues had it that Mama Sere's late husband, the baron, who had disappeared some years ago, had run off with a dancer from Sadler's Wells. More knowing opinion had it that the baron's bones had become part of the newly paved road that ran from Sans Souci.

Other opinion held that an unrecognizable corpse that had been found floating offshore had been the baron himself, albeit in altered form. In the dwarf's judgment the story simply did not hold up. As everyone knew, the dwarf maintained, the baron could not swim a stroke, let alone float!

Whatever the stories, there was common agreement that Mama Sere's villa had the most voluptuous girls in Caribe.

The pink and white villa, cooled by the sea, was a world apart from the squalor and swelter of Port-au-Grasse. The villa, as jitney drivers would point out, was a pleasure dome for the rich and powerful.

By custom, the villa was closed to the public on Thursday nights. On that night Barras and a few intimates had the place to themselves. For Barras it was a night to drink, play cards and whore to exhaustion. Since Barras worked hard seven days a week, often eighteen hours a day, in the service of his people, few begrudged him his night off, least of all his wife, who had his respect, if not his attention.

Undoubtedly Mama Sere herself was the most incredible sight in the villa. Of mixed breed and almost white, Mama Sere was singularly fat—not merely fat but *fat!* Estimates on the kind side put her weight at over 150 kilos. In the dwarf's reckoning, however, these estimates would hardly account for the weight of her stomach alone.

The dwarf, always in attendance wherever Barras was, also spent his Thursday nights at the villa. From time to time he would chat with Mama Sere, usually in her room where she lay in bed with her dachshund, Wilhelm, by her side. Her immensity was such that the dwarf often feared she would roll over forgetfully and squash the poor beast like a grape.

Now and then with a wink Mama Sere would tease the dwarf, inviting him to her bed. The dwarf, though, was wary of her; he had heard frightening tales. It was said she had a thatch that scowled, actually scowled. A thatch so formidable that she could swallow you whole, suck you right up, shoes and all—*poof!*

The participants in the card games that took place each Thursday night would vary according to invitation. Tonight Barras had with him only Dufar, the unsmiling chief of intelligence; Salant, minister of justice; and Latour, his *valet extraordinaire.*

As usual the card game was held in a gilt salon in the east wing of the villa. By early evening the dwarf was far ahead in his winnings. Dufar suspected him of using marked cards, which was true.

New cards were brought in and carefully inspected, yet the dwarf continued to win with annoying regularity.

Barras himself was in an expansive mood. He had had enough to eat and drink, and upstairs the exotic Ninon waited for him. But there was more to it than that, Latour knew. Barras and the others were waiting in anticipation of favorable news, expected shortly, of a mission that had recently been put into motion.

Within the hour Ligny arrived. No one had expected Ligny himself to come; in fact, Ligny had never once set foot in the villa. His arrival now, the dwarf could guess, had to mean that the expected news was bad; and indeed it was. The mission had failed, utterly and abysmally.

Ligny, commander of the *armée*, was a formidable man. His face was a coppery hue, his cropped hair streaked with gray. A specialist in tank warfare, Ligny was, by common consent, the only man who could stand up to Barras one to one.

Ligny's recent bitter quarrel with Barras had by now been patched over. In his absence one of Ligny's subordinate commanders had been summarily executed and later hung for display outside the Fortress. When Ligny heard of the barbaric act he hurried back and had it out with Barras. In the end Barras had to back off. He had to admit he had overstepped Ligny's authority; on the other hand he offered no apologies.

After the quarrel, which took place in Barras's study, the dwarf saw the two of them emerge arm in arm. In parting, he saw them embrace each other, comrade to comrade. Whatever else was between them they had one common purpose, one aim, the destiny of Caribe; and it had been that way since Valmy. That night at Valmy, the three of them—Barras, Ligny and Sorge—had struck back at the generals who had conspired against Barras. It was a time of terror and triumph against the high command under Fouché, one of the few who had escaped the awesome bloodletting of that night.

The report Ligny had brought to the villa was brief. It concerned the latest failure to assassinate Fouché. Earlier attempts had been made by M-5 under Dufar. By order of Barras, the latest plan had been under the command of Ligny, who had taken the assignment with reluctance. He was, Ligny told Barras, a soldier, not an assassin. Yet he did as he was ordered for the sake of the mission.

When Barras heard the report he stood up from the card table, sweeping away cards and chips with a tidal fury. Everyone present could understand his anger and frustration. For years, as they all knew, Fouché had been the bone in Barras's throat.

Fouché. Former commander of the army, former rival, now agitator, pamphleteer, the focal point of unrest against Barras. Fouché, an exile in Mexico City, still dreaming of a return to power and former *gloire*. Fouché, the mind and backbone of the insurrection against Barras.

It was, of course, a situation that had but one solution; yet that solution, in its execution, seemed impossible. In all, six attempts had been made on Fouché's life, each one failing to penetrate the guards and barriers surrounding Fouché in his fortified villa. It soon became apparent that in exile Fouché still had access to the inner secrets of Caribe, even to the highest councils; access that allowed him warning and time for countermeasures.

Ligny's report strongly suggested a leak in security. Fouché's men, it turned out, had been ready and waiting to intercept the lieutenant who had been assigned to the assassination.

Barras stood before the group. "How did it happen?" he cried out with rage. "How? *How?*"

Barras fixed each of them in turn, saying, "How did it happen? Only five of us knew. I knew. And *you*, Ligny. *You*, Dufar. *You*, Salant, and *you*, Latour!"

They all looked at each other uneasily until Dufar spoke out, saying, "There was someone else who knew."

"Who?" asked Salant, who had the juiceless face of a cadaver.

"We forget that Sorge was also privy to some of the arrangements."

76

"The plans were later changed," Barras asserted. "Every detail was altered."

"Nevertheless," Dufar insisted, "Sorge knew enough. Enough, I say, to betray us."

Barras remained silent but his eyes were alive with thoughts.

"No," said Barras with emphasis, "No, it cannot be Sorge. Anybody else, but not Sorge."

Barras began to walk off, out of the room, and Dufar knew that further discussion was useless. The matter of Sorge cut to the core of Barras's trust.

In the hallway Barras turned once to the others. Through the open door, in a voice that bellowed and reverberated throughout the villa, he cried out, "It's not Sorge. I tell you, it is *not* Sorge!"

He stood where he was, alone and defiant in his towering rage.

Later, in a corner alone, the dwarf kept thinking of what Ligny had reported. There had been a leak, obviously. As everyone knew, Port-au-Grasse was like a sieve. Not even Dufar, with all his instruments of terror, could stanch the leaks. At any point a secret could go astray. A clerk in a cipher room, a chance remark, a tapped phone. Perhaps even on higher levels. A disappointed cabinet minister, an embittered general, perhaps a ranking officer in M-5—who could say? Who knew all the wheels that turned within wheels?

The dwarf waited for Barras, who was now upstairs with Ninon, spilling out his rage. Ligny had left and the others had crept away. The dwarf was impatient for the night to end. He began to browse around, inspecting corners, keyholes, ratholes. Mama Sere's girls, of course, did not stir him; it was a lack of interest, he suspected, that was part of his abominable curse. On the other hand, what could one expect of a body centuries old? But that was not to say he was uninterested in women. He was indeed curious about them, and perplexed; at times he had had idyllic notions about them.

He remembered. Once, long ago, he had become enchanted

with Michelle, a girl from Dijon, with whom he had picked butter-cups during the Terror. In small ways she was kind to him. In turn, he wrote poetry for her, which he slipped under her door. These idyllic moments ended, however, when her brother, an idiot, bru-tally sodomized him, while Michelle sat in attendance, knitting and smiling an angelic smile. Latour was outraged by the affair. Mi-chelle, obviously, had misunderstood his poems.

Then there was Anna, mistress to Ivanov, the great swordsman, whom the dwarf had served as valet.

In his own way the dwarf worshipped Anna from afar. Latour played for her haunting melodies on a balalaika while she made love to Ivanov on a lumpy bed in the next room. There were many nights and many melodies, each more haunting than the last; and it all continued until one night Ivanov was set upon by six ruffians dis-patched by Anna's husband, a count of small renown. While Ivanov held off his attackers, cutting them down one by one, Anna took refuge under the bed. Lying on the floor and stimulated by the blood and ferocity of combat, she writhed with an ecstasy she had never before known. Later, when the ruffians, all of them, had been put to the sword, she still lay there under the bed, bathed in the after-math of an incredible rapture. The great Ivanov took offense and reproached her, exclaiming, "Couldn't you wait? Even a whore would have waited."

The dwarf, in retrospect, sorely regretted the incident. Particu-larly painful for him was the loss of his balalaika, which had been stomped on by one of the ruffians, obviously a lout with no ear for music.

The dwarf returned to his corner in the villa, waiting for Barras. His stomach was beginning to churn. Awful memories now began to crowd his mind, and there was more to come before the night was over. Memories of terror, savagery, cruelty that he had to witness over and over each night. When would it end? He had been given a sign. Someone unknown to him had been doomed; someone had been cursed to take over his burden of unending life. But when? How much longer must he wait?

In the morning, at about eleven, Catherine kept the appointment she'd made with her doctor. She'd gotten up with a migraine and had to pull herself together to be on time. On her way by cab she had felt drained and depressed, in a gray mood.

In the doctor's office she waited with impatience as the doctor, an elderly man with rheumatic fingers, wrote out a prescription for her. That done, he began to leaf through her file. She knew what he was looking for.

"Didn't it come back?" she asked, unable to constrain her anxiety.

"I had it here," the doctor said, fumbling with papers, annoyed at the misfiling.

"It *is* negative, isn't it?"

The doctor looked at her curiously. "I'm sorry," he said. "I thought you knew. Your husband—"

"My husband?"

"Yes, he called. I assumed . . ." he did not finish.

She understood. Smithy had called, pretending to be her husband.

At last the doctor found the slip and she stared at it, unable to speak. Her mind was numb, resisting what she already knew.

Afterward, outside, she almost vomited in the newly fallen snow.

Later she called Smithy's answering service and left a message —"Muriel. Call back." Varying names had different meanings, Muriel being a code for urgent.

Catherine went back to her apartment to wait for Smithy's return call. She did not know how long she'd have to wait. She began to drink and she smoked one cigarette after another, caught up in a ganglia of nervous moments. Her migraine pulsed without letup.

An hour later Smithy called.

"I have to see you," she said almost at once and with urgency.

"When?"

"Today. *Now.*"

"Okay," he said and began to tell her where to meet him. His words were cryptic, unintelligible to an outsider, but she understood his directions. When he was done he hung up abruptly, as he always did; he was never on line longer than necessary.

She got to the Half Moon ahead of time. She sat in a booth near the back, facing the rear. She had some tea with lemon, and felt nauseous. She had hurried here, taking two cabs and walking several blocks, a procedure Smithy always insisted on.

She was dismayed that she was pregnant. Last month she'd been with Smithy, and he'd had his way with her, as he always did, in some anonymous hotel room. It didn't happen with any frequency but when it did she invariably gave in; she never thought to say no to him. She gave in with a distaste and a passivity she had to conceal from him. She gave him nothing really, she would tell herself. She liked to think of it that way; it made it easier for her afterward.

Smithy was always generous to her, never with gifts, only with money, hundred-dollar bills, usually clean and unused. When he'd have her there'd always be some money left behind in her coat pocket, and it made her feel like a whore. From time to time he'd send money by mail. There was never a note with the money and, of course, never a return address. Since she made little as an actress and always needed money she took what he gave her. Once, years ago, to get rid of her dependence, she took a job as a waitress, not minding it, rather liking it. When Smithy found out he became angry.

"Don't do it again," he warned her. "I'm taking care of you," he told her. "Don't insult me that way again."

Smithy's pride in caring for her was important to him, she knew; and rather than face his anger again she let her dependence continue, but not without a passive resentment.

She was remembering the intensity with which she had once loved him; it was a feeling hard to imagine now. It was over with; it had ended four years ago, she remembered. She had become pregnant with his child and had had a miscarriage. The pregnancy had been an ordeal for her; she had been afraid of it, fearful she would die. She could not remember the miscarriage; it was blocked from her mind. Smithy afterward never spoke of it, nor could she ever bring herself to ask him about it. As it turned out, the ordeal had left its mark on her and she had come to feel dead inside, her body dry and cold, as from residual fear.

As she waited she thought she felt a movement inside her. It wasn't possible yet, was it? She felt anxious about the life, Smithy's life, growing inside her. She knew she'd have to rid herself of it.

She continued to wait, thinking of Robert now and recalling the miracle that had happened to her with him. For a long time she had been empty, yet last night with him she had begun to feel again the stirring of her body. She felt once again alive. How had it happened? She hadn't expected it; she had been years without expectation; yet last night it was there. Out of deadness, a spark. Out of coldness, warmth again. Out of dryness—

She was suddenly aware of Smithy standing beside her and sitting down, facing the front as he always did. He was on time. Whatever else you could say about him he was always on time. He was like a machine, Smithy.

Smithy, she noticed, wasn't wearing the horn-rimmed glasses he'd recently gotten. His eyes seemed milder but not much so.

He ordered toast and milk, and when the waitress was gone he asked, "What's wrong?"

"You know what's wrong."

"What do you intend doing?"

"Whatever has to be done," she said.

"It's ours, you know."

"Why can't you just let go?" she said, her voice low but rising.

"I never wanted it to be angry between us."

"But it has to end," she insisted.

"It'll end," he said. "When I'm dead it will end."

She looked away feeling cold to the bone. Her hands were clenched under the table, and she could hear herself saying to him, "I need some money, Smithy." It was as if someone else had said the words. She hated asking him but she had to ask.

"Money for what?"

"You *know* why."

Smithy was thinking about it and not saying anything.

"It has to be," she insisted, aware of Smithy's reluctance.

"Are you sure it's what you want?"

"Yes. Yes, very sure."

Smithy shrugged. "All right," he said evenly. "If that's what you want—do it."

She was taken aback that Smithy had given in so easily. It had to mean he wanted something from her—but what?

"I'll have the money tomorrow," she heard him say.

"You could mail me the money," she suggested, anxious to avoid another meeting. "You do know where I'm staying, don't you?"

He nodded, yes.

Of course he knew! She'd known that last night.

"We'll meet tomorrow, in the morning," he said. "I intended seeing you anyway," he added.

She was suddenly wary.

"See me? Why?"

"I'm going away for a while."

A pause.

"How long?"

"A half year or so."

She could feel her heart beat.

"More likely a year," he said.

A year? A *year*? She could feel the tension draining from her. Smithy later arranged their next meeting. When he was done he rose and walked away with hardly a good-bye, merely a nod. It was always that way with Smithy; he came and went abruptly. You could never count on knowing his next word or his next move.

When Smithy was gone she felt relieved and began to smile; she couldn't help smiling. She began to plan ways of celebrating her good fortune with Robert. A year was measurable, yet at the moment it seemed almost forever. She wanted to cry out with her joy, and suddenly she was aware—her migraine was gone.

Robert had called to say he'd be late and Catherine waited for him like a young girl on a first date, expectant and nervous, wanting everything to be just so. She had put on the blue sheath dress that he liked. Her throat felt hoarse and she drank to ease the rawness, taking scotch and water as she waited. Once she thought she felt a movement within her womb and she became anxious about it. It wouldn't be right, she felt; nothing would be right until that was over with; and she drank some more to ease her tension.

When Robert came in her anxiety was suddenly gone. He came to her with that serious look of his, and he kissed her deeply, holding her and saying with wonder, "You're beautiful."

She hugged him tightly. "I thought you'd never come," she said to him.

"You hungry?"

"A little, but let's stay in. I bought some champagne for tonight."

He was holding her hands and looking at her eyes, saying, "You've had more than enough already."

"You were late and I—"

"You don't have to explain."

"But I want to. Tonight's special."

"What's the occasion?"

"Open the champagne first," she said, an impish smile in her eyes.

With a shrug he went to the table, where he opened the champagne. He was curious, she could tell, but he was trying not to show it.

When he had poured the champagne, he asked her, "What do we drink to?"

"To Smithy," she announced, knowing he'd be surprised at that. And he was; he couldn't hide that.

"Why Smithy?"

"Shh, all in good time," she said, feeling full of surprises, bubbling with things she wanted to say. She took his hand and led him to the open space in front of the record player. They sat down on the floor facing each other. She sipped from her glass, and he from his; then she exchanged glasses and they sipped again, his lips on the imprint of hers, and hers on his. It was all so perfect, she felt, and she could feel herself wanting him.

She put on the record player and sipped some more, feeling soft and warm.

He asked, "Did you see Smithy?"

"Shh," she said softly, putting him off.

"What happened?" he was asking.

"You'd hardly believe it."

"Believe what?"

"Smithy." A pause, a mischievous pause. "Smithy is going away."

"Away—where?"

"No, you don't understand," she said. "The *where* is not important. It's the *time*. Smithy will be gone a year—a whole, long, everlasting year."

"He called to tell you that?"

"Yes," she said, knowing it was a lie, but it was such a little, little lie it didn't matter, did it?

"Where's he going?"

"Away. Just away."

"Did he say where?"

"Please, Robert," she beseeched with a smile. "Please don't be Mr. Detective. Not tonight."

He said, "If he called, then he must have followed us here the first night."

"He knows I'm here, yes."

"Does he know about me? I mean, who I am?"

"Am I under suspicion again?"

"I'm sorry," he said, and she could see the thoughts turning in his eyes.

"What's wrong?" she asked.

"I don't care what you have with him . . ."

"But you're angry all the same."

He let it pass. She was right and he was right, but it made little difference now which was which.

She lit a cigarette and leaned over to change the record player, feeling a tension again. For a time she listened to the melancholy beat of the music and looked at him quietly through a haze of smoke.

"I had such a wonderful night planned," she said ruefully. "I was saving up all the things I wanted to say to you, and do and think and feel."

He put out his hand to her in a conciliatory gesture.

She took his hand.

"I wanted to hold hands with you," she said to him. "I wanted to touch what you touch. I wanted to make you sorry for every day you didn't know me. I wanted to say . . ."

He waited.

". . . to say I love you."

He was silent and she waited for him to respond, to say something, anything.

She looked into his eyes.

"Robert."

She waited.

"You do believe me, don't you?"

"I want to, except . . ."

"Except what?"

"You saw Smithy today, didn't you?"

She didn't answer.

He said, "You didn't just get a call, did you? You *saw* him."

"Yes. Yes, I saw him," she conceded.

"He called and you came."

"Yes, he called and I came," she said.

"Now it makes sense," he said. He had dragged from her the little lie and now she could see it was out of his system.

"Are you angry?" she asked.

He shook his head.

"Is the interrogation over?"

"It's over, yes."

"What do we do now?"

"Listen to the music."

There was a quietness now, listening, looking at each other, the tension gone.

She leaned back against him and he held her, kissing her hair, and it was all she wanted for the moment.

In a while she said, "I did mean what I said—I mean, about how I feel."

She paused, then continued.

"I didn't expect it, wasn't looking for it, but there it was. Last night, out of nowhere—"

"Last night you were angry at Smithy," he said.

"Let's not talk about him, please."

"Did he say where he was going?" he asked, and she could tell he wasn't letting up.

She shook her head.

"Did he ask you to go with him?"

"I'd tell you if he did."

"Did he ask about me?"

She turned to face him, saying, "What's bothering you?"

"It doesn't make sense," he said.

"What doesn't?"

"Smithy—going away without you."

She lit another cigarette, and she could see the unsettled look in his eyes.

She gestured with her cigarette, saying, "I just told you I love you, and all you've done is cross-examine me—why?"

"I want it to be open between us."

"It is."

"Then tell me—why am I here?"

"What?"

"What did you want from me?"

"Help. I needed help."

"What kind?"

"I don't know," she said. "I just wanted to be free of Smithy. I needed someone—"

"Why did you hold back about him?"

"I wasn't sure of you."

"Are you sure now?"

"Yes. Yes, I'm sure."

"Then tell me about him."

"No, don't ask me, please."

"Why not?"

"It doesn't matter now, does it? He's going away."

"Tell me anyway."

"Please, Robert."

"Are you afraid—for *him?*"

"Let it go, please."

"What are you afraid of?"

"I just don't want you hurt," she said.

"Me? You're afraid for *me?*"

She saw the look of disbelief in his eyes.

"You don't know how he is," she said.

"What does he do?"

"I don't know. I never knew."

"Does he carry a gun?"

"No." She hesitated. "No."

She began to cough then. Her throat was raspy and she sipped some champagne to ease the rawness.

In a while she said to him, "I just don't want trouble, not for him, not for you. He's going away. Let him go."

"And when he comes back?"

"It'll be a whole year we'll have—you and me. Isn't that enough for now?"

"Sure. Sure, it's enough," he said, and she could tell he didn't mean it.

He reached out and held her hand now, then embraced her. There was silence once more, listening, touching, kissing, saying words without words. He was caressing her gently and she became aroused. She had to withdraw somewhat, saying to him, "No, not tonight. Just hold me."

She saw his curious look and she had to say to him, "We'll have to wait a few days. You don't mind, do you?"

"It's all right."

"You're an awful liar," she laughed.

"There'll be other times."

"I'll make it up for you," she said, holding him tightly, feeling the power in him and wanting him, yet she had to say no to him now. She felt unclean inside and it wasn't right now, not with

Smithy's life inside her. She tried not to think of it and she kept saying to him, "I love you, I love you." She wanted to say it and for him to know it and to feel as she felt.

And she thought, in time she'd be able to come to him whole and clean with nothing between them. They'd have a year together; it'd be like a lifetime. It was a year, wasn't it? It wasn't a trick Smithy was playing, was it?

"Robert, hold me," she was saying. "Hold me. Hold me!"

Later she began to cough again, a hacking cough that shook her.

"That sounds bad," he said to her. "You ought to be in bed."

While she undressed and got into bed, he heated up some soup and tea.

She had the soup sitting up in bed with her robe around her. She was beginning to feel tired and drowsy. Afterward she had some tea with honey, sipping it slowly. Her face was flushed.

He was sitting by her on the edge of the bed.

"I feel awful," she said to him.

"Go to sleep."

"Will you stay?"

"I'll be here."

"When I'm asleep you can go."

He took her hand.

"I wanted tonight to be so perfect," she said.

"It is."

"I wanted to love you—"

"I know."

"We hardly touched the champagne."

"You need some sleep."

"I don't want to sleep. If I sleep you'll go."

"I'll be here."

She finished her tea and honey and presently her drowsiness deepened and soon she fell off into sleep.

He took off her robe. She was naked and he covered her with the blanket. He kissed her cheek; it was warm with a rising fever.

Her sleep was restless. Now and then he heard her cry out with an incoherence of words. He kept holding her hand. Being with her now, sitting by her, was in itself an intimacy he had never before felt.

He wondered—*did* she love him? Did she herself really know? It didn't matter, he felt; with her, he had had the only feeling of love he'd ever known.

Yet, what *did* she feel? Did her feelings have meaning only in, or out of, Smithy? Smithy had called and she had gone to him. She had lied about that, and you had to ask—what other lies were there? If you turned over the stones what would you find? And yet, even that didn't matter to him now.

He kept wondering. She was with him now, with him yet apart. As he sat here watching over her she seemed remote and inaccessible, existing within a web of secrecies. How long would it last? A day, a night, and how many more?

He heard her cry out again in her restless, broken sleep. He kept sitting, holding her hand, listening to her feverish outcries that had meaning only in the buried recesses of her being.

Smithy came to his mind again. Smithy—suddenly leaving—*why*? Was something about to happen? Or had it already happened?

In the early hours of morning he rose and put on his holster, and before he left he kissed her once more, saying to her, I love you, I love you, wanting her to know and feel it. He looked back once and saw her as she was now, asleep and curled up like a child with a fragile beauty that he wanted to keep from harm against the world. It was an image of her that he wanted to hold in his mind.

Catherine waited for Smithy on the mezzanine of a bookshop off Broadway. It was late morning. She wore a cloth coat with a scarf and a woolen hat. Her throat was raw and she felt weak. She had gotten up late and had to hurry to get here, with hardly time to pull herself together. She felt disjointed and unfocused.

In a while Smithy appeared. He came out of nowhere, it seemed, and there he was, standing near her, taking a book from the shelf and scanning its pages.

"There's been some trouble," Smithy said to her in a low voice, talking into the book he held.

She didn't quite know how to take it. Everything in Smithy's life had always seemed under control. Now something had gone wrong.

Smithy spoke again, his voice barely audible.

"I've been marked for death," he said to her. His words were formal, almost archaic. He seemed like a machine malfunctioning but unable to feel it.

She stared at him, wondering if she had misjudged what he had said.

"Who?" she finally said, almost whispering.

"The people I work for."

In the past Smithy had mentioned he worked for some governmental agency; she'd taken that for granted. Now she wasn't sure.

"Who are they?"

"I can't talk here," he said. "Meet me at this hotel," he added, giving her a sealed envelope. She could feel a key inside.

She hesitated, reluctant to get involved. Smithy waited patiently for a reaction from her. Finally, grudgingly, she nodded. In the end she couldn't say no to him. She never could.

She left the bookshop first. Outside, in the street, she pulled her coat tightly together. The sharp, gusty air made her draw closer within herself. Later she read the message but did not discard the notepaper. Smithy, she knew, had always been strict about leaving papers behind.

Once she looked around to see if Smithy was behind her. There was no sign of him but she knew he was there somewhere.

She got to the hotel room first; Smithy would come in afterward—that was his procedure.

The hotel room seemed unused. In the closet, she was sure, there'd be no more than two suits with the labels removed. There'd be no papers around either; Smithy kept everything in his head. Wherever Smithy stayed, it was always the same, an unidentifiable existence.

She kept her coat on, sitting on the edge of the bed, waiting for Smithy. She felt chilled.

Smithy came in a few minutes later; he saw her sitting in her coat, her hands clenched together.

"Want a drink?" he asked.

She nodded.

He got some scotch and water for her; he had been prepared for that.

She took a few deep sips of the scotch and it eased her tension somewhat. She waited for Smithy to say something.

He stood near the window, wearing a black suit with a thin knit tie. His hair, she saw, was several shades darker than it had been yesterday.

Finally she asked, "What are you going to do?"

"I don't know yet," he said. "I'm waiting for a call. When it comes I'll know what to do." He paused. "Could you stay a while?"

She looked away.

"I mean until the call comes," he said, and it was as close to begging as she had ever seen him come. He'd always been hard and self-sufficient, but here he was now, needing her. You could almost feel sorry for him.

She waited, sipping the scotch. It all seemed unreal, the clock pulsing and Smithy sitting now, waiting, saying nothing, as if he were just waiting for time to pass on a gray winter day.

She was unsure of what was happening. As a young girl she

had always felt that way, unsure of herself; for her, life had always trembled with uncertainty.

She remembered Mobile where she had lived for a time.

Mobile. Dead residue of the past, and the loneliness there. You felt it at night, alone in your room, with all the sounds outside not belonging to you. It had a sound, loneliness.

She remembered the day Smithy had come to Mobile.

A fog was sweeping in over the bay, with gulls going in and out of it, and she was walking, going back to a house that wasn't hers, to an ugly room, to people who didn't care or want her. Nothing was hers. She had had to live with strangers, relatives of one sort or another. There'd been a younger sister, Jenny, who'd died in an orphanage, and a brother she'd never seen. He'd been in trouble, she'd heard, and he'd died in some shooting that people used to hint about.

She was coming home from school, she remembered. She was skinny and pimply, and suddenly there he was, this paratrooper or whatever he was, with medals and shiny boots and blond hair. He came up to her and began talking to her—to *her!* She almost wet herself being near him and hearing him say, "You on your way home, Cathy?"

She couldn't speak. He *knew* her. He knew her name!

"Would you like a malt?" he asked.

Would she? With *him?* God, would she!

When they went to a hangout on the corner she was dying for some of the girls to see her with him.

He told her his name. She liked the sound of it, Smithy. She kept saying it over and over to herself.

Once he asked her, "You like where you're staying?"

"I hate it," she blurted out.

Then he asked, "Did you hear about Jenny?"

She was surprised. "Did you *know* her?"

"I saw where they buried her," he said. "Nobody gave a damn.

You could hardly find the grave. She was seven and she'd never talked. She cried but she couldn't talk. All she knew to do was cry."

That's how it began. Smithy, her brother, had come back. She'd heard he was dead but here he was. He was family, real family.

She remembered how she had cried when Smithy told her about Jenny, but Smithy didn't cry. The bitterness was inside him; it couldn't come out.

"We're all that's left of the family," he told her later. "Just you and me." The way he said it made her feel sad.

"From now on *I'm* taking care of you, Cathy. You come with me. You don't have to look back, not once."

Later they took a cab to the train station. It was the first time she'd ever been in a cab. With Smithy everything seemed to be the first time, walking, breathing, being alive.

On the train, sitting next to Smithy, she felt an incredible excitement just being with him. Sometimes it seemed too much and it all spilled out of her with words that hardly stopped.

Once she asked him, "Is it true what they say?"

"About what?"

"About you killing someone."

"It's just talk," he said, and that was all he said about it.

They took the train to New Orleans, where they registered at a hotel and had their meals served in the room. Shrimp and steak and pie so thick you could hardly imagine.

Afterward she took a bath in foamy suds, and Smithy came in while she bathed, and it was exciting, him being there watching her. When she got out of the tub he took a great big towel and rubbed her dry. The touch of his hands made her feel oozy and she didn't want it to end, not ever.

Catherine kept waiting with Smithy for the phone to ring. The room was quiet; time seemed not to move.

She asked, "Do you think he'll call?"

"He'll call."

"Isn't there anything—?"

"We just have to wait."

And it continued, the waiting, the silence.

She lay down on the bedspread; she still wore her coat. She was thinking of Robert now, feeling the need for him, to be with him in mind and heart. She was becoming drowsy and her mind began to drift into a dream. She was away with him somewhere in the warmth of a summer afternoon and he was holding her gently. She was at peace. Gradually the dream began to fade. For a time she held on, saying his name until there was nothing.

When she woke she had to focus on where she was. Her mouth was dry and cakey.

Smithy was sitting near the window.

"What time is it?" she asked him.

"Almost three," he said tonelessly.

She was under the covers of the bed; her coat was on a chair.

"Did your friend call?" she asked.

Smithy nodded; he said, "Yes, but there's a call we have to make now."

"A call?"

"If you don't feel up to it—"

"You want *me* to make the call?"

"Yes, later. Tonight."

She thought about it a few moments.

"I'll come back later then," she suggested.

"You can't go back to your place," he said.

"But I have to change," she said. "Look at me. I feel so—"

"You can't go back," he repeated.

She was suddenly wary.

"Why not?"

He came closer now.

"Your place is being watched."

"Watched?"

He came still closer; she sat up stiffly.

"Who've you been seeing?" he asked.

She could feel her heart beating.

"How did you meet him?"

"Why?"

"Did he approach *you?*"

"Yes. Yes, of course."

"What's his name?"

She hesitated.

Smithy waited, his expression insistent. "What's his name. I have to know."

"Dempsey. His name's Dempsey."

"His first name?"

"Robert," she said with reluctance.

"I knew it," Smithy exclaimed, slapping his fist against his palm. "I knew it!"

"Knew what?"

"I knew it was him—Dempsey!"

"You know him?" Her heart was going faster.

"He operates out of Houston," Smithy said. "They sent him here. He's a killer."

"It's impossible," she exclaimed.

"He's one of *them.*"

"It can't be. It just can't be."

"He's been using you to get at me."

She shook her head, resisting what she heard.

She stared up at Smithy who was coming still closer.

"What did you tell him about me?" he asked.

"Nothing."

"Has he asked about me?"

"Why should he ask?"

"Were you followed this morning?"

"I took a cab—two cabs."

"Why did he move your things?"

"I asked him to."

"Does he carry a gun?"

"A gun?"

"Yes, a gun."

She shook her head; she didn't trust herself to speak lest her voice betray her.

Smithy kept questioning her and she kept resisting, lying defensively. Smithy, she felt, must be playing some game. Whatever he found out he'd use later.

Once, unconsciously, she glanced at the phone.

Smithy saw her eyes and said to her, "Use the phone if you want to. I won't stop you."

She stared up at him.

He went on. "Use it," he said, "but if you call and question him he'll know that you know. He'd have no alternative but to get rid of you. If you call you're on your own. I won't be around to protect you."

She felt numb with indecision.

"Call him," Smithy said. "Pick up the phone and call," he insisted.

She was looking at the phone and remembering the ugly gun Robert carried. The phone now seemed like a fearful instrument.

She felt chilled to the bone, and she had to get up and pour herself another drink. God, what was happening? Everything was suddenly grotesque and disjointed. It was crazy—*crazy*. It wasn't true, not a word of it, she told herself, yet she couldn't bring herself to pick up the phone.

Later Smithy began to explain to her the call she had to make. He kept from her the identity of the man she'd be calling. All she knew was that the call involved a man Eddie, who was dead, and an envelope he had left behind. As always, Smithy kept things to himself, telling her only what he felt she had to know.

For several hours Smithy rehearsed her over and over. She felt weak and sick but she kept on, holding herself together, passively doing what Smithy wanted. She had no will of her own now. For her, Smithy had become her only reality, the only thing she could count on.

At 2120 hours, as Smithy reckoned time, he put through a call, then handed her the phone. He listened in on an extension.

She heard a man's brusque voice: "Yes?"

"I'm a friend," she began nervously, disguising her voice as that of an older woman.

"Yes, what is it?"—impatiently.

"I'm a friend of Eddie," she said carefully, playing her role.

The ensuing conversation, with Smithy prompting her, was a tense experience for her; but when it was over she knew from Smithy's expression that she had done well, and she knew it too. It had been a part played almost to perfection, and she felt a quiet exhilaration now.

Smithy came to her then with a drink and she took it eagerly, needing it. As she drank she saw him putting on his overcoat, and he was saying, "I'll be back. I won't be long."

She began to feel drowsy and her head was spinning. She sat down on the bed, unable to stand, and then lay back. Smithy was fading from her and the room was hazy, her eyes were closing, and she was drifting off into a deep sleep.

Catherine had been sick when Dempsey had left her the night before, so he did not call her until late the next morning, not wanting to disturb her sleep.

His call—two rings, a hangup and a call—was a simple signal he had arranged so she'd know it was he calling.

There was no answer. That could mean she was out, perhaps

to a doctor or druggist or on some small errand. It could mean too she was seeing Smithy again.

Afterward, at intervals, he kept calling her. There was still no response; and that, he reasoned, eliminated a visit to a doctor or some minor errand. The possibility of Smithy remained and that now became an unsettling irritation in Dempsey's mind.

Shortly after three Dempsey got a message to report to Martin's office. It probably had to do with Scapa, he could guess. The Scapa matter, he knew, wouldn't go away, not easily.

When Dempsey got to the office Martin offhandedly asked him to sit down, but Dempsey remained standing, waiting for what was to come.

Martin fumbled with some papers on his desk and cleared his throat. "It's been suggested," he began, "that you take a leave of absence." Martin looked up now, waiting for a reaction.

"Is that an order?"

"It's an order, yes."

"Yours?"

"No, but it is now."

Dempsey waited.

"Is that all?" he asked.

"There's been a lot of heat," said Martin, "and people upstairs are remembering the Muller case all over again. I told you that before."

"I was cleared of that."

"Sure, but it keeps coming up. There's been a pattern—"

"What are you saying?"

"I'm saying we need time for things to cool off."

"How long do I cool?"

"As long as it takes."

"I'm on the Burry case."

"Sheldon will handle it."

"It's not a simple case."

Martin shrugged.

"Maybe not," he said, "and maybe you're reading too much into it."

Dempsey understood. The Burry case didn't have much of a priority. Burry was a cipher. No one had even come to claim his body. He was dead and no one gave a damn except to close the book on him.

Dempsey persisted. "There's more to it than just Burry."

"Yeah, what?"

"It wasn't a casual killing. There was a careful setup in place. Who would have gone through all that just to kill someone like Burry?"

"What's your guess?"

"I don't know yet."

"What *have* you got?"

"Not much."

"Seems like a cold case to me," Martin commented dryly.

"It's been that way up to now," Dempsey said. "Krone's clammed up and no one else saw, or knows, or says anything. The killer was seen but no one remembers him. The manager at the apartment house was *this* close to him, face-to-face, but all he remembers is an average-looking man. I questioned the manager three times and all I got from him was a vague description. It's like having nothing."

"Think he's holding back?"

"I'm sure he is."

"How sure?"

"I talked to him once about Turner, just testing the water. I made some comment about the kid's hair, a casual comment, and right away the manager was correcting me. I could tell right there he had a good eye for detail. The point is, he doesn't want to get involved, not in a murder case."

Martin shrugged. "He's not the first witness who's run scared."

"I need more time with him."

"You don't have that time," said Martin. "Sheldon will take it from here."

"He's too new."

"That's not your problem. Just see to it that he's briefed."

"Anything else?"

"Yes, Turner's being reassigned."

"When was that decided?"

"When you get back someone else, someone with more experience, will work with you."

"The kid learns fast," said Dempsey. "I'd like to bring him along."

"That's not the point. You're a high risk, Dempsey. You keep losing partners. No reflection on you, but—"

"I see."

"It was a mistake in the first place letting Turner team up with you."

"Maybe you're right."

"I was there when we buried the kid's old man," said Martin, remembering. "I'd hate to be around to bury the kid."

And that was it. Martin was kicking two problems under the desk at one time, and that was only the beginning, Dempsey felt. Later he'd probably be assigned a desk job, out of the way, forcing his resignation. Whatever Martin's personal feelings, he had a department to run and wasn't looking for unnecessary problems. You couldn't fault him for that.

And maybe it *was* time to quit, Dempsey later reflected. He'd never considered it would end this way, being eased out a back door. He'd always felt the end would come in a moment of sudden violence. For him it had always been only a matter of time, a matter only of how and when.

It had been that way too during the war, a matter always of how and when.

The war, in retrospect, was impressed on his mind as frag-ments, as images without meaning.

The steaming heat.

A carcass, with birds picking at its unwondering eyes. Carts and implements smiling in the sun and beginning to rust.

You look for meanings. There is meaning in the intoxicating movement where one moment predicts nothing of the next, but what is the meaning?

Stad, the sniper, remembering last actions seen through his sights. He is a collector of sorts, collecting sudden, irretrievable moments.

Meaning. A direct hit, a body almost unrecognizable, leaning against a young tree, both almost black with the ferocity of earth hurled at them, gaping holes in the body with twisted roots blown into the wounds, implanted there like strange wild growth.

You know fragments. A road that goes somewhere to a secret time and place, a fragment of a road. You know bits of a man, part of time. The rest slips by unknown and lost. You never had it.

Scorched trucks, crumpled armor, useless hulks. Dumb, silent chaos. It's open to see yet it has its own secrecy. You look but understand nothing.

Bodies rotting in hidden places. You can hardly come near them. They have names you wouldn't want to know. The rot pollutes even that.

And you wait. You had to wait.

On leave after months of combat, his unit was quartered for a time near a squalid town by the Mekong.

One night he entered the town. He was alone, for what he had to do he wanted to do alone.

He went directly to an old church, which was empty and standing as a shadow among shadows in the moonlight. Around the back he approached a stairway leading to the cellar vaults. Descending, probing with a flashlight, he came to a heavy door that was open. In a small room that was like a penitent's cell, a small candle provided a flickering light. In the room he saw a young girl sitting up in bed. She had straight hair and unkempt bangs. He had heard of her. She was an orphan, only twenty, with no youth. When she opened her mouth you saw three front teeth missing. She had come to this town to find some relatives but had been told they were gone, so she found her way to this place. She had had with her, when she came, some few pieces of fruit, some rice and a torn picture of her family. It was said that the war was impressed on her mind as one incident—her father, an official, and her mother each hacked to death by irregulars when government units withdrew from the town near the coast where her parents had lived.

The young girl was fearful of authorities, and so she kept to herself. For a time she lived as a prostitute; she was ugly though and without grace and her earnings were meager. In the end she came to this underground place where she lived on the charity of the church, living a solitary life underground where huge rats scuttered with ravenous hunger and where monks had once fasted with a hunger more fierce.

Dempsey had a basket with him. In it was a puppy. One of the men had found it in a field. It was a frightened creature and it ran clumsily, seeking any shadow to hide in. The puppy had a defect; it could not bark. Sometimes it seemed to cry but no sound came from it.

When he set the basket down in front of the girl she seemed uncertain. He indicated to her that the dog was hers now. Hesitantly, she began to pull the basket upward toward her, doing it slowly, as if haste would upset her good fortune. Then she lifted the puppy out of the basket and held it to her face, caressing it with the wonder of life.

The next morning he went again to see the girl. He felt uneasy as he descended the steps to the cellar.

When he came to her room he found it in darkness. He heard the sound of sobbing. He struck a match and he saw her grotesque face of grief. As the match died out he saw a splotch of blood on her hand. Lighting another match he saw the blood once more. He followed his match to the basket, to the small dog. He saw a saucer and some tins of milk, and the puppy. A horror shivered through him. He lit another match and saw the creature again, its throat mangled where some wild rats had torn at it, one eye socket gnawed deep.

He stared at the mutilation as if the obscenity had its meaning in him. He touched the girl's hand to comfort her but she recoiled from him. She shrank back, hunching over within herself, a pitiful figure, suddenly small and shrunken and quivering as if some giant hand had struck her.

He felt numb, unable to move. In retrospect now he understood what had been. He had reached out to the girl; in a deeper meaning he had reached out to God, as he had in a time long past. It had been a useless act, he knew. He could cry out, he could beg, grovel, eat dust; but in the end it was useless.

In the darkness he heard the sobbing of the young girl, and he felt repelled by the obscenity that lay at his feet. It was meaningless, yet it had meaning for him. It would end this way, he knew; end with an obscenity. And in that cell of a room, out of the pit of his anger, he cried out with rage. He had to cry out; it was all he had left, rage and defiance. Yet even that, he knew, was meaningless.

Later that summer, on a mission up north, he was captured by a group of regulars and taken to a camp where he was bound, beaten, tortured, interrogated; he was for days without food or water, without sleep, but he did not break. His resistance angered his captors. Day by day he was ground down. There were weeks of isolation, moments of kindness and torture again, until he felt himself within the vortex of the irrational. The worst of it was to wake up and know where you were. You were caught in the web of another day. You wanted to cry out but there was no ear to hear.

For a time his captors left him alone; and one day, with three others, he made his escape. The others, one by one, were caught and cut down. Alone, he managed to survive, impelled by rage. Rage had become his strength and his weapon.

Deep in a heavy woods, soaked in an oppressive heat, he paused once in his flight. Ahead of him were several squads searching the undergrowth. He began to circle back, prepared now to meet his end face-to-face. He moved deeply into the abyss of the unknown, passing from reason to unreason.

He came behind one soldier and began to stalk him. The hunted had become the hunter. When he closed in on the soldier it was over in a few moments, the soldier dropping to the ground, his neck cracked.

Dempsey, armed now with a rifle and some grenades, moved ahead, guided only by instinct. Two soldiers began to converge on him, and he cut them down at a distance with the rifle. His aim was unerring; there was no reprieve from his sights. He was in possession now and invulnerable, it seemed—godlike and anti-God.

Later he ran out of ammunition and he had to pause again. He was covered with sweat.

For a time he took refuge in a shack to rest. In a corner was an axe.

Two of the enemy approached the shack, kicking open the door, raking the room with automatic fire.

To the side of the doorway Dempsey had been waiting for them, the heavy axe gripped in his hands. When they rushed in he staggered them off balance with a violent thrust. With a cry of ferocity that came from his depths he swung the axe. It descended, catching the first soldier in the neck, cleaving downward at a diagonal through the spine. Blood rushed out in spasms.

As the other soldier regained his balance Dempsey kicked him backward, knocking his rifle away. Dempsey reached for the axe buried in the body. As he wrenched it out of the body the other soldier cried out in horror.

Dempsey paused, waiting for the soldier to reach for his rifle. Nothing moved; the moment was frozen.

Dempsey began to pick up the rifles and ammunition, hardly bothering to look at the soldier.

In a while the soldier began to relax; the danger for him had passed. He lit a cigarette and began to smile a bit. Dempsey had seen it before, after combat, men eating ravenously and laughing, as if that and being alive were the same.

Dempsey bound up the man and left. There was more to come. It was a long way back to his lines, and he had to enter again into the killing ground, into the abyss of unreason. The ferocity of his anger was not yet done. He was deep in enemy territory, surrounded and with little hope. As he moved out he looked upward once. He was still in possession; and however the day would end he would ask nothing, give nothing. Whatever the outcome, this day, this one day, would be his.

Almost two weeks later he emerged back to his own lines. Behind him thirty-one of the enemy lay dead.

In a base hospital, utterly spent, he slept through a day and a half. Later, a depression began to settle in his mind and marrow.

He remembered. On the first day of his escape he had gone beyond the permissible; he had gone there with unreasoning rage and defiance—a defiance against God. And for that day, he knew, there could be no forgiveness, not in heaven nor on earth.

Yet, incredibly, he had survived; inexplicably, he still lived— but why? What more was there to be? Death was a simple matter, and pain could be borne—in heaven or earth then, what else was there to be?

* * *

Later that evening Dempsey caught up with Turner. The kid was in his car down the street from Christy's, a plush steak house.

Dempsey got into the car and sat down beside Turner.

He asked, "How long has Krone been in there?"

"About an hour," the kid said.

"We're off the case, you know."

The words had a sudden impact on the kid.

"What happened?"

"Sheldon's taking over."

"What went wrong?"

"Forget it," said Dempsey. "Go home. Nothing will happen tonight."

"Maybe it will."

"Forget it. I said, forget it."

"Suppose you didn't see me," the kid suggested.

Dempsey thought about it. The kid was hanging in, hating to let go. He wanted one last shot. Maybe nothing would happen but he wanted the shot.

"You'd have to be careful," Dempsey said.

"Krone won't know I'm on him."

"I mean about Sheldon or his partner."

The kid understood.

"You'll be on your own," said Dempsey.

It was snowing and the windshield wiper was running.

The kid asked, "What happened? Was it something I did?"

Dempsey didn't answer; he was watching a limousine drive up in front of Christy's. In a few moments a pudgy figure in an overcoat emerged from the restaurant.

"That's him, Krone."

"I know," said the kid, leaning forward.

"Call me later," Dempsey said.

"Sure."

Dempsey got out of the car. On the street he observed Krone

getting into the limousine. In a few moments the limousine began to make a U-turn in the snow and head west.

The kid had turned on his ignition. As he began to move out Dempsey was saying to him, "Be careful . . ." but the words were lost in the sounds of the motor.

Dempsey stood there watching Turner drive off. The kid had begun to grow on him, and he felt protective. He wondered why he had called out a caution. It was, after all, only a routine surveillance.

That evening Krone had his usual table at Christy's. For the years he had come here he'd always had the same waiter but had never bothered to ask the man's name.

Krone looked at his timepiece, which he carried on a chain that bulged over his stomach. The watch had a gold cover with initials on it engraved in Cyrillic script. The initials, he liked to tell, were his father's, a general once in the Imperial Army and bearer of the Order of Suvorov. A still earlier version, which originated during his two years in Lewisburg, told of a card game in postwar Vienna in which young Krone, pitted against a cunning speculator, came away from the table with a quarter million in pounds sterling and the watch to boot.

With his pudgy fingers he snapped the timepiece shut, a motion like the snap of a jaw.

Krone pushed his coffee aside. His recent meeting with Sorge had left him unnerved and sour in the stomach. The loss of the shipments would be a heavy setback; he had money tied up in a half-dozen depots. Sorge had given him two days to find the leak but Krone hardly knew where to look, and time was running out.

Later, when he left Christy's, he took his limousine back to his townhouse. Madame Krone was waiting for him in the drawing room.

"Trouble again?" she said, seeing his face.

He shook his head.

THE DESCENT

His mother crossed her legs unhurriedly, her movements like little ceremonies. There were few wrinkles on her face, which was lean and dominating; her body was still supple.

"You're sweating again," she said, not letting him pass without a comment from her.

He kept walking; he was in no mood for words.

Upstairs in his bedroom he stood by the window, looking at the snow falling on the city. Sorge preoccupied his mind.

Through his open door he could hear his mother coming up the stairs. In a while he heard her drawing her bath.

His hands sweated. His mother always had a way of knowing this and letting him know she knew, always in a demeaning tone. She ran the townhouse, *his,* where she held court for a remnant of old émigrés who came to feed off his crystal and tell trivial old stories and lies; after a while it was hard to tell which was which, even for them. They were relics, all of them, dying off one by one, gathering at sad little funerals. His mother, of course, would survive them all. It was what she did best.

During the thirties it was she who had held the family together. Her husband, a minor functionary in the Austrian bureaucracy, had fallen to pieces, and when he died she survived in one way or another in a hundred illicit beds.

When Krone was ten he ran errands for her. Once, at a hint from her, he stole a necklace. That evening, before she got ready to adorn herself, she let him into her room. She let him watch as she sat naked on her bed, powdering her legs, raising them one by one toward him.

He always remembered that night. It had become for him an erotic memory that was evoked over and over, its clarity never fading. Even now, many years later, the image remained of a body wantonly naked and creamy.

Krone was lying down, fantasizing, when he was startled by

the ring of his phone. His private number. He was annoyed by the intrusion. He picked up the phone. "Yes?"

He heard an elderly woman's voice. "I'm a friend," she began. "Yes, what is it?"

"I'm a friend of Eddie," the voice said with a hoarseness.

Krone was instantly alert. Eddie—Burry's first name.

"I have an envelope," he heard her say.

"An envelope?"

"Eddie left it with me in case . . ."

"In case what?"

"If something were to happen to him I was to give you the envelope. You would understand."

"Who are you?"

"A friend. Just a friend."

"Where are you now?"

"I can't say. You see, my husband—"

"Yes, but the envelope."

"I could mail it to you but I lost your address. Sometimes I'm so—"

"Could we meet tonight?"

"I could mail it to you tomorrow."

"It may be important," Krone insisted.

"I'm at the Taft—oh, dear, I shouldn't have said that. You will be discreet, won't you?"

"Of course."

"I could leave it at the desk."

"Wrap it in another envelope in the name of—of Doctor Stacy."

"Do you spell that with an *e?*"

"Yes, *Stacey* with an *e,*" said Krone impatiently. "I'll pick it up in half an hour."

There were more words said but Krone hardly listened. When the woman hung up he quickly dressed.

When he was ready he paused. He was convinced there were

detectives downstairs in the street, observing the townhouse. He thought about it for a few moments. Presently he went to his chauffeur's room.

Wearing an overcoat and his chauffeur's cap, Krone approached the desk in the lobby of the Taft Hotel. Waiting for him was an envelope addressed to Doctor Stacey, with an *e*, wrapped in an outer covering of Christmas decorations.

At the far end of the lobby Smithy sat reading a newspaper. He lowered the paper a bit to watch Krone at the desk, Krone swallowing the bait.

Smithy began to notice a young man in an overcoat near the entrance. The young man was observing Krone as he picked up the envelope.

Krone held his patience until he got to a bar on 47th Street. At a table he ripped open the wrapper. He recognized Burry's crude, cramped writing. Opening the envelope Krone saw a Xeroxed manifest. There was a listing of "Machinery and Spare Parts"—a coded tabulation of a cargo of 60-millimeter mortars and automatic weapons. There was a transmittal slip in Burry's name for ten thousand to the Banque Suisse. The cargo, Krone knew, had left Huerta on a weekend. Two days later Burry had deposited ten thousand into a Swiss account.

As Krone put the papers back into the envelope he noticed a phone number in a corner of the envelope—again, in Burry's own crude scrawl. Krone recognized the number; it was that of Sorge's answering service.

It was clear from the papers that Sorge had been involved in diverting the cargo ship. But how did Burry fit in? Had he been blackmailing Sorge? It was hard to say; there was not too much to go on, and Burry was dead. It wasn't much but here was the first bit of evidence. A piece of luck. Not much, but enough to link up Sorge for the moment.

In a booth at the bar Krone put through a long distance call to

Caribe, reversing the charges. He finally got Dufar, chief of intelligence, on his private number.

"Maxwell," said Krone.

"Yes?" was the reply in precise English.

"About the shipment that was mislaid. I have a copy of the manifest. It turned up unexpectedly."

"I see."

"Our mutual friend was involved. I'll send you details."

"Yes, at once," said Dufar. "We'll straighten out matters here."

"I'm sure you will. Now about the shipments—"

"Yes, of course. Proceed as usual."

When Krone hung up, he was elated. The shipments to Caribe would begin again. The flow of arms would continue as usual.

The next day, under an assumed name, Krone arranged for an afternoon plane to Miami. He wanted to be out of Sorge's reach for the time being.

It was clear from Dufar's words that Sorge would be recalled to Caribe for "discussions." Under the circumstances Sorge would be walking into a cold steel trap.

On the plane Krone began to feel uneasy. He had fallen into a piece of luck, but was that luck what it seemed to be?

Krone began to sweat again.

It was snowing heavily when Dempsey stopped off at Catherine's place. He managed the lock easily and let himself into her apartment.

The rooms were as he remembered them. Catherine's suitcases were in the closet; her clothes still hung there. The bed was unmade.

He searched the bureau but could find nothing, not a letter, not a scrap to indicate the whereabouts or even the existence of Smithy. Wherever he looked it was the same.

He went through the closets again. Once he reached out to touch her blue sheath dress.

He opened a near-full bottle of scotch she had. He began to drink and to wait.

She had been gone a whole day now. She was with Smithy, he was sure of that. She'd have to come back though, at least to pick up her things. He wasn't sure what he would say to her or what lies she would tell him when she came back.

He kept drinking and thinking of her. She was imbedded in his mind with remembered touch and taste and feeling.

He had to wonder—had she gone back to Smithy willingly or not? It was hard to tell; the threads were elusive.

He waited, standing by the window in the darkness, watching the snow fall. From time to time he wondered how Turner was making out, not caring one way or another. He was thinking too of his soured meeting with Martin. Things seemed to be breaking up and out of joint. Nothing was clear, nothing whole. There was not much to do except wait it out.

Turner had taken up watch on the side street near Krone's townhouse. The snowfall had stopped for a time and a frozen stillness lay over the city.

Earlier he'd watched Krone get out of his limousine while the chauffeur drove the car to the garage. Then he saw the chauffeur, wrapped in an overcoat, walking back to the side entrance of the townhouse.

Turner was hoping something would happen. He hoped for some event, some information to give to Dempsey. He wondered what had happened downtown. Probably had to do with Scapa, he figured. It would blow over, he felt, and in time things would get back to normal. It wasn't easy with Dempsey, but being with him was being with the best—what more could you want?

Somewhat later, about a half hour later, Turner became aware of the chauffeur coming out the side entrance, wearing his cap and a heavy overcoat. There was something different about the chauffeur, Turner felt. Was it his shape or the way he walked? It was dark and hard to tell at this distance.

In a while Turner saw the limousine emerge from the garage; it turned down toward Madison, then south. Turner followed at a distance. There was not much traffic and he could afford the lag.

The limousine made several turns, obviously to shake off a possible tail. Turner held back to avoid being seen. Near Broadway he saw the limousine turn into a public garage.

Quickly following into the garage, Turner saw the chauffeur waiting for the attendant, and it was then that he recognized who it was—Chrissake, it was Krone!

Presently Krone left the garage, turning toward the avenue, and glancing back once. On the avenue Turner observed Krone entering the Taft.

Turner followed him in and from a position near the entrance he saw Krone pick up an envelope at the desk. Krone put the envelope inside his coat and quickly moved past Turner out the entrance into the street.

Turner followed. He felt he was on to something important; he didn't know what.

As he followed Krone through a thin flow of people he became aware of a figure to the side of him, just slightly behind.

The figure cut in front of him and he saw the face then, a cold face with a slightly beaky nose and eyes like carbolic death.

On his way back to the Edison, Smithy went over in his mind the night's happenings.

Predictably, Krone had picked up the envelope. Within a day its contents would reach Barras in Caribe, triggering off a harsh, swift reaction. The fuse had been lit.

His plan had held up so far, except for one matter. Krone had been followed. In his eagerness to get to the Taft, Krone had let his guard down, and Smithy had had to deal with the situation on the spot. With that out of the way, his plan was still on mark and unaltered.

The man who had followed Krone, as Smithy had learned from his papers, had been a young detective named Turner.

When Smithy got back to his room he saw Cathy on the bed; she was still out from the sedation he'd given her.

In a while he took off her clothes and covered her gently with the blanket. His only regret was that it had had to be this way.

He began to focus on tomorrow—a critical day. Each day now had to be held together in delicate balance. Whatever he did he did for her. He and Cathy were all that was left of the family. She was all he had.

For a time he watched her quiet breathing, and he touched her hair with a tenderness. It'll work out, he said to her in his thoughts. It'll be like it used to be, you and me—just you and me.

In his study Barras was having his usual late-night meal. The dwarf was pouring wine for Barras when Dufar came in with an urgent matter. Barras paused in his meal while Dufar related the phone call he had had with Krone a few minutes earlier.

Dufar added, "We'll know more tomorrow when we get the papers."

Barras went back to his meal, cutting at his steak, while Dufar stood there, taken aback by the lack of concern shown.

Dufar said, "I think—"

"I know what you think," said Barras angrily, cutting him off.

Dufar could only shrug and wait. The dwarf too waited for Barras to react. The news had dismayed the dwarf, but he tried not to show it.

Barras was chewing, saying nothing; but his eyes were focused in thought.

Finally he looked up, saying, "I think . . ."

"Yes?"

"I think it's time to recall Sorge."

Dufar allowed himself a hint of a smile.

"If you permit me, sir—"

"I want Sorge back."

"It may take time—"

"We don't have time."

"—we've lost contact with him," Dufar admitted nervously.

"In that case, perhaps your fumbling mice would allow me to guide them."

"You *know* where he is?"

"I've a cable from him."

"Where? Where is he?"

"At a motel, on some business, he says."

"A motel?"

"It's called the Five Palms," Barras told him. "Do you know Newark?"

Dufar shook his head.

"Then I suggest you find out. And one more thing, Dufar."

"Yes?"

"I want Sorge back. If you fail me, Dufar . . ." Barras left his threat hanging.

Barras drew from his desk the cable from Sorge and turned it over to his chief of intelligence.

"I want him back, Dufar."

Dufar nodded and shortly left in haste to do what had to be done. It was the moment he had waited for, and you could see the glow in his eyes.

Afterward Barras went back to his meal but did not continue for long. At one point he stopped eating and began to stare at his plate, his eyes brooding, until suddenly with a cry of anger he swept the plate from his desk.

116

The dwarf patiently bent down to clean up the floor of the study. His stomach was in an awful turmoil.

Later the dwarf went back to his room, where he took some powders to relieve his distress.

For a time, near a guttering candle, he sat on the floor, leaning against a coffin that was of a size fit for a potbellied child. Years ago the dwarf himself had constructed the coffin, and he kept in it some of the things he had collected from time to time. It had been his hope to be buried in his coffin; it had been his hope to be rid of his abominable curse, and to die a decent death. It was his due, was it not?

He contemplated once again the vision he had had of the stranger who was to come to take up his burden. It was true, he told himself. It had to be true. There had to be an end—even a bug could look forward to an end.

Opening the lid to the coffin now, the dwarf looked inside where his body would eventually lie.

Within were his things. At the sides, where his earlobes would rest, he kept a variety of herbs and potions. Near the position of the armpits was an assortment of passkeys certain to open whatever human ingenuity could lock. Up a sleeve were cards with subtle markings and dice of uncertain warp. Near the brow rested a zodiac and head map of a hairless phrenologist. Deep in the orifice of the corpse, if one dared venture there, one found perfumes of the sort that had bedeviled that old whoremaster, the late King Louis. Near the toes were letters patent to the ducal throne of Sysk, a principality uncharted on any map, bearing a seal unknown to man or beast.

In a rash moment some time ago Latour had promised to leave his possessions to those gypsy dwarfs who roamed the hills like scavengers; but of late he had had second thoughts.

On the occasional evenings when the gypsy dwarfs came down from the hills, he would drink wortwine with them around a boiling caldron and recount stories of what he had seen in his time. Often his tales had a moral; but what with his drinking and all, more often than not he would forget the point of his tale. It made little difference, really. The gypsy dwarfs were a raffish lot—clods, all of them. While he spoke they yawned and drank and made rude noises. They thought him odd or mad or both. Even their scruffy cat, which had pretensions of being a black cat, would often smirk at him. The cat, however, had sense enough to keep its distance from Latour, who lost no opportunity to stomp on its insolent tail.

Later, with a sadness, the dwarf closed the lid of his coffin and began to wait, as he did each night, for the horrors of memory to ravage his mind.

For a time he sat there, leaning against the coffin, thinking of Sorge. Sorge, he recognized, was unlike the others around Barras. Over the years Sorge had never tried to use him or seek small favors; Sorge had never jostled for position, as did the others who were close to Barras.

Occasionally, when Sorge came back from a trip, he would bring a gift for Latour, perhaps a box of splendid cigars, or a straw hat or some bonbons. In truth, Sorge had always treated him as a man among men rather than as a freak of nature.

Latour began thinking of ways to warn Sorge of his danger. There had to be a way, but how? There was so little time and he had no means. Gradually it came to him that there was indeed no hope of forewarning Sorge except a fool's hope. In the end, it seemed certain, Sorge would be brought back for interrogation in the lower chambers of the Fortress. An interrogation there by M-5 had only one meaning—torture by the meat-rackers in their black butcher smocks until a man was broken and beyond repair.

Dempsey woke up the next morning in Catherine's apartment. He was aware she had not come back.

He rose from the armchair he had slept in all night. His suit was rumpled and he was unshaven. An irritation was settling in his mind.

He wondered about Turner, and he called the kid's number. There was no answer.

Again—still no answer.

He made a few more calls, then drove to his own apartment for a shower and shave.

The stinging cold shower cleared his head, and as he dressed he began to plan his morning, his mind sifting out thoughts and turning over probabilities.

He was ready now; and, as always, he checked his .38.

Husler met Dempsey in Catherine's apartment. Husler was on his day off. He owed Dempsey for a past favor and Dempsey was calling on it now.

Dempsey did not waste time. He held out a photograph of Catherine.

"Her name's Fleming. Catherine Fleming. When she comes back I want to talk to her."

"Detain her?"

"Just tell her I want to see her."

"Do I wait here?"

"No, downstairs."

"How long?"

"Till I let you know."

"What else?"

"There's a man. Name's Smithy. Medium height, thin, horn-rimmed glasses, medium blond, Caucasian, a slight beak on his nose."

Husler was soaking it in. "What else?"

"If he shows up with or without her, stay on him. Don't lose him. I want to know where he stays. I want to know anything, everything. You let me know. I'll take it from there."

Husler nodded.

"And be careful," said Dempsey.

"Is he armed?"

"Consider him armed."

"Anything else?"

"Yes, keep it under wraps."

"Sure," said Husler, pleased that Dempsey had let him handle a private matter for him.

They left the apartment and Dempsey drove off alone. He had confidence in Husler. Husler was experienced; he was steady and low-keyed, and you could count on him.

From his desk Martin looked up at Dempsey with a puzzled expression; his jaw jutted.

"I don't understand," he said.

"The kid's missing," Dempsey said again.

"Why come to me?"

"The kid was on a stakeout last night."

"Where?"—brusquely.

"Krone's place."

"On whose orders?"

"The kid wanted one last shot at it."

"And you let him?"

"Yes, I let him."

"I thought I told you—"

"I know what you told me."

Martin was mulling it over.

"Did he get home at all last night?"

"No."

"Did he call in?"

"I've asked around. No."

Martin thought about it further. He reached for his phone, not bothering to conceal his irritation.

When the call was over and he'd hung up, Martin said to

Dempsey, "That's it. Not much there. Sheldon had a man there last night. Nothing happened. Krone went home and stayed there. The only thing that moved from the house was the chauffeur. On an errand. He was back in an hour or so."

"Did Sheldon's man follow him?"

"He had orders to watch Krone. That's exactly what he did."

Dempsey persisted.

"What about the tap?" he asked.

Martin didn't answer.

"The tap on Krone," said Dempsey. "It's been in place two months."

"I don't know about any tap."

"Sharkey's handling it."

"What about it?"

"Maybe there was a call last night—"

"You're beating a dead horse, Dempsey."

"Maybe. Maybe not."

Martin was looking at him closely.

"What did you tell the kid last night?"

"That we were off the case."

Martin shrugged.

He said, "Maybe the kid took it personally. Maybe he got drunk; maybe he's sleeping it off with some girl. Maybe anything."

"The kid doesn't drink."

Martin was turning it over in his mind. "Okay," he conceded raspily. "I'll give it a shot, but you and me, we're not finished yet."

Dempsey nodded. He'd deal with that later.

Martin said, "Check the hospitals."

"It's being done."

"And his car. Put out a—"

"It's been done," said Dempsey. The machinery was in motion; all you could do now was wait.

Martin reached for the phone again.

* * *

There was some delay but the tape arrived and Dempsey quickly clicked it into the tape recorder on Martin's desk.

Martin was still skeptical.

The first call was a wrong number; it seemed authentic enough. The second one was between Madame Krone and a friend. An ordinary call; two old friends chatting.

The third one, a call to Krone, was from a middle-aged woman. She was a friend of Eddie, she said, and she had an envelope Eddie had left in her care.

When the conversation was done Dempsey replayed the tape, fixing each word. The tone in the voice quavered, he noticed.

He turned off the playback.

"Eddie. Do you know who Eddie is?"

"How should I know?"

"It's Burry's first name."

Martin was surprised.

Dempsey said, "The chauffeur going out had to be Krone. The kid must have followed him."

"It's a good possibility, yes."

"And that voice—"

"What about it?"

"The woman has a cold."

"I noticed that, yes."

"There's one more thing."

"What's that?"

"That's not her natural voice," said Dempsey.

Martin was staring at the tape machine. The Burry case now had suddenly taken on a new dimension.

Dempsey got on the phone.

"Matt?" He waited for a reply. "Matt, pick up Krone. Now." His words exploded. "I want him *now*."

Dempsey hung up abruptly, and he was on the phone again, calling, questioning, issuing orders. Without a word being said,

Dempsey had begun to take charge of the Burry case again, and Martin did not for a moment interfere.

When Catherine woke she felt queasy, and she became aware of Smithy standing near her.

"Something's happened," she heard him say.

She sat up startled; he had caught her in the vulnerable moments of awakening.

She tried to clear her head.

"What's wrong?" she asked him.

"The situation's more serious," he said to her. "For *you*," he added.

"For me?" She felt chilled.

"You'll have to get away."

"Away? Where?"

"If you don't," he told her, "you'll be dead in a few days."

She rose, feeling weak.

She wore only her slip, and that too made her feel vulnerable.

"But where would I go?"

"I've already made the arrangements," he said.

"You knew?" she reacted. "You knew about it before?"

"I didn't want to alarm you," he said quietly. "I thought I could work things out."

"But why me?" she asked, trying to focus.

"Because they think you know too much."

"Know? What do I know?"

"It's what they think you know," he said.

"Oh, God," she exclaimed. "What's happening?"

He came closer.

"Right now your apartment's being watched," he told her.

"By who?" she asked, yet dreading to hear the answer.

"It can happen anywhere," he said. "On the street or here, if we're traced."

She could feel her head pounding.

"We don't have much time," Smithy was saying. "He's already killed one man. The one you called about."

She was shivering.

"Will you be coming with me?" she asked.

"No, you have to go alone," he told her. "You'll use the Calder passport. It's the only one I could lay my hands on in a hurry. There's a reservation for you at the Aristos Hotel in Mexico City. There'll be a message at the desk, telling you where to go next. I'll meet you in ten days."

"Yes, ten days," she said, repeating the words numbly.

"If you don't hear from me in two weeks, consider me dead," he said in an ordinary way that made the words more chilling.

She tried to steady herself.

Through the next few hours Smithy guided her, instructing her in what she had to do.

In the bathroom she dyed her hair black, consistent with her photograph in the passport. Later she applied dark-toned makeup which Smithy had already gotten. She remembered the Calder passport; it was the one she'd used years ago on a trip to Basel she'd made for Smithy.

Smithy had her empty her purse of all identification. In turn he provided her with a new driver's license, credit cards, all in the name of Elizabeth Calder. He gave her a plane ticket and five thousand in cash. From the closet he brought out a traveling bag that was ready and packed with clothes and whatever else she might need for her trip. It had taken a lot of effort, she knew, to pull this all together in such short time; it was something Smithy had always been good at.

Through it all Smithy remained calm. It was that calm, his sureness, that held her together now, and she was grateful for that. The familiarity of it all was helpful too. She'd learned a lot from

Smithy, about schedules, passports, visas, foreign currencies, mail drops, time differentials, a thousand details he had made her fix in her memory. He had trained her in makeup and in cover, in voice training, some of it fitting in with her career on the stage.

She was remembering her first overseas assignment, a trip to Cairo to pick up a package from a man who had only a first name. Then a flight to London to deliver the package to another man with a first name only, whom she met in a museum. For the trip she had used a forged passport and a new identity. It was government business, Smithy had told her to reassure her; but even if it hadn't been that it wouldn't have mattered to her. She'd been in love with him then, crazy in love, and would have done anything for him.

Smithy had always managed everything. On her trips Smithy had always held her on a short string. Often she'd know only her first destination where a message would be waiting, telling her where to go next. Or she'd have to wait somewhere for Smithy's call before she knew her next stop. With Smithy everything was held in airtight compartments. If something went wrong in one place, he once told her, it wouldn't spill over to the next. But nothing ever did go wrong, and in time it began to seem so ordinary, always so easy, always without a hitch. She tried to hold on to the feeling that it was all so ordinary, even now.

In the cab to the airport Catherine felt herself almost without a will of her own. Whatever she did she was doing through Smithy; his will had become hers.

Near the airport she had a mental block. She had forgotten the name of the hotel in Mexico City. She wanted to write it down but Smithy cautioned her. "Don't write anything. Keep it in your head. Remember it—the Aristos."

It was almost two when they got to the airport.

There was a delay in the flight. Over the loudspeaker came the announcement that the flight would be delayed an hour.

Catherine was grateful for the delay. She felt safe as long as

Smithy was with her. The thought of being alone, without him, filled her with anxiety.

Glimpses of Dempsey kept recurring in her mind, always with a focus on his gun in its holster.

She tried to shut it from her mind.

Turner was traced to the Roosevelt Hospital. He had been slashed in the abdomen. He was found without identification in an alley where he had been covered with rubbish in the snow. He was in a coma, barely alive, holding on to life by a thread.

Martin was putting on his coat, ready to go to the hospital. He paused to look at Dempsey, who was still at the tape, playing it over and over, listening to nuances and voice patterns, concentrating on phrases and words. Another word, another phrase, intonations, cadences, Dempsey oblivious to all else.

"Coming to the hospital?" Martin asked.

"No. No, not now."

"What are you after?"

Dempsey didn't answer.

Martin said, "When we find Krone—"

"He's not the key."

"We'll find him."

"It's not Krone."

"Why not?"

"A knife's not his style."

Martin said something more but he was aware that Dempsey had drifted from him and was submerged again in his world of tones and phrases uttered by an unknown woman speaking in a voice that was not her own.

As Martin was leaving he heard again the familiar phrase, "I'm a friend of Eddie . . ."

The voice had a slight quiver, a trace of nervousness.

* * *

There was a further delay of more than an hour in the flight to Mexico City. Smithy took Cathy to a bar where she had several drinks to soothe her nerves.

Finally the call for boarding came. Cathy did not rise at once. She lingered with Smithy until the last call, and she held on to his hand until his fingers slipped from hers.

On the ramp, looking back, she saw that Smithy was not in view; she felt suddenly cut off.

Smithy took a cab back to the city. It had been a cruel but necessary hoax he had had to play on Cathy; it was regrettable only in that she would have to live with the fear of it until he was together with her again. He'd make it up to her, he thought. *If* he survived. He'd planned carefully, but luck, he knew, irrational luck, was an incalculable factor in any plan.

On the way back to the city a thought began to nag at him. Had Cathy left behind any papers in her apartment? A diary? She had once kept one, he knew. If she had one now there was no telling what was in it, perhaps some entries linking her to him. No real harm in that, considering the distance he had maintained between them. Yet the thought of leaving tracks, however remote, went hard against his grain. He'd seen it before, small details, carelessly neglected, becoming dangers. There was always the chance . . .

Smithy had the driver let him off at an intersection two blocks from Cathy's apartment. It was early evening but already dark.

When Martin came back from the hospital he found Dempsey at his desk. The tape had been turned off.

"The kid won't last," said Martin.

Dempsey seemed not to hear.

"I said, the kid—"

"I heard you," said Dempsey sharply.

Martin let it go.

"Find anything?" he asked.

Dempsey was staring at the desk.

"By the way," said Martin. "There's a guy outside. Wants to see you."

"What about?"

"Says his name's Simpson. Says it's important."

"Simpson? He's the manager."

"The guy who couldn't remember?"

"Let him in," said Dempsey.

In a while the manager was brought in. He wore a tie and hat and was carrying an overcoat.

He stood there nervously.

"I've been thinking about it," he began. "I mean—"

"Your memory's come back? Is that it?"

"Yes, I began to remember—"

"Remember what?" Dempsey shot back at him. "You remember he had a small hook on his nose?"

"Why, yes."

"And he wore horn-rimmed glasses?"

"Yes, that's exactly—"

"Get out!"

The manager hesitated.

"I said, get out," Dempsey said angrily. "Get out!"

The manager, shaken up, turned and hurriedly left the office without shutting the door.

When the manager was gone Martin closed the door behind him and turned to Dempsey.

"What's that all about?"

Dempsey was glaring at the tape. "The woman," he said, "the one on the tape—I know who she is." Dempsey did not look up nor did he allow his feelings to surface.

"Tell me about it."

In a voice kept under control Dempsey began to brief Martin

128

about his involvement with Catherine and of what he knew about Smithy. The briefing was detached, almost devoid of emotion.

Later, other bits of information began to come in. Turner's car had been found in a garage near Broadway; on the seat of the car was a half-eaten candy bar. It had been established earlier that a man in a chauffeur's cap had picked up an envelope at the desk of the Taft. The man who had left the envelope there was identified as average-looking.

It was a good guess, Dempsey reasoned, that Smithy had been at the Taft and had intercepted Turner near the hotel.

"It was a setup," Dempsey said to Martin. "My guess is, Smithy couldn't give the envelope directly to Krone. Whatever the reason—maybe authenticity—the envelope had to seem to come from Burry."

"A dead Burry?"

"Yes, that's why he was killed."

"A damn small reason, isn't it?"

"Not if we knew what was in the envelope."

"Is that what it's all about?"

"Yes, a damn envelope wrapped in Christmas decorations."

Martin was aware of the calm in Dempsey's manner; it was a surface calm, Martin knew, and it had to explode. It was only a matter of when.

It was numbing cold but Husler did not break the continuity of his surveillance except once to urinate and once to call in to Dempsey.

He wondered how long he'd have to wait until Dempsey showed up. He'd have to call Leah, else she'd worry, waiting up for him, as always, no matter what time he came in. When he'd get home he'd pick her out of bed and carry her to the kitchen. She'd sit with him while he warmed some soup or whatever he'd fixed in the morning, and they'd talk for hours, he and Leah. She was frail, like you could touch her and she'd fall apart. It'd been that way for ten years, Leah hanging on and he dreading the day he'd come home and find her—God, it wasn't right. Anyone else, but why Leah?

When she'd finally drop off to sleep he'd sit and watch the late show, Alan Ladd in Macao or somewhere, it didn't make much difference, he wasn't watching anyway, just mulling about a life gone down the drain.

Dempsey and a few of the brass had covered up for him for the one mistake he'd made. They'd done it for Leah, he knew; but from that time on he was through, with nothing left except a few years till retirement and, after that, waiting to die. Funny, you felt dead inside but you had to wait to die.

It was after dusk when Husler became aware of a man walking into the entrance. He noted the man's precise walk. An average-looking man wearing a coat and hat against the cold.

Later he saw a light go on in Catherine's apartment on the fifth floor. Suddenly for him the numbing, daylong waiting was over.

It was dark, a winter dark, and he was concentrating on what he had to do. The man was alone and possibly armed, and as Husler entered the building he knew he was going in against instructions, but he had to go, as always feeling he had to prove himself over and over to retrieve the one bad moment of his life.

Martin had asked him, "Where's she now?"

"Probably with Smithy," said Dempsey. "She's not at her apartment, I know."

"How do you know?"

"Husler would have called."

"Husler?"

"He's been at her place all day."

Martin shot a look at him. "Why?"

"I was worried about her."

Dempsey was putting on his coat.

"You going to her place?" Martin asked.

"There may be something I missed before."

"I'll go with you," said Martin.

"I'd like to handle it alone."

"I know, but I want it cool."

Later, as he drove with Martin, Dempsey kept thinking of Catherine. The call she had made was a deliberate act. You couldn't get around it, and that was the sticking point, he knew.

Martin saw his expression.

"Don't let it get personal," he said.

Dempsey kept staring ahead; his face was a piece of rock.

It was dark and chilled on the street, and Dempsey was looking for Husler when he heard the sounds of gunfire—two shots and a shattering of a window.

Dempsey motioned to Martin, who began to race toward the building entrance.

Drawing his .38, Dempsey ran across the street toward the construction site there, quickly making his way in the darkness around to the back entrance of Catherine's building. Ascending the steps, he opened the door and moved into the hallway. In a low crouch, his body in balance, his .38 at ready, he waited.

He heard a muffled shot. Some moments later the door to the stairwell opened and he saw a figure turning toward him at the front of the hallway near the lobby. It was Smithy and he had a gun.

Dempsey pulled his trigger as a shot slapped past his shoulder and bit into the door behind him. He heard the impact of his own shot splatter against metal—Smithy's gun.

As Smithy dodged behind the wall of the lobby, Dempsey's second shot missed its mark.

He edged toward the wall. He heard the sound of a firing pin but no shot came. Smithy's gun, he guessed, had been disabled.

Dempsey began to move forward; he had the entrance covered.

He heard a side door open from somewhere in the lobby. He heard Smithy's voice—"Get inside—quick!"

Dempsey rushed forward and when he got to the door of the apartment at the side of the lobby, he found it shut. He stepped back and shot at the lock. He kicked at the door; it sprang open.

In an instant he was focusing on Smithy and a middle-aged woman near the window. Smithy had a knife at her throat; his useless gun was on the floor.

Smithy glanced at Dempsey's gun. "Drop it," he ordered.

Dempsey, seeing the woman's horrified eyes, knew he had no choice; he dropped his gun.

"Kick it over here," Smithy ordered.

"No," said Dempsey, resisting the demand. "You can go out the window. You'll have a few seconds start. That's all you'll get. Make up your mind."

Smithy, appraising the situation, was beginning to raise the window with one hand.

Dempsey said, "You may get away, Smithy, but I'll find you, and when I find you I'll—" He stopped abruptly, aware of the ferocity of his anger, the image of Catherine tearing across his mind.

The window was fully raised now. In two quick movements Smithy shoved the woman toward Dempsey and sprang out the window into the construction site a short distance below.

Momentarily impeded by the woman's body, Dempsey did not waste time retrieving his gun. He sprang out the window but by the time he hit ground Smithy was already halfway through the construction site heading toward the back fence there. Dempsey could hear Smithy's quick footsteps in the dark. There was a pause now —Smithy, he could guess, was climbing the fence. Dempsey took his chances in the dark and went after Smithy, but by the time he got to the fence and over it, Smithy was gone, swallowed up in the night.

When he got back to the street, Dempsey saw Martin, who had

been wounded in the shoulder. Two police cars were converging on the street. Dempsey briefed the men quickly and they fanned out toward the adjacent streets.

Later Martin had his wound treated. His arm was put in a tight sling and in less than an hour he was back again with Dempsey.

Husler, it turned out, was dead.

Dempsey put together what had happened. For some undetermined reason Smithy had gone to Catherine's place. Husler had surprised him there. Smithy was unarmed, except for a knife, yet he managed to disarm Husler and use his gun against him. On the stairway coming down Smithy intercepted Martin and caught him in the shoulder with a shot that spun Martin around into the bannister, knocking him unconscious for a time.

Martin said to Dempsey, "You did a good piece of work."

Dempsey shrugged it off. In the end all that counted was that Smithy had made a clean escape.

When Dempsey thought about it later he had to admit that Smithy's escape had been astonishing. Few men could have pulled it off. Fewer still could have carried it out with Smithy's icy nerve.

Dempsey began thinking of Catherine again; he felt empty. He had given her what he had given no one else; he had loved her more than had seemed possible for him. Yet she had gone back to Smithy; she had resisted but in the end she had gone back. And tonight she would be with him as once she was; they would be together again, lying in a bed of lies and corruption—what words would she say to him in the hollow of night? What were the words, the whispers and intimacies that would pass between them in that ungodly bed?

Later that night Martin went once again to the hospital to see about Turner. As he entered the corridor upstairs he came upon Dempsey, who was sitting on a chair, hunched over, oblivious to what was around him.

Martin approached but Dempsey made no sign of awareness.

Not wishing to intrude, Martin proceeded down the corridor toward Turner's room.

Outside the door stood Father Balsam, a spindly priest with sorrowful eyes, a perceptive man without pretension.

"The doctor's with him," the priest said quietly.

Martin nodded and remained silent. There was much to say, yet nothing to say.

Dempsey was sitting, bent over. He felt empty without being empty, and he was thinking that whatever he touched he hurt. He reached out and whatever his hand touched became withered. Maggie and Husler, and now the kid, almost dead; and all he could say was, I'm sorry, I'm sorry, saying it over and over until it was without meaning.

Once, in a child's world, he remembered, there had been magic and promise. The word of God had been in him and all things seemed possible. The child had walked with the grace of wonder. He had known the unutterable and touched heaven itself—where had the child become lost?

He was thinking of Turner now; he wanted to cry out, he wanted to say—Take me. Do with me what you will but let him live. God—God, let him live!

The priest was observing the figure hunched over in the chair down the corridor.

"That's Dempsey there," said Martin.

"Yes, of course."

The priest was silent a few moments, then said, "I passed him before. I would perhaps want to talk with him."

"Now?"

"No, not now, later," said Father Balsam. "At the moment I would be interfering."

"With what?"

"With his prayers."

"Dempsey? *Dempsey* praying?"

"Yes," said the priest. "When I passed him before I could feel him praying. He's been crying out to God."

"I wouldn't have thought—not Dempsey."

"He is what he is," said Father Balsam.

"And what is that?"

"I don't know. I'm only a priest. What is in him is between God and him alone."

Sometime later the nurse came from the room, and from her expression Father Balsam knew that Turner was dead.

Dempsey, bent over, with his hands covering his face, felt a vitality suddenly drain from him; and he knew then in his own way that Turner was dead. He looked upward, and he knew what he had known for a long time, that it was all useless. In his coming in and his going out, in his waking and sleeping, in his breath and mind, it was all useless. Damnation was the only permanence of his being; it was in him like breath and blood and life itself.

On his way out, Father Balsam passed near Dempsey. The priest could see the tears in Dempsey's eyes, and the anger there.

The priest said to him gently, "You must forgive—you must forgive even God."

In a motel on the outskirts of Newark, Smithy waited for Dufar's men to arrive from Caribe.

As he lay on the bed he recollected the unexpected encounter he had had with Dempsey. He had known, of course, that Cathy had taken up with someone. It had ruffled him, to be sure, but he had done nothing to interfere. Time itself, he had felt, would take care of the matter. And yet that one factor, that unforeseen element, had turned out nearly fatal.

He was sure Cathy must have known that Dempsey was a detective. It was a matter she had kept to herself, obviously reluctant to reveal her indiscretion.

As for the surveillance of her apartment, that in itself seemed natural enough in the circumstances. She'd been away from her place without a word, and you had to assume she had told Dempsey more than she should have—enough, in any event, to provoke curiosity, if not suspicion of one sort or another. Yet, despite it all, Smithy was convinced that Dempsey could not have penetrated much beneath the surface; but there was no telling how much he did know.

It had been close. Dempsey had come within a hair of cutting him down, and Smithy knew that he was alive only by the grace of a deflected bullet.

At any rate it was over with, and for the time being it didn't matter. Dempsey was sealed off from what was happening. Dempsey's existence, however, by its unknown possibilities, was an unsettling factor; but there was no way of dealing with it now.

Smithy had planned to meet Cathy within ten days; but her connection to him, now established, had rendered her contaminated. For the time being he'd have to treat her with extreme caution.

Once, years ago, he could have counted on her without question; but that trust had ended when she had become pregnant and the child she bore had died. He remembered how it had been then. She had been fearful and depressed by her pregnancy. Cathy had been ridden with guilt; she had felt she would not survive her term or that the child would be born malformed with incestuous taint.

As it turned out, a boy was born. It was born without mishap and well formed. Yet Cathy afterward had remained tense and depressed. At the hospital she never once asked for the child. When it was brought to her she hardly dared touch it.

Later he took Cathy and the child to a summer cottage that he had rented near the sea. He had gotten things for the child and had arranged for a woman to come during the day to help.

That first evening at the cottage, he remembered, he'd brought some wine and flowers for her, but it was a joyless evening.

At night when the lights were out the child woke and began to cry persistently. Cathy's mind was aflame. She lay in bed, listening, shunning the child.

In time he got up and attended the child. He felt tender toward it. He prepared milk for the child and afterward soothed it, humming, improvising. The sight of the small body with its tiny squeezed face and groping fingers entranced him. Here was a life—*his.*

He said nothing to Cathy; he wasn't angry either. He understood how she felt. Here, with her, was the child, an embodiment of the guilt she felt.

Later Cathy tried to sleep but couldn't. All night the wailing persisted until Cathy was close to screaming. In the morning she awoke haggard, worn out and distraught.

The woman he had arranged for did not come that morning; she had called in sick.

The child started to cry again and Cathy had to hold her hands to her ears, her fingers like trembling claws.

He took the child and held it for some time until it fell asleep. Afterward he called a service for another helper. Later he went to the village store for milk.

When he got back he saw Cathy sitting up in bed. Her face was chalky. It was quiet. He went to the sink to wash his face. He said to her, "Can't you sleep?"

She seemed not to hear him.

There was an unnatural quiet in the room. Cathy was staring at the bassinet.

He went to the child. He saw a tangle of sheets around it, tightened, twisted. He unloosened them, uncovering the child's face. It did not move.

"What happened?" he cried out.

"It's dead," she said in a flat voice.

He picked up the limp body. A tremor ran through him. "What happened?" he cried out again.

She stirred. A wild terror came to her eyes. "I didn't do it," she shrieked. "God, I didn't do it!"

He moved the body to induce some breath of life, but there was no movement. The child was limp, its naked little body lifeless with twisted strangulation. He began to breathe into its mouth, kneeling there by the bassinet. It was no use.

Cathy was lying in bed now, curled up facing the wall. Only silence now. He did not reproach her; he understood even that.

Later he went for a doctor, and when he got back Cathy was gone. She had come to herself, he guessed. She had found herself alone with the dead child and had fled in terror.

Afterward he came across her again in the city. Cathy, he found, had put the child's death completely from her mind. For her, the child, buried in oblivion, had died of a miscarriage.

In the course of the autopsy Smithy had learned that the child had not died of strangulation, as he had assumed, but of other, natural causes. Yet he and Cathy never spoke about it. He kept what he knew to himself; he did not want to open up old wounds. In the end Cathy drifted away from him. He saw her from time to time but there was a coldness in her body, like remembered fear. Smithy was aware that one day she would remember the child again; and that day, he was sure, would be for her a day of chaos.

Dufar's men, Smithy had calculated, were due to arrive at the motel within eight and a half minutes. They had called from the private airport, ostensibly to bring him word from Barras.

The second phase of Operation Bluebird was now in being. It was, perhaps, his last job. His reflexes, though still responsive, had begun to lose their fine edge. It was only a matter of time, he felt, before he'd have to quit or his luck ran out. The money itself that was involved in this last piece of business was, of course, considerable; but it was the game itself, the grand scale of it, that truly intrigued him. In a way, he found it irresistible; if he pulled it off, it would be a feat long remembered in the secret archives of Caribe.

At 2122 hours he became aware of movements outside his door.

At 2125 there was a knock on the door. He had no need to look at his wristwatch. Within each hour his mind was trained to register minutes within a ten-second variance. He was ready now.

He took his time going to the door. No need to hurry. Everything revolved around him. Others might act but they acted only in response to his own initiatives.

The two men who entered were unknown to him. No doubt they had been handpicked by Dufar. The telltale nuances of their mixed blood were faint.

One of them addressed him. "Sorge?"

Smithy nodded.

"Your names?" he asked. His French was brisk, his inflections approximately correct.

"Monserrat."

"And you?"

"Beloit."

"Who has the message?"

The two men looked at each other uncertainly. Monserrat had a thin mustache; Beloit wore a loose, mousy suit.

"We have orders for your arrest," Monserrat finally said, and waited for a reaction.

"On whose authority are you acting?"

"Colonel Dufar's."

"Show me the orders."

Monserrat displayed a document, signed by Dufar and by Salant, minister of justice.

Smithy dismissed the document with a gesture. "I'm under the authority of Barras," he said. "Without his signature these orders are quite meaningless."

"We have our instructions."

"I'm prepared to return to Caribe if—"

"We must search you."

"As you see, I'm unarmed."

"Nevertheless—"

"You must take my word," Smithy said.

Monserrat stepped forward.

"It's necessary—"

"If you touch me you touch Barras," Smithy said, standing his ground.

Monserrat paused at the implied threat.

Smithy said, "Obviously there's been a mistake. When I get back I will clear my name. Meanwhile you must accept my word."

Monserrat stood there, momentarily frozen with indecision.

"If you wish it we accept your word," said Monserrat, conceding the point to break the impasse.

Smithy nodded with an easy smile, and he said, "I'm surprised Dufar sent only two men."

"There are four more outside."

Smithy was amused. "Only six in all?"

He took a few steps toward the door, then turned to Monserrat.

"You may consider yourself lucky," he said to the agent.

"Lucky?"

Monserrat found himself looking down at an automatic in Smithy's hand. There was a moment of fear.

Smithy smiled.

"Here," he said. "You hold it. Next time follow your orders. You'll live longer that way. Now get my coat, and you, my attaché case."

Both agents breathed with relief and did as he ordered. Smithy put on his coat and strode to the door, the two agents following behind like servants.

As he entered a limousine that was waiting outside, his bearing was one of cool arrogance. If he lost control, he knew, his chances of survival would melt away.

The limousine arrived at the private airport. Before long he would be back in Caribe. He was still in control. Despite some malfunctioning and rearrangements his plan was still intact, more or less as he had planned it initially almost a year ago, revising and fine-tuning as he went along.

It was a certainty that Krone had informed Dufar of the envelope linking Sorge to Burry and to the cargo diverted into rebel hands. That information would be quite enough to give Dufar a cutting edge. That had been the point of it, to give Dufar an edge that cut deep enough but not enough to destroy. A fine line, though, for in Dufar's hands any edge was a butcher's tool.

PURGATORY

Caribe.

Caribe occupies the northern half of Dominica, the second largest island of the Greater Antilles, the southern half being occupied by the Republic of Hispaniola.

The peasant's life is short and harsh, but he has a saying: **Bon Dieu bon**—*God is good.*

"The army, my invincible sword."

—BARRAS

In a floppy hat and culottes that came halfway to his shinbones the dwarf, Latour, waited at the airport in Port-au-Grasse. It was past midnight, but not too late an hour for the dwarf, who had the habits of a night creature.

In and around the airport were militiamen and a scattering of *cagoulards* in their familiar black hats and dark glasses. Dufar, like an obelisk in his thin, white uniform, stood in the background, smoking a Splendid.

The airport, showcase of the republic, had runways for jets, with sleek roads to three points of the compass. A fourth road, still unfinished, led to the Bienville housing development, which itself was unfinished, the first spade having been turned three regimes ago with great fanfare, as a gesture toward the unwashed poor, who, as far as the dwarf's nose could determine, still stank of poverty.

On coming to power five years ago Barras had ordered construction at Bienville and scores of other projects halted. Funds, hitherto appropriated, were summarily diverted to the military budget. In one stroke, by the will of Barras, the army, under Ligny's command, had become the principal instrument of the nation's destiny.

When the plane approached the tension began. Standing on the hood of a jeep the dwarf saw the plane land and taxi toward the terminal, which was completely sealed off.

Sorge emerged from the cabin, his hands manacled. He was quickly taken to a waiting command car that drove off into the night.

The dwarf's jeep, driven by a corporal, followed the escort vehicles from the airport. Except for the procession nothing stirred on the road. Under edict the city had been shut down tight as a drum.

Latour observed the command car turn and enter the main gate of the Fortress. Surrounded by six paratroopers in green battle dress, Sorge was hurried through the huge gate, along a gloomy corridor, down humid stone steps to the dimly lit third level. On the third level—you couldn't go lower except to hell, as the saying went—maximum security prevailed.

Latour followed the paratroopers to the third level, his credentials allowing him access there.

At the end of the corridor one of the guards opened the iron door to a cell. The guard had a brutish face hardly distinguishable, in the dwarf's opinion, from the other humanoids comprising the prison cadre.

Sorge was thrown into cell 325X and the heavy iron door was

slammed shut. The paratroopers, part of an elite detachment, took up guard in twos at intervals along the corridor.

To the dwarf's knowledge, cell 325X was the only cell with an X affixed to its digits. Prison archives disclosed no significance to the X; it existed like an irrational afterthought.

The Fortress itself was constructed in the years 1805 to 1807 under L'Estrange, a former slave and self-proclaimed emperor. Originally the Fortress had been designed as a citadel by its architect, a modest scholar who had written a definitive thesis on dungeons; his paper being a model of meticulous research.

The Fortress, admittedly, borrowed heavily from French and English concepts, of a time when torture had reached exquisite heights. The prison's instruments of torture, however, as a keen eye could discern, were adaptations of later times—interpretations, for example, from Slavic influences, circa 1930; and variations translated from later Teutonic experimentations.

As a matter of curiosity the dwarf had once inspected cell 325X after the removal of a political corpse from its confines. The cell was small, windowless and of very thick black stone, its ceiling not over three feet in height. The floor, as always, lay under seven inches of water that crawled with things—just "things," Latour had noted, not having bothered to examine them by microscope or otherwise. The cell had no bed, no toilet, not even a Judas hole to peer through. When the door was slammed shut not a speck of light nor sound penetrated the cell. An occupant had only the choice of lying down in the foul water or sitting crouched over in a soundless, tomblike existence.

In the normal course, after daily interrogations that involved lacerations of the flesh of one sort or another, the prisoner, who was often unable to stand, would be thrown back into his cell, where his untreated wounds, exposed to the noxious slime, would begin to fester and rot.

Prison archives, Latour had noted, disclosed that no occupant of cell 325X had ever survived for more than eleven days, the record-holder being a scrawny, toothless deaf-mute who died without trial on Ash Wednesday, 1868.

Later that night the dwarf reported to Barras his observations of the night's events. Barras wore a simple blue tunic buttoned to the neck. Behind him on the wall was a huge war map of the island.

"Sorge is in 325X," the dwarf said glumly.

Barras nodded knowingly. "Dufar, I see, is out for blood."

The dwarf felt an urge to protest, but he kept his silence, knowing his place.

Barras said, "Dufar's a butcher, I know—"

"Sorge may be innocent."

"Dufar will determine that."

"Sorge won't last a week."

"Dufar's methods may be crude," Barras shrugged, a gesture of regret, "but I can't allow myself to interfere. If you wish, Latour, you may sit in on the interrogations."

"Me?"

"Dufar's reports, I'm sure, will be exact, but it would be helpful, you understand, if I had *your* impressions."

The dwarf understood. His presence at the interrogations, as the eyes and ears of Barras, would put a subtle restraint on Dufar, though perhaps not for long. If matters had gone this far it had to mean the evidence in Sorge's dossier was damaging, if not conclusive. It was obvious that Barras's concession toward Sorge was merely a gesture, a remembrance of Valmy when Sorge had stood with Barras against Fouché and the high command.

Presently, as Latour got ready to go, Barras stayed him, saying, "Ah, Latour, one more thing. The commander—"

"Vernier?"

"Yes. Tomorrow you are to make arrangements with his widow. His children will need care." Barras was referring to the commander of the ambushed troops, who had been executed for the disaster in the hills.

"I had to do it," Barras explained as an afterthought. "I had to set an example."

The dwarf was bewildered by the conciliatory gesture, but then it dawned on him that perhaps Barras was paying in advance for the agony that would be inflicted on Sorge.

Barras put his hand on the dwarf's shoulder. "You may go, Latour. We've had more than enough for one day."

For a moment then there was a sense of camaraderie between them. It was odd, their relationship. Barras had ministers and aides and officers of rank at his call, yet in the early hours of morning it was to his valet, a dwarf, that he would confide his innermost thoughts and doubts. Sorge had once been in that intimate circle of confidence, but Sorge was now in 325X, his life hanging by a thread.

Later, with a heaviness, the dwarf went to his room. Tomorrow the brutality against Sorge would begin.

It was late at night when Catherine got to the El Aristos where Smithy had said a message would be waiting.

At the desk she inquired about the message. None had come. Later, in her room, she ordered up scotch and began to drink. She wondered—would there be a message for her tomorrow? If not, what then? She felt drained and uncertain, and her migraine began again.

She slept badly that first night. She had frightening dreams but could not recall them when she woke the next morning.

She felt unsettled. She dressed and put on her sunglasses. Downstairs at the desk she spoke to a clerk whose name was Ramirez—a runt of a man with a thin mustache and a tight black suit. Ramirez checked around and confirmed that there was, indeed, no message.

Had it been mislaid? she asked him.

Ramirez shrugged, his rabbit teeth framed in a smile.

"But there has to be a message," she persisted. "Could I see the manager?"

Ramirez hesitated. "The manager—he is not here," he said.

"Will you ring me when he comes in?"

"*Si, si,*" said Ramirez, his smile gone.

Later she changed some currency into pesos and picked up a newspaper and magazines at the stand.

Ramirez was in a sweat. He remembered seeing a letter in an airmail envelope addressed to Elizabeth Calder with a notation—*Hold for Arrival.* It had come two days ago, he remembered. He had held it in his hands and had laid it on the desk, and that was the last he remembered of it.

He was upset. There'd be trouble, he knew. These tourists always made a fuss. Every other day some complaint, with the manager giving him a hard time. It was a joke with the others but not for him, worrying about his job and being pressed for money —getting in deeper and deeper with Antonio, who always came around with a big smile but was nasty about money.

It'd be another bad day, he felt. Lately every day was a bad one.

Wearing a blue suit and white, pointed shoes, Antonio sat in the lobby of the El Aristos, smoking a panatela and watching Ramirez at the desk. That deadbeat Ramirez seemed to be having a fuss with a tourist.

Antonio observed the woman in sunglasses. He watched her change some currency and pick up a paper and magazines. An American, he could tell at a glance. She had a nice figure, and he liked the way her thighs moved.

Later he approached Ramirez. The clerk became tense.

Antonio smiled. "Trouble again?"

"No, no," said Ramirez quickly.

"What did she want?—the one with the sunglasses."

"Oh, nothing. Just a letter."

"Is she here alone?"

Ramirez nodded.

"Room 302," he said, leaning over the desk confidentially, "Calder. *Elizabeth*," he lisped.

"Might be interesting," Antonio speculated.

Ramirez was momentarily relieved. It had been a small favor he'd done and Antonio, he felt, would be off his back for a few days.

Nicky had bought the newspaper in the lobby of the hotel in Miami. He always got the New York papers when he was out of town. Miami was okay but for him there was nothing like New York. Even the broads smelled better up there when their juices were running.

In the lobby he sat reading his paper. He wore a snap-brimmed hat and felt sharp. Out of the corner of his eyes he noticed a blonde giving him a look. Too bad he couldn't stay around, but he was here on a quick job, in and out. The job hadn't come through the usual connections, but the money was sweet.

Nicky had had it figured at first that it was something personal —a guy getting back at Krone for fooling around with his wife. Didn't seem like much, this guy; but when you looked in his eyes it was like looking into something dead. You figured Krone was crazy messing around with a guy who had eyes like that.

Anyway, it was a sweet deal with a lot of waiting around at first, but when things broke they broke fast. Before you knew it you had to catch a plane for Miami, almost missing it by a hair.

It was in all the papers about Burry, and by this time you had it figured there was more to it than Krone fooling around with this guy's wife.

Nicky folded his newspaper and made his way toward the elevators. Krone was upstairs, alone in his room.

An easy hit, Nicky thought. No sweat to it.

Martin was with Dempsey when word came that Krone was reported a suicide in Miami. An eight-story drop. Window open. No sign of a struggle.

Martin mulled it over. "Suicide?"

"Doesn't make sense," said Dempsey.

Martin agreed. "That's four dead," he remarked. "Where does it end?"

"When Smithy's dead. It'll end when he's dead."

Martin sat down. He'd been to see Leah. Leah in bed, a string of bones. Her only connection with life had been her husband, Husler. When Martin had told her about his death she merely stared at him for a time. Then tears came and she began to cry softly, turning her head into the pillow. You couldn't hear or see her crying, but her frail bones kept quivering, and what could you say to her?

Dempsey was saying, "McNulty can handle the Canadian end," referring to Krone's Toronto operations.

Martin was remembering his encounter with Turner's mother. She had seen her husband die. Now her son was dead. A family of three, two of them dead. Her family had ceased to exist. It had been too much for her. She had screamed at Martin because he was there, screaming obscenities and anguish until in the end she collapsed on the floor with heaving sounds and wailing.

Dempsey was saying, and Martin was barely listening, "Coombes can handle the loan-sharking end of it."

The papers, Martin was thinking, would tell of two men who had died in the line of duty. What it came to, though, was two women crying and two bodies you had to bury. Martin wanted to say something but he didn't trust his voice not to crack.

Dempsey said, "I'll take the depots—the shipments." Martin could guess that Dempsey had judged that end of it the most promising. Maybe it was only a hunch, but that's all you could go on for the moment.

Martin composed himself now.

"I've got to clear you for the job," he said to Dempsey. "It may take time."

"We don't have time."

Martin agreed. "You go ahead," he said. "I'll cover for you. I won't ask questions. Just get me Smithy."

At the moment, with Leah still on his mind, Martin would have dealt with the devil; but when he saw the expression in Dempsey's eyes, he began to wonder whether or not he had already made that pact.

That night Dempsey began to put his affairs in order. He prepared some few notes to leave behind in the care of Martin, and then he was ready.

He went to pay his respects to Turner's mother, and stayed with her for an hour or so. She talked about her son; she talked and she cried until she was empty of both words and of tears.

Once she said to him, "He's in God's hands now." It didn't mean anything, he thought; but it had meaning for her, and that was its meaning.

Later he saw Leah. She was sitting up in bed, and with her were two neighbors with Gothic faces watching over her. One of the women offered him tea with biscuits; and he sat there with them in the early afternoon. Leah, her face bony and drawn, and often crying, kept glancing at the door, as if waiting for her husband to come home—and what could you tell her that really mattered?

Still later he walked to the zoo and watched the polar bears in the snow. The trees in the park were bare and stark against the motionless sky. His mind had few thoughts; it was as if his mind were clearing itself of thought and memory.

He bought some chestnuts from a sidewalk vendor and ate them as he walked back to his place.

His anger had been drained off and what remained was a cold residue, deeply buried. He felt as if, for him, there were no past or future.

He began to clean and oil his .38; he was quietly relaxed. His mind was cut off from all ties; it was free and without restraint, ready for what had to be done.

When he had reassembled his gun he tried the trigger, feeling its response, which was finely honed and attuned to his own acuity; its rhythm and feeling were his; he and the gun were now one.

It was early morning and the dwarf lay on the bed in his room, dreadfully exhausted. He began to vomit but nothing came up except sour bile.

Last night he had had to witness in his mind his days in a death camp in 1942. The remembered stench of bodies had become so vivid that his room now seemed to exist within that abattoir.

In his years he had witnessed endless atrocities. The rack, the wheel, the knout; spikes, burnings, decapitations. Boiling oil, pincers, iron hooks, scorpions; flayings and floggings. The stake and the garotte; caldrons, poleaxes, roastings. The auto-da-fé; St. Bartholomew's night; the Inquisition and the Holy Crusades.

He had seen murder and butchery, children dismembered, thrown from windows, their heads cracked open like melons—and what does a child's blood write in the gutter?

He had witnessed gas chambers and dissection tables; he had been in the Crimea and at Verdun; he had seen the desperation and anguish—and at night in his room, prodded by an unnameable compulsion, he had to witness these horrors over and over until mind and soul became suffocated. His pores stank of these evils, his body retched until he longed to be rid of body and mind and of existence itself.

In the early hours of morning, when the horrors had abated, he began to huddle in the corner of his room where his coffin lay. He ran his hand longingly over the rough grain of its wood; and he wept, but without tears, for he had been given no tears to weep.

The dwarf thought once again of the signs he had seen. At night, in the flames of the candle, it had been given him to see what could not be seen, to know the unknowable. The signs had been tenuous, but clear enough. Someone had been condemned to become what he had become, to live as an Ishmael serving others, doomed to witness whatever was hideous and obscene. Upon someone—someone he did not know—an unspeakable curse had been laid. Someone had been cursed to take up his burden—the signs had been clear to the dwarf. Out of someone's doom was to come his own salvation.

The dwarf kept wondering about the matter for some time. It seemed grotesque to him that out of someone's agony would come his own peace. It was a joke, of course, he told himself—a cosmic jest, surely. Truly an affront against reason—even a fool, a desperate fool, would have to acknowledge that the signs were but a warp of mind, a bit of hallucinatory nonsense.

The more the dwarf thought about it the more his hopes began to disintegrate until, in the end, all hope was gone—gone with the clear light of morning and of reason.

A deep depression began to settle upon him; and as he rose to go his way, he was what he was, a dwarf, perhaps mad, perhaps sometimes foolish; a dwarf nevertheless, who had to face once more another day, bereft of hope or even the hope of hope.

Alone in his study Barras stared at the huge war map on the wall. The map for him was alive with the shifting complexities and the reality of two nations existing on one island like two cocks in a pit. To the north, Caribe. To the south, under the dictator Acosta, was Hispaniola. Two nations on one impoverished island, each arming for an inevitable day of reckoning.

For five years now, Barras reflected, he had deprived his nation to forge a weapon of revenge against the Hispaniolans for the shame at Massacre River.

Massacre River.

For generations, ten of thousands of illiterate blacks from Caribe had migrated southward illegally into Hispaniola to find back-breaking work in the cane fields at meager wages to feed the hunger of their families—work the Hispaniolans found demeaning and onerous.

In time, fearful of a "weakening of the national blood" by the migrant blacks, Acosta ordered their expulsion. The army began rooting the workers out of their *bateys*. As the migrants fled northward across the border at Massacre River, an incident occurred. A Hispaniolan soldier was found dead, gutted with his own bayonet. In retaliation Acosta unleashed the army; and in two savage days thousands of cane workers were butchered on the banks of the river, their rotting bodies lying for miles along the river.

There was an uproar in the foreign press. Later, on camera, his pancake makeup wilting, Acosta denied all knowledge of the incident. Off camera, he offered indemnity at the grudging rate of twenty-five gourdes per body.

The Committee of Five, then ruling in Caribe, accepted the offer. Fearful of provoking war, the committee had done nothing to prevent the slaughter; now, in silence, they swallowed their shame.

But for Barras the infamy was not one that could be paid for in gourdes; it was an affront that could be wiped out only in blood. After Valmy, when he had come to power, he had already begun to plan for that day of reckoning, for the time when he would hurl Ligny's armor across the river into the plains beyond to wipe out that day of shame.

* * *

At the gate of the Fortress the dwarf was subjected to a close body search and his credentials examined by Captain Derac, commander of the paratroop detachment that had taken temporary control of the Fortress. The old procedures, tight as they were, had been screwed even tighter. Under a new directive, nothing could move in or out of the prison unless Dufar personally approved. Even the dwarf's credentials, signed as they were by Barras himself, had to be cleared through Dufar.

When the dwarf arrived at the interrogation room Sorge and Dufar were already there. That morning Sorge had been rousted from his cell quite early. After a breakfast of watery gruel, his hair was clipped to a stubble and he was given a gray, oversized prison uniform.

The interrogation room, as the dwarf noted, was almost like a set piece from M-5's interrogation manuals. Sorge was sitting on a plain, hard chair, his hands and feet manacled. A high-intensity spotlight was directed at his face but he did not avoid its glare.

In a swivel chair Dufar faced Sorge from behind a desk that was devoid of even a scrap of paper. On a protruding ledge of the desk was an intercom phone.

The dwarf took a chair in the far corner behind Dufar to observe the proceedings.

The room itself, like the others in the interrogation section, was somewhat narrow. Conforming to examples of simplicity set by Barras, Dufar's room was not one centimeter larger than the others; yet it had an aura of its own, vested as it was with Dufar's awesome power as chief of intelligence. As the expression went, Dufar's room was equal but more so.

The other rooms were painted a dirty brown to absorb spatterings of blood; Dufar's room was a harsh, chalky white without a hint of violence. Softening procedures were assigned to the other rooms, to those interrogators known as "meat-rackers," who wore black leather butcher smocks.

The dwarf's stomach was knotted with apprehension.

Dufar rose now, coming toward Sorge, extending his silver cigarette case. "Cigarette?"

"You must know I never smoke," Sorge said coldly.

Annoyed by his error, Dufar clicked the case shut and retreated to his swivel chair. Sorge's presence had thrown him off balance and he had reacted like a novice at his first interrogation.

Dufar sat in silence, merely waiting. Time, he knew, was a weapon in his hands. Finally he said, "You have been informed of the charges, have you not?"

Sorge nodded—an almost imperceptible movement.

"What do you say to the indictment?"

"As you must know, I am innocent. The charges are part of a conspiracy against me, against the state and against Barras himself."

"It is *I* who bring the charges," Dufar said dryly.

"In my trial—"

"This *is* your trial."

"Who are my accusers?"

"*I* am your accuser."

"Then I must protest," Sorge said. "Let my protest be in the record."

"As you see, no records are kept."

"Latour is my witness."

"Latour is merely an observer. Nothing outside will intervene between us. You and I alone will settle this matter."

"Then I demand to see Barras."

"Your request has been denied beforehand."

Dufar paused.

"Before we proceed," he said, "it may interest you that the police in New York are searching for someone answering your description—"

"It's of no interest to me."

"—in connection with the murder of a man named Burry and

of two detectives," Dufar continued. "There is also a warrant out for a woman, an actress, as an accessory to the crimes."

"You're wasting time," Sorge said. "If you want the truth you can get at it without this nonsense."

"How would you suggest we proceed?" asked Dufar, his tone ironic.

"Inject me with Sodium Pentothal."

"What?" Dufar had been caught off guard.

"Yes, under a doctor's supervision, with a witness present. A simple injection, and the truth will emerge."

Dufar exhaled cigarette smoke. "I alone will determine procedures," he said. "Not you."

"Let Barras decide after he's heard the tapes."

"Tapes?"

"The recorder in your desk—it's still there, is it not?"

Dufar stood up abruptly.

"That will be all for now," he said. "Before our next meeting you'll have time to reflect on the needless pain you'll inflict on yourself by your denials. You are guilty, Sorge. We don't need truth serums to determine that. In the end, in one way or another, you'll die. If you confess it will be a quick death. That's the best you can hope for."

The interrogation was over and Latour was relieved it had ended without violence.

The first session clearly had been in Sorge's favor. His unexpected request had gotten him a reprieve while Dufar thought out the situation.

There was hope now, the dwarf thought. Even if Dufar refused Sorge's request, Barras surely would accede to it.

The dwarf left the interrogation in a hopeful mood.

When he reported to Barras he found Barras listening to the tape that Dufar had already submitted to him.

Barras turned off the machine; he pondered.

"What do you think?" he asked Latour.

"About the drug?"

"Is Sorge bluffing?"

"That assumes he's guilty."

Barras shrugged. "It would prove nothing," he said. "If he's eager for it, it could mean he's prepared himself."

"Or that he's innocent."

"It doesn't matter, one way or another," Barras said.

"Even if he's innocent?"

"Matters have gone too far," Barras said. "Once we brought him back it was the end for him. Even if he were innocent, as you believe he is, could we let him go? There are too many secrets in his head. Considering everything, do you suppose we could count on his future loyalty?"

The dwarf was dismayed. Barras's logic, harsh as it was, was unanswerable. For a time Barras had been reluctant, but once he had given the order to bring Sorge back, the outcome was inevitable.

The dwarf went back to his room. His stomach and mind felt wretched, and later that night, in the solitude of his room, he was compelled to witness again the execution of Damiens, which had occurred in the spring of 1757.

In the morning, as the dwarf began to remember, Damiens had been put to the rack. The executioner's assistants, using forceps, tore indiscriminate chunks of flesh from Damiens, and poured into the wounds molten lead from a brazier, which merely whetted the appetites of the spectators.

In the afternoon Damiens was hauled to the Place de Grève. His crime, it was said, was an attempt on the life of Louis XV. The streets near the site of execution were suffocated with festive crowds.

Naked and mangled, Damiens was bound on a platform with iron rings attached to his limbs. Four horses, huge beasts, were strapped to chains held by the rings. Damiens looked on the proceedings with the curiosity of a bystander.

The horses, stirred by prods, began to strain in opposite directions. The limbs of the victim were stretched violently out of their sockets, but held to his body. Damiens screamed at the violence done to his body.

Suddenly, with a sucking noise, the left leg was torn loose. Damiens raised his head, astonished. Then an arm was wrenched away. Those bystanders who possessed a subtle ear for agony, together with those who collected last words, leaned forward so as to lose neither a cry nor a word.

Another arm tore off abruptly, and Damiens stared at his remaining limb, dismayed by its stubbornness. At last, even that remnant was wrenched away, and there remained only a stump and lifeless head. The executioner, with the airs of a *seigneur*, now held up his hand and announced with a shout that Damiens was dead. The executioner bowed and the crowd churned with a hoarse swelling roar that came from its bowels and loins; and that afternoon there began monumental orgies and feasts that lasted the night.

Afterward the remains were burned and the ashes scattered to each of the four winds by a nervous flunky newly in charge of ash scatterings.

The dwarf woke early in the morning, feeling drained and wretched. Today would be another day to be lived, a day of feeling, seeing, knowing; a day of new violence.

Today was to be the second interrogation, and he was sure that today would begin the savaging of Sorge's body. Another day of dread to remember.

As he walked down the palace hall he began to think of the keys he had in his coffin. Perhaps one of them might fit the lock on cell 325X; if not, one could, with some ingenuity, fashion one such key. Yet how was he to get past the guards and paratroopers? Like everyone else he was carefully watched and subjected to a close body search; perhaps even more so than others, for Dufar was quite aware of his feelings about Sorge.

As he came near the door to Barras's study, the dwarf felt a twinge of guilt; for what was in his mind was in itself an act of disloyalty toward Barras. Yet guilty or not, his mind continued to turn over new and intricate schemes, none of which, he knew to his dismay, had a prayer of hope.

Barras was up early that morning. There was a heavy schedule before him. In the morning, long budgetary meetings. In the afternoon, longer meetings with Ligny and endless planning. Up at five and a hectic pace until late at night. Yet there was never enough time for all the problems, many with no clear solutions, others insoluble.

He was rankled by the festering insurrection in the hills. It was Ligny's estimate that it would take a year or more of heavy losses to root out that canker of rebellion. A harsh cost, but one that had to be met before the day of reckoning with Acosta. The timetable for the assault against the Hispaniolans had already been set; further delays would upset the balance and work in Acosta's favor.

Barras stood at his window, which overlooked the white-washed courtyard with its slender palms. The morning was quiet, a city awakening. Beyond the city lay the provinces, the cane fields, the gashed hills and small farms, too many of them drained of vitality by centuries of misuse and erosion. All in all, an uneducated land: its tongue Creole, its religion Christianity blended with the mysteries of voodoo. A land of five million beings, festering with poverty and unrest. Out of the sweat of the people he had forged the national weapon; out of their mouths, Ligny's armor. In time, like a sickness, the fester of unrest had erupted into an insurrection in the hills, a sickness that was kept at fever pitch by the money and supplies gathered by Fouché from his exile in Mexico City—Fouché, the will and the backbone of the rebellion.

Barras stirred with impatience. There would be no rest for him until Fouché was dead. With Fouché dead, the rebels would be weakened and their destruction less costly in men and matériel. But if it was to be done it had to be done soon, he knew.

The image of Fouché burned in his mind. Fouché, that stubborn little man who would not die.

After the first interrogation Colonel Dufar had summoned Mercier to his office at Command Center. A potbellied oldtimer, Mercier was chief medical officer of M-5.

"Mercier, a question came up . . ."

Mercier listened attentively.

"Does a drug exist," asked Dufar, "which would nullify the effects of Sodium Pentothal?"

"Not to my knowledge, no."

Dufar was not satisfied.

"This is important, Mercier."

"There may be unpublished research—"

"Yes, yes, I understand," said Dufar impatiently. "Now tell me —to your knowledge, are the effects of Sodium Pentothal invariably conclusive?"

"In most cases, yes, but it may be . . ."

Mercier went on, but Dufar waved him away.

Later that night Dufar received a disturbing cable from Communication Center. Krone, his chief witness against Sorge, was dead —a suicide in Miami. His death had occurred during the time that Sorge was in a motel near Newark. Dufar rejected the idea of suicide. But if it wasn't that, it had to mean Sorge had others acting with him. If so, how many others were there? How wide was the net?

Sorge's demeanor this morning had unsettled Dufar. Sorge had been aggressive, as if it were he, Sorge, who was determining events. Sorge seemed to be playing a game. Yet, in the circumstances, what game was possible? There was no way out for Sorge, no escape—or was there?

Dufar sent for Captain Derac and questioned him closely about procedures within the Fortress. The procedures, Dufar had to admit, were extremely tight, yet he was not wholly satisfied.

Derac, a tall, splendid figure in battle green, stood at attention.

Dufar said to him, "I want you to conduct a search of cell 325X. I'm holding you personally responsible for its security. I want the cell examined stone by stone—at once."

In time the captain reported back to Dufar. Every stone within the cell had been minutely examined, he said. Nothing and no one could get in or out except by the iron door, which was secure. Six paratroopers stood guard around the clock. Escape from the cell, the captain concluded, was impossible.

When the captain left, Dufar was still on edge. With Sorge, he knew, one always had to expect the unexpected.

There was an open question too about the woman, Catherine, who was reported as missing. What was her connection with Sorge? Dufar had ordered reproductions of her photograph that had appeared in the papers. Copies were sent to all agents and diplomatic listening posts, particularly in Mexico City. Considering that Sorge was now in complicity with Fouché, there was a good possibility that the woman, if indeed she had fled, would likely seek refuge with Fouché in Mexico City, or use his villa as a stopping-off place.

Dufar's instructions to his agents had been brief—*Detain subject pending further notice.*

Dufar began to busy himself with paperwork, but he was uneasy. He felt himself on a tightrope. If he erred, if something went wrong, Barras's wrath would be unforgiving. Dufar knew he had to be careful—but of what?

In cell 325X Smithy was Sorge again, thinking, feeling and being Sorge. With one purpose—survival.

His wrists and feet were in irons and chains; and to Sorge, the cell was not a confinement but a problem to be managed. The cell was a tomb; in it you couldn't stand nor could you lie down in the fetid water covering the stone floor. You had to sit bent over somewhat, careful not to chafe against the irons. In the putrescence of the cell wounds never healed but grew corrupt and gangrenous. In any event, you couldn't count on the ministrations of a doctor.

Privy to procedures, Sorge knew what to expect. In the cells on the third level, the political level, you had to sit near the iron door. In the mornings, when the guards came, you had about a half minute to get your daily rations. If unable to get to the door, you had to manage the day without rations. If you didn't respond for two days running the guards would investigate. Usually they found a corpse.

For Sorge the crucial problem of survival was the fetid water on the stone floor. Before tomorrow was over, he was sure his flesh would be ripped open in one way or another by one of the meat-rackers; afterward he would be thrown back into his cell with his open wounds. He had prepared himself with shots and antibiotics, but there was no way of knowing how much, nor for how long, these measures would help.

Later that night, he was hauled out of his cell and thrown into another nearby cell. Subsequently he was brought back to 325X. He was aware at once of a crucial difference. The deadly seepage had been drained away, and the stone floor scrubbed clean with harsh antiseptics.

Sorge understood what had happened. In an excess of caution Dufar had ordered the cell examined. The men who made the examination—probably paratroopers under Derac—had had the cell scrubbed clean by attendants before entering that odious tomb. The examination, of course, had been unnecessary. As Sorge knew, cell 325X was escape-proof.

Once the rank water had been removed, his chances of survival, of course, had improved. His plan, piece by piece, was now falling into place.

By now Dufar, no doubt, had already questioned Mercier and had decided against the use of Sodium Pentothal. By this time too, one could guess, Dufar would have had a meeting or two with Barras. Barras's attitude, of course, was predictable—it would be a hard one. You could imagine Barras, like a suspicious peasant, questioning Dufar about security procedures, putting him on the defensive until Dufar felt himself on a tightrope.

All in all, everything was in order except for Cathy. He had no reason to doubt Dufar's statement that the police were searching for her. It was probable too that Dufar had his own men on the lookout for her.

By now she had already gotten his message at the El Aristos, and was on her way to Veracruz—or was she? For one reason or another she might have stayed over in Mexico City. But it was there that Dufar had a dozen or more agents, a special unit, keeping a close surveillance over Fouché. There was a possibility that one of these agents might stumble across Cathy, penetrating her disguise —a remote possibility, to be sure, but one that was disturbing.

Later, Sorge prepared himself for the night, breathing evenly, his mind within a cool center, his pulse gradually slowing; and he continued his withdrawal until awareness ceased.

At 0600 hours Barras summoned the General Staff to the War Room. Ligny, the aggressive commander of the *armée,* sat in his customary place to the right of Barras.

The dwarf, as usual, served coffee to the officers.

Abruptly Barras rose and strode toward the map. With a pointer he jabbed toward Massacre River, that turbulence which gushed down the steep ranges toward the sea.

"Here," he pointed, indicating a point due south of the river. "Acosta is massing here and *here,*" he jabbed with emphasis.

"The usual winter maneuvers," said Ligny in a calm voice. His coppery, powerful head and his eyes commanded attention. "Intelligence reports—"

"Intelligence reports?" Barras snapped back. "The enemy is massing and we—*we* sit and read reports. Yesterday, five reconnaissance planes sweep over our airspace. Something is happening, Ligny."

"We're keeping close watch—"

"That's not enough. I want the Third Tank Battalion moved to Tournée and the Seventeenth to Gônave. I want every unit on red alert."

"As you wish."

"I want it done now—today."

Later, dismissing the officers, Barras asked Ligny to remain behind. Barras approached him. "We're alone," he said in a conciliatory tone. "Tell me, friend to friend, what do you think?"

Ligny shrugged, "Perhaps we're overreacting," he said quietly. "In any event, if you wish to proceed, I'd suggest no more than an orange alert and that we leave the Seventeenth where it is."

"Agreed," said Barras. "Do it your way."

"The Third will be in Tournée before nightfall," Ligny assured him, and Barras nodded his agreement.

"I know you don't see eye-to-eye with me," said Barras, "but my nose tells me something is out of joint."

"It may be," said Ligny, cognizant that Barras, at his core, had a peasant's sure instinct. Today perhaps he had overreacted but you could overlook that. Sorge's return had put everyone on edge, especially Barras, who had trusted him more than most.

On his way to Command Center Ligny had misgivings about the move to Tournée. That action would probably provoke Acosta to countermoves of his own. A cool grip would be needed to keep matters from getting out of hand.

* * *

Later, alone in his study, Barras lingered over the war map again, observing the coastline, aware of every weakness, every port and coastal gun. The Hispaniolans had naval superiority, but it was on the plains, the flat plains rolling down from Massacre River, that the issue would be decided by Ligny's armor.

Picking up the intercom now he called Dufar.

"Yes, sir," Dufar responded.

"Arrange to have the X102 ready for coastal inspection. Proceed through usual channels."

"Usual channels?" said Dufar. "Under those conditions it would be difficult, as you know, to ensure secrecy."

"That's exactly what I want," said Barras. "I won't be using the launch. I'm going to Tournée with Ligny. Make arrangements with him. Use Security One conditions."

"Yes, sir."

"One more thing. I want to be informed directly of anything unusual—anything. Put your agents on alert. Take nothing for granted."

"Of course."

"Especially with Sorge," Barras added. "Sorge has been back two days and already things are stirring. Keep your eyes open. I'm holding you personally responsible, Colonel."

The machinery was beginning to move, thought Barras. You could count on the Third Battalion being in Tournée before the sun had gone down. You could count on it too that the Hispaniolans would have intelligence reports on the move within two hours. Before the day had passed Fouché in Mexico City would know about it. There were few secrets in Caribe. Secrets were like commodities bought and sold in the marketplace. In Caribe, leaks in security were a way of life. Countermeasures turned out futile; it was like trying to hold back the sea.

Barras thought about Ligny, that battering ram. Give him a

column of tanks and you could be sure he'd slice through anything. Dealing with the rebels was another matter.

The rebels had no fixed points. They appeared and disappeared like smoke in the sprawling hills that covered three provinces. They scattered into the marrow of the villages, feeding on the peasants' mistrust. Barras himself had sucked that same mistrust from his mother's breasts. It would leave him only when life itself was gone. To generations of peasants the government had always been the enemy—demanding much and giving little. There was not much he could do about it. He could promise them only years more of austerity. Out of their unwilling sweat he had to forge the national weapon. For that purpose the nation had to swallow much. There was an old saying—"When the anvil, suffer. When the hammer, strike!"

Ligny was his hammer but Ligny's strength was slowly being sapped by the insurrection in the hills.

At precisely 0900 hours the second interrogation began. Sorge had been brought in under heavy guard.

Latour sat again on a chair in the corner behind Dufar.

Sorge, his face covered with stubble, was placed in a hard chair facing the glare of the spotlight in the semi-dark room.

"What had you to do with Burry?" Dufar began in a conversational tone.

"Nothing."

"Was he blackmailing you?"

"I had no dealings with Burry."

"Who, do you suggest, killed him?"

"A bungler, I would say."

"Why do you say that?"

"Six shots at close range? One or two would have been enough."

"I see. You thought of that too—to put that idiot Dufar off track."

Sorge shrugged. "If you want to know about Burry," he said, "discuss it with Krone. I'm sure you're in close contact with him."

"Krone? We both know he's dead, of course. Whom did you use? Fouché's men? From Mexico City? You've always been one step ahead, Sorge. It's time, I think, we catch up. Now tell me, *who* is Smithy?"

"I don't know anyone by that name."

"According to police reports his description fits yours exactly. Do you have any comments?"

"No."

"You and I both know who Smithy is."

"You're wasting time, Colonel."

"I agree. Do you wish to confess?"

"There is nothing to confess."

Dufar lit a cigarette.

"You'll have one minute to decide."

"The minute is quite unnecessary," Sorge said.

At the end of the time Dufar rang a buzzer. Two guards entered.

"Take the prisoner to room eight," he ordered.

As Latour had observed, the interrogation had been quite pointless, really only a matter of form. Both Sorge and Dufar seemed to know it. The real interrogation, it was apparent, would be conducted down the corridor by one of the nameless meat-rackers.

Dufar's report gave an accurate account of the savaging of Sorge's body. Sorge had been bound up and lashed with a wet bullwhip until consciousness left him. During the whole time he had not cried out once. Later his unconscious body, like a side of meat, was dragged along the stone corridor down the steps to the third level where he was thrown back into that soundless tomb, cell 325X.

When Barras had finished the report his only comment to Latour was, "He's a stubborn fool, Sorge. What has he to gain by it?"

The dwarf felt depressed. The cruelty in room 8, even in the reading of it, had cut to his core.

That afternoon, having an hour to himself, he went to his room and took some herbs to settle his mind. He felt green inside, anticipating the next interrogation which would probably involve shocks of steadily accelerating voltages in room 5—the shock room.

There was, it seemed to him, a terrible stir of violence in the air. It was in the Fortress, in the city and at the border, where units were being reshuffled. The border itself was like an open wound that never healed. Along the ranges and eastward was a *cordon sanitaire* of barbed wire, pillboxes and scorched earth.

How the enmity between the two sides began, no one could really say, least of all the dwarf, who was dismayed by the violence. The enmity between north and south had existed from generation to generation; and by all accounts the bloodiest encounter between the blacks and reds, as the sides were indicated on their respective war maps, took place at Kleber Pass. Latour himself, having served at the time as orderly to General Jussac, had witnessed that awesome bloodletting.

In Port-au-Grasse, historians still talked with awe and incomprehension about that battle of annihilation, which pitted the north under Jussac, who commanded a regiment of Napoleon's garrison, against von Brecht, a mercenary, commanding a conglomeration of Spanish grenadiers, freebooters from the Baltic and some barefoot natives hastily stuffed into uniforms.

Von Brecht, commanding the southern forces, was a bloat of a man, renowned for the plunder and rape of villages by the cluster and towns by the bushel. Jussac, on the other hand, had never tasted battle, having been held in reserve from Marengo to the field of Austerlitz.

On the eve of battle, having analyzed enemy dispositions, Jussac was elated. Tomorrow would be his first taste of battle and of victory. With jubilance he leapt upon his horse, his cape flaring like a giant bird, his sword annihilating the air. Latour, his orderly, had to remind him, "Not yet, *mon général.* Tomorrow."

As by fate, a mist descended at dawn into Kleber Pass, a mist denser than any ever known to man. One could see no more than a few meters or so ahead. Nevertheless Jussac, thinking to take advantage, ordered the advance, maneuvering his troops across the wide part of the pass, which had many arid ravines and turns. Riding up a knoll to have a command view of the coming battle, Jussac watched his army disappear into the inscrutable mist.

As the forward column advanced, a drummer boy took a wrong turn at one of the ravines and the rest of the column followed blindly, hearing only the tattoo of the drum. The forward commander, sensing the wrong turn, upbraided the drummer boy, who began to cry. The commander ordered the forward column to retrace its steps. In so doing, the front and rear elements began to fire at each other, cavalry units hacking down their own grenadiers, cannon cutting to pieces their own mounts. Even camp followers and dogs snarled at each other in the confusion.

Hearing the sounds of combat within Jussac's army, which was furiously committing suicide, and alarmed that his own men were being cut up, von Brecht called retreat and fled. In the retreat to the south, von Brecht's men razed three hamlets and a score of farms. With lances used for boar hunting they skewered at random some hapless peasants whom they had missed before; and they paused now and then to rape women and children and an unwilling assortment of sheep and cows.

Meanwhile, within Jussac's army, which was engaging itself like a madman at his own throat, huge masses of foot soldiers, artillery and cavalry began to melt away. The army beat at itself, bled itself, carved itself up until it was one macerated ball of anguished flesh, which became smaller and smaller until there were only scattered remnants of crazed men fleeing into oblivion.

Waiting impatiently on the knoll, Jussac heard the sounds of battle, but could see nothing. Each messenger he dispatched into the impenetrable mist failed to return. Sensing something amiss, Jussac began to ride toward where his army had disappeared.

As the mist began to lift, Latour, who was nearby, saw a strange sight. Astride a horse was a wild-eyed figure with wilted plume and what appeared to be a toy sword. It was Jussac, in the masquerade of a general, it seemed. In the distance were the remnants of his army, two drummer boys leading ghost columns, approaching each other. When they met they began to quarrel over the drums. Later, exhausted, they began to look for food, and became friends.

The dwarf, having keener eyes than most, had witnessed the battle from a cave halfway up the side of the pass, where he had sat, toasting herbs over a fire. Afterward, untethering his ass, the dwarf rode down into that pass of corpses and stench.

Amid the heaps the dwarf saw a scavenger, a peasant who seemed fat beyond belief. The scavenger wore several uniforms one over the other, and on his head were three military caps, each at its own rakish angle. Several swords jangled at his belt, along with watches, crucifixes, pendants and trinkets of all sorts. Each pocket bulged with spoils; and, as the scavenger walked, he gave off sounds like a sad tambourine.

One soldier, barely alive, called out to the scavenger for water. Approaching, the scavenger, who had a brutish face, stared for a time at the soldier's ring. While the soldier cried out, the scavenger squatted, trying to work off the ring. Unable to remove it, the scavenger sliced the finger off with a knife and walked away, pleased as a dainty hippopotamus.

The dwarf dismounted and carried water from a stream to the dying soldier. Huge, ugly flies began to gather. The sun burnt implacably over the rising stench and unmoving horror.

The scavenger moved on. It was a scavenger, one of those humanoids of the world, the dwarf thought, who would have the last word. Indeed, who was more appropriate to break wind over the last rites of battle?

In time, mercifully, the soldier died. Latour closed the dead man's eyes and placed herbs on them, as a remembrance.

In his room in the palace, all the years of violence began to close in on the dwarf's mind. Violence, he knew, was in man's blood like a madness. Neither reason nor all the saints could change that. Only in death was there peace, when earth covered over the hate, the hurt, the pain and brutality.

In his time he had been hung, shot, stabbed, garotted, poisoned, kicked, mauled, sodomized, mangled, piked, gassed and beaten by an assortment of humanoids, cretins, lords and beggars, churchmen and others; but he could not die. By divine providence he could not die.

From place to place endlessly he had sought out help from learned men and holy men. Most of them turned from him, shunning him. Once he had consulted a Jesuit. After reading books on the matter the Jesuit felt compelled to exorcise the dwarf out of existence, an attempt which solved nothing except for the Jesuit, who came to an untimely end, drowning in a vat of vinegar.

In later years, an Encyclopedist, in two closely reasoned articles, each more erudite than the other, proved the dwarf to be nonexistent—ab initio, at that. Before the articles were published, the Encyclopedist, it happened, developed monstrous boils on his scrotum and went mad at Charenton, side by side in a ward with the equally erudite Marquis de Sade.

In all his years of seeking, the dwarf found no one to help him. For his efforts he was hounded by the Inquisition in two countries. In Rome he had an unfortunate encounter with one of the Borgia popes, who mistook him for a moneylender. From a monk, who had flagellated himself for thirty-three years, the dwarf received a hair shirt stinking of sweat. From a miracle worker, who could turn water into wine, the dwarf went away with a half cup of rancid water. From a Calvinist preacher he received five admonitions. From a guru, merely the vacant eyes of infinity.

For the dwarf there was no reprieve from the doom of life. Everywhere he was treated with scorn, disbelief, contempt or indifference. Nowhere, not in all the years, did he find someone who could help him.

Yet he had continued to hope. It was a hope, though, which reason rejected; for he believed neither in man nor in God nor in the fables of man.

This morning, in the clarity of the early morning light, he had seen his hopes vanish like mist. Yet now, like Lazarus from the grave, hope had begun to rise once more. To be sure, that hope was a fragile one, yet it was hope nevertheless, enough to sustain him for one more day and one more night.

The second night at the El Aristos Catherine slept badly. In her dreams she heard the sound of a child crying, and she could not shut it out.

In the morning she felt drained, and later she vomited in the sink. In time she pulled herself together and dressed. Wearing her sunglasses she went downstairs to the desk. Again, no message. She'd almost expected that, as if it were something that had to be.

In the dining room she had a light breakfast, some tea and a half slice of toast.

She felt isolated, uncertain. She knew she'd have to see a doctor soon; she couldn't let too much time pass. Yet she had to wait for Smithy's message, which would let her know where to go next. It would probably be her final destination, and when she got there she'd have time enough to—yet what if Smithy's message never came?

Upstairs in her room, sitting on the bed, she began to wonder about Smithy's intentions.

She was remembering how it had been in the years after her miscarriage. Her feelings toward Smithy had turned, and she began to feel relieved when he was away.

Once, when he was gone for months, she began to go out with other men. It started that way, casually, out of loneliness, out of a need to be with others. There was no permanence, though, in any of it. She avoided sex, and the affairs for her became dry and joyless.

She began moving from place to place but always, somehow, Smithy managed to find her, usually through people she knew in the theater. He began to intrude into her life. Whenever he showed up, whoever she was seeing at the time would drop out of sight. Calls began to dry up. She was hardly aware of what Smithy was doing until the affair with Bart was broken off.

Bart had fallen in love and wanted to marry her. He'd made money on Wall Street and had been all-American at Tulane. She didn't love him but he was better than most, and she kept seeing him until one day Smithy came back from one of his trips; and that was the last she ever saw of Bart. Later she found out he was crippled with a broken neck in a hospital out of town. When she called, Bart refused to talk to her. She remembered then what she'd heard about Smithy, that he had once killed a man. She hadn't believed it before, but she believed it now.

Was Smithy now playing one of his games again? Was it possible?

She found herself looking at the phone near her bed, and she wondered whether to call Robert. She was hesitant, yet anxious at the same time, to know what was true or not true. But how would she be able to tell? And if she called, and it was true what Smithy had said, what then? The call, she knew, could be traced; and Smithy's plans, whatever they were, might be jeopardized.

In the end she didn't call. Whatever he was, she had to trust Smithy. She was convinced his instructions would come; he had never failed her before. The message *would* come, she told herself. It had to come—*had to.*

That night at a back table in a bar, Antonio had tequila and lemon with Mendez, his contact, who looked like a barrel with three chins. Earlier the barrel had called him for a meeting.

"Something important," the barrel had informed him, sounding like a funeral organ. The barrel was like that. He could sniff up at the sky and say, "It looks like rain," and make it sound like a catastrophe.

At the bar the barrel put a copy of a photograph in front of Antonio—a bad reproduction of a woman's face.

"Here it is," said the barrel.

"Here is what?"

"The woman my people are looking for."

"Who is she?"

Mendez shrugged. "I'll know more later," he said.

Antonio expressed a mild curiosity.

"How interested are your people?"

"The orders come from high up."

"I mean, how much is there in it for *me*?"

"More than you can count."

Antonio leaned closer to the three chins.

"Is she here?"

"It's possible, yes."

"What's her name?"

"Here, on the back," said the barrel. "But she could be using another name."

Antonio looked again at the bad reproduction.

"Mendez," he said quietly.

"Yes?"

"You're crazy, you know. How can you find someone who looks like an ink smudge?"

"It has top priority," the barrel persisted.

Rising, muttering to himself, Antonio put the reproduction into his pocket; and almost before he reached the door the matter passed from his mind. Remaining behind, the barrel felt let down. Later, gorging himself on two dozen tortillas, he became more buoyant.

Dempsey took an early plane to Washington for his meeting with Cunningham, a middle-echelon functionary. The meeting had been arranged by Martin through a State Department aide.

There were the usual preliminaries as Cunningham, his face creased with age, took time to light a pipe, relate an anecdote and settle back comfortably. He had a casual look. Tweeds and vest. Behind him on a shelf was a replica of a sloop. A dog-eared dossier lay on his desk.

"I understand you're interested in Krone," said Cunningham, getting down to the matter at hand.

"That's right."

A quiet puff.

"Anything in particular?"

"What's in your files?"

"Some of it, of course, is classified."

"I thought clearance had been arranged."

"To a point, yes. Beyond that—"

"The point for me," said Dempsey, "is four dead bodies. The answer may be in that file on your desk."

There was a glint in Cunningham's eyes. "Reminds me of an amusing story—" he began, but Dempsey's intense expression cut him short. "Now then, where do we begin?"

"I'm interested in Krone's exports."

"The arms shipments, I gather."

"He had depots in Mexico. Know his contacts there?"

"We have a few minor names."

"Where did he ship to?"

"In the last few years? Caribe."

"Know his contact there?"

"I understand his contact was in New York."

"You have his name?"

"Yes. Sorge. A cover name, I imagine."

"What do you know about Sorge?"

"Not too much. Rumors, undigested hearsay. Few hard facts."

"But no address. Is that the bottom line?"

"On the contrary," said Cunningham with a hint of a smile. "I can be quite specific about that. Sorge, it happens, in in prison—in Port-au-Grasse."

"What else?"

"On charges of treason," Cunningham added.

"Anything more?"

"From what we hear, a shipment of arms, one of Krone's own shipments, was diverted by Sorge into wrong channels. At least, that's what the charges specify."

"Who was on the other end of that treason?"

"As we hear it, someone in Mexico City."

"Anything more specific?"

"Yes, a general in exile—Fouché."

"When did all this happen?"

"Quite recently. In fact, Sorge was recalled to Caribe only two nights ago."

Dempsey seized on that.

"*Two* nights ago?"

"Yes, why?"

"Two nights ago two of my men were killed. We're looking for someone named Smithy. Know what Sorge looks like?"

"He's said to be rather indistinguishable. I'm afraid that's all I can tell you."

"Indistinguishable? You mean, average-looking?"

"I suppose it could mean that."

"Could your people run down a better description?"

"It's possible, yes."

"There may be a photograph around," Dempsey said.

"We'll do what we can, of course. Are you suggesting Sorge could be Smithy?"

"Smithy fits that general description, average-looking."

"I see."

Dempsey shifted his position.

"Fouché? Is he French?"

"No, a mulatto, born in Caribe."

"Know where he is?"

Cunningham hesitated.

Dempsey asked, "Any problem?"

"I'd suggest no contact with Fouché."

"Why not?"

"Unless, of course, you get higher clearance."

"I'll get it," Dempsey said firmly.

Cunningham leaned back, withdrawing from Dempsey's intensity. He said, "You may never find out, you know."

"Find out what?"

"Whether Sorge *is* Smithy. From what we hear it's not likely Sorge will be alive for long."

"Is that rumor or fact?"

"Merely a matter of probability," said Cunningham, and you had the impression he knew more than he was telling.

Later, the meeting nearly over, Dempsey said, "That photograph. You'll get it, won't you?"

"If one exists, yes."

"It's urgent," Dempsey pressed.

"I understand."

"If there's any problem let me know."

"There may be a photograph around. Somewhere."

"Just let me know," Dempsey said, pressing, and Cunningham knew that in one way or another Dempsey would get what he was after.

Later, when Dempsey was gone, Cunningham still felt his presence in the room. Cunningham could understand. Dempsey was carrying four dead bodies in his mind, and you could tell that some of those bodies were a personal matter. And he was carrying the bodies with him through a solitary hell.

Back in the city, waiting out time to hear from Cunningham, Dempsey kept the day open for himself.

Late that morning he began to work out at the gym, taking his time, pacing himself with an easy rhythm. In turn, he had a sauna, a massage and cold shower; and he dressed without haste. The day, he felt, was his and his alone.

On his way to the park he stopped off for a shine, and had small talk with Nat, the old bootblack at the stand. In the park he went to the zoo, where he fed the monkeys, watched the yawning lions and the polar bears slopping around. He bought a yam from a pushcart vendor. The yam was warm in his hand and the taste and smell of it were good.

He went past the empty mall and around the edge of the lake, past the benches to the playground where kids in overcoats and scarves played the games kids play. He absorbed the movements, the colors, the shouts and sounds, and breathed in the clean sharp winter air.

For a time he watched a small boy who was alone and quietly observing a squirrel in the snow. The boy wore a knitted wool hat and you could see his bangs and the wonder in his eyes. Dempsey was reminded of himself as he once was, a small boy in an isolated village in a time long gone. He remembered the bangs he had had and the woolen mittens his mother had made for him. Remembered a boy who carried in him an unutterable promise that was like a cry in his throat; for he was the son, the begotten son, with the covenant of the Father within him.

Yet on a morning never forgotten, that world, and its innocence, was forever destroyed, broken by a mindless savagery that mangled and corrupted the purity of a heart and mind. And what could you say to the boy? Even now, with the years washed over, what were the words that would make him whole again? You carry his dead remembrance like broken glass in bleeding hands. In the night he cries out to the Father, and what do you say to him? Where are the words of the Father for his son?

Dempsey was remembering now again those graceless days after the war, in the heat of that first summer. He had begun to stay up late at night and wake up late; gradually time for him became reversed and useless. He ate in cheap cafeterias. He remembered the tile walls, the antiseptic smell of mops and the paint—a slopbucket white. He mingled with derelicts, merging in with them, descending slowly without will to stop the downward drift.

One day then he gathered himself together and took a room in a cellar near the beach.

In the room night or day made little difference. One day replaced another imperceptibly so that gradually the days seemed to merge without form. Time moved but did not pass.

At night he listened to the sounds of the bay. The night had its own sounds and thoughts.

He remembered—an inertia had had him rooted. Once he had gathered himself and thought—I have to get out. But it seemed such an impossible thing to do, merely to get out, to pass through an open door. He had to get out, but he couldn't get in either.

Time had a drawn-out passivity that was unyielding. He tried to read but the words had no meaning.

He had brought little with him for his fast. He did not eat but he drank from time to time; and as the days passed, his mouth became sour and coated.

Nausea came and, later, a parched feeling. From time to time he walked around in his cell of a room to stimulate his circulation.

His fasting continued past the first week. He remembered a time of inflamed boils that suppurated and healed over. A time of phantasms, and later a boredom—a devouring emptiness.

On the twenty-seventh day, the fast was over. Natural hunger had returned. He felt its urgings in his mouth.

He felt clear, remarkably clear and light. His tongue was clean and sweet. The body, he knew, had cleansed itself.

It was time to leave, he knew; nevertheless he felt he had to stay; he was not yet done here.

The waiting began.

His hunger increased. He tried to concentrate but his thoughts were fragmented.

His body was gaunt with emaciation. Hunger was in him with a rage; it seemed to be all there was.

The fast was over and he was undergoing starvation now. His body was beginning to devour itself. In time, he knew, he would approach the absolute margin.

Days passed by, and weeks.

His body ached to the bones. He began to lose the clear buoyancy he had had at the close of the fast. It became difficult to walk to the sink for water. In time too it became an ordeal to sit up in bed.

His flesh became sensitive. His mind turned inward. There was nothing here, he told himself. Yet he waited—for what?

He was living on his own life now. His whole body was beset by weakness. He could sit up only by leaning against his pillow.

He prayed, as he had prayed each day, and his prayers now were like tears. He felt he hardly controlled them.

He waited for a sign, for a word; but there was only silence in that sunless room.

The next morning there was a knock on the door. He did not answer.

Go away, he thought.

The knob turned and he heard a woman's voice saying, "Are you there?"

He did not answer.

"I must come in," the woman insisted.

Finally, with reluctance, he managed to get to the door and open it. The woman came in. She wore a nurse's uniform; she was quite thin.

He stood there, a sheet about him.

"You'd better get back to bed," she said.

He began to walk, barely managing.

"What's wrong?" she asked.

"I'll make it," he said.

"Let me help you."

"I can manage," he insisted.

When he got back to bed, she said to him, "The old man upstairs was worried. He hadn't heard from you for weeks. Yesterday he looked in your window—"

"Tell him I'm all right," he said to her.

She was observing his sunken eyes and face through which the skull obtruded.

"You need a doctor," she said to him.

"No. Just get me some salt water and clear broth. I'm not sick."

I'm not sick, he thought. *I'm not sick.*

The fast was over, he knew. From the moment he had answered the door he knew that the fast was over. It had been meaningless; he knew that too.

He had brought himself to the abyss, to the edge of death; he had prayed, wept; he had endured pain; he had cleansed himself; yet it all came to nothing. There had been no word, no sign, no grace —nothing, except an oblivion of silence. He had prayed at an empty altar; and he knew, as he had known for a long time, that for him the altar would be empty, forever empty.

He was remembering and walking, and he kept walking. He was on Madison Avenue now, looking at windows, aimlessly moving, reading a headline at a newsstand, giving a dollar to a panhandler, chatting with a tout he knew, browsing in a bookshop, leafing through books—Dostoyevski, Willa Cather and *The Stranger* by Camus with its incredible opening—"Mother died today. Or, maybe, yesterday; I can't be sure."

Walking again. A movie on Third Avenue, milk and donuts later in a coffee shop, doing ordinary things in an ordinary way, feeling, touching, tasting, smelling, being alive, as if each taste and touch and smell were the last of its kind. At two in the morning he began to go back to his rooms, with memories crowding in on him —Turner and Leah, and Catherine. He had not wanted to go back to his place but he began to know that for him the day and night were over. The ordinary day, his small respite from time, was over for him. When he got back to his place the images of death and of violence began closing in over him.

Later, at a table, sitting on a hardbacked chair, he began to disassemble his gun once more. It had no need of cleaning but he cleaned it nevertheless with ritualistic care; his mind submerging inwardly into a smaller and smaller existence until he was at the center of a vortex that became only he and the gun.

For a time the images came back—the park, the snow, the small boy with a wool knit hat. And in his mind the boy began to cry, and it was like a crying in him.

In his room he looked upward now and said in his heart—what

more must there be? I gave you all. I reached out and you gave me emptiness. In my prayers I heard only your silence. I would give you breath and tears and life itself—what more must I give?

He waited; for a long time he waited; but in the end it was as it had always been; for him there was no remission. And he knew what he had already known. He had been damned, inexplicably damned, for some unknowable cause; and neither tears nor prayers nor the rage in his being could alter what was meant to be.

And he said then what had to be said:

"Pain is easier to bear than thee. Do what you must. I go as I go; I beg no more."

In time then he began to reassemble his gun; it was cold in his hands. The day, and the night, were over; and he knew that for him there was no going back.

Crouched down, Fouché tended his garden in the courtyard of the villa. It was late afternoon and getting cooler. Fouché, a rather thin figure, wore a wide-brimmed straw hat that threw a shadow over his narrow face with its flecked goatee and steel-rimmed glasses. He wore a khaki jacket. Though he customarily worked in his garden without tie, his shirt as always was buttoned to the neck.

Looking up now, Fouché saw Ari approaching.

His aide, heavily built, with a bull neck, wore a loose cardigan. Born in Crete, Aristedes had been with Fouché for four years as aide, watchdog and factotum.

Ari waited for the general to speak first.

Cleaning his trowel on a brick, Fouché rose from his crouch into a stiff, lean military posture.

"Any further news of Sorge?" he asked.

"Not much more," said Ari with the manageable French he'd picked up in Caribe where he'd been a dealer in commodities. Branded a speculator by the new regime, he had thrown in with Fouché; and like the general, he too waited out time, dreaming of a return to Caribe, to position and power.

They began to walk.

"It's time for a sip," Fouché said.

In his study, a plump Mexican woman with fuzz on her face served them iced tea and English biscuits.

The study, lined with shelves of books, pamphlets and military manuals, was windowless, having been bricked up years ago.

On the wall of the study was a map, identical to the map in the War Room in Caribe.

In a wicker chair Fouché sat stiff-backed. His eyes, never at rest, had a cold, critical look.

"It looks bad for Sorge," Ari commented.

"It seems he reached too far."

"Why did he wait to let himself be trapped?"

Fouché shrugged. "It's a pity," he said. "We might have made good use of him."

"*I'd* never trust him."

"It's not necessary to trust a man to use him," Fouché said. "Once he took our money he was in our hands."

"The fifty thousand? It was hardly worth the risks he took."

"It was more than fifty thousand he was after," said the general. "Think back. After the negotiations for the shipment, what was it Sorge asked you?"

"As I remember, he asked if we could handle another matter for a quarter of a million."

"For information."

"Yes, he wanted to sell us information."

"*Exactly,*" said Fouché, almost pouncing on the word. "And if you analyze it, that is precisely why he didn't run, why he hung on."

"But he didn't have the information. If he had it he would have come to us with it."

"Perhaps it's not here. Ask yourself, if not here—where? In Caribe?"

"He had to go back for it?"

"That's the point," Fouché exclaimed with a logician's triumph. "That is exactly what Sorge did in allowing himself to be brought back to Caribe."

"At such a risk?"

"He was arrogant enough, it seems, to think he could manage it. But he'd been away too long. He lost touch; he miscalculated his influence with Barras."

Ari stood up, his eyes betraying a stubborn resistance to Fouché's reasoning. Fouché did not pursue the matter. Ari, he recognized, was useful but limited in imagination. In the long run Ari was hardly more than a minor footnote in his plans.

Fouché waited now for Svensk to come, to explore with him the further possibilities in this matter of Sorge.

Fouché remained in his study, out of which emanated a network of insurrection reaching out toward Caribe. The villa itself was like a fortress sealed off from the world by a high thick wall. At the front gate two armed men stood watch within bullet-proof turrets. The windows of the villa were protected by iron bars and mesh wire against grenades. All approaches were electronically wired. Within and without, guards and local police were on alert around the clock against assassins.

Fouché took off his steel-rimmed glasses, rubbing the bridge of his nose. He thought of Barras, that former peasant who now held power in Caribe. In time that would change. The regime seemed impregnable but a mounting unrest was draining its strength.

Fouché knew it would be a hard road back to recover what had been lost in one night at Valmy to that primitive, Barras. Two or three years more were needed to bleed the regime until it was ready for the kill.

In his mind's eye he saw himself in an armored car at the head of a triumphal procession entering Port-au-Grasse amid the acclaim of the populace. The old regime would be swept away, and Barras himself would become only a memory, a discard in the junkheap of history.

Fouché had late dinner with Svensk, his contact, who used as cover an export-import firm of heavy machinery. Svensk, with his round bald head and black suit, had the air of a mortician about him. It was Svensk who had been behind the scenes during the secret negotiations between Sorge and Ari for the diversion of the shipment of mortars and automatic weapons.

After dinner and plum liqueur, Svensk began peeling an apple, leaving the skin continuously intact.

"I'm being asked awkward questions," Svensk commented.

"About my report?"

"In last week's initiative your people took casualties at an unacceptable level."

"I can't agree with your appraisal," Fouché said sharply.

"At that rate they'll bleed themselves to death."

"What we need is more matériel and less critiques," said the general. "My last request for funds is still on someone's desk in Moscow."

"These things take time," said Svensk, impassive as always.

"If we don't act decisively we may lose the initiative."

"It's not a simple matter. There are other, complex considerations to be taken into account."

"What I need is a commitment—"

"It's being considered."

"—a firm commitment before spring. I intend personally to take to the field."

"We're aware of the situation," said Svensk dryly.

Fouché shrugged. You couldn't push Svensk. Like those bureaucrats in Moscow, Svensk himself moved with glacial caution. Fouché understood; he was aware of the concern over his abilities. His fall from power at Valmy lay like a pall over their considerations. They held back, cautiously evaluating each step, doling out funds in careful measures. Eventually he was sure he'd get a firm enough commitment. Even an apple-peeler could recognize the significance of a foothold on the island. There'd be more haggling and delays, to be sure, but in the end they'd come around to him. It galled him, though, that for the time being he had to deal at this, a mortician's level.

Later when he brought up the matter of Sorge, Svensk looked at him curiously. "Sorge? He's as good as dead. What's there to discuss?"

"The situation."

Svensk paused midway through a slice of apple.

"What situation?"

"Do you recollect the matter Sorge brought up—concerning information?"

"Yes, the quarter of a million. But what could he have had that could possibly be worth that much?"

"We had the same question then—what could he have? Codes? We've broken every code. Military dispositions? It's all an open book to us. Sorge was aware of that."

"What else is there?" Svensk popped a slice of apple into his mouth.

Lighting a cigarette, Fouché took his time, letting Svensk wait.

"Tell me," Fouché said at last, "would it be worth a quarter of a million to know the present intentions in Barras's mind?"

"Are you suggesting Barras can be bought?"

"Of course not. Nor can Ligny or Dufar be bought."

"What are you suggesting?"

"A defection."

Svensk became alert. "Whose?"

"Ask yourself, who would be worth a quarter of a million?"

Svensk thought about it.

"Except for Barras, Ligny or Dufar—no one. But what's the point? They can't be bought. We agree on that."

"There's a fourth possibility," said the general, playing out his hand bit by bit.

"Someone on Dufar's staff?"

Fouché shook his head.

"Ligny's staff?"

"Higher."

"There's no one higher except Ligny himself."

"I mean higher than Ligny's level."

"You must be joking. Only Barras is higher."

"No, there's a step between."

"There is no such position," Svensk argued.

"Think again," said the general. "Who more than Ligny is at Barras's side? Who attends every staff meeting? Late at night, when all the others are gone, who is with Barras? Whom does Barras confide in?"

Svensk's mouth was agape.

"You mean Latour? The dwarf?"

"Why not? Why else, do you think, did Sorge go back to Caribe?"

"He didn't *go*—he was caught. We both know that."

"No. No, as I see it he *allowed* himself to be caught."

"Allowed himself?"

"Yes, to get Latour out."

"How did he think to get *himself* out?"

"He must have counted on his influence with Barras. He miscalculated, of course, but that's not the point."

"Even if you were right, what *is* the point? Sorge will be dead within a week."

"Yes, but Latour's still alive, and if Latour was willing to defect . . ."

"Yes, of course," said Svensk, caught up in the speculation.

"An interesting possibility, don't you agree?"

"On the other hand," said Svensk, retreating to his mortician's role, "it may all be just a dream."

Fouché shrugged, a gesture of exasperation.

For the time being he let the matter drop. In the end, he knew, he'd win out. In the end, despite Svensk and his kind, Barras's carcass, rotting in the sun, would be his, Fouché's, vindication in history.

Ramirez, the desk clerk, came across the missing letter in a drawer of the back office, where it had gotten mixed up with other papers.

Working late and finishing off the day, Ramirez had gone through the drawer, sorting out and discarding papers. It was then that he had noticed the ripped envelope among the discards. There it was—an airmail letter to Elizabeth Calder, postmarked New York, with no return address. On the side was a notation, "Hold for Arrival."

Ramirez wondered how he could explain the torn envelope to the woman in 302. If she made a fuss about it, he was sure he'd be blamed as he was for almost everything else that went wrong.

The envelope, Ramirez noticed, contained a folded slip of paper. Luckily it hadn't been torn. There wasn't much on the slip except a typewritten name—Hotel Emporio, Veracruz.

Ramirez thought about it. In a while, using a blank, Ramirez began typing out an exact duplicate of the torn envelope. Then prying loose the postmarked stamp Ramirez glued it to the new envelope. There was one flaw, though—the postmark was cut off at the edge of the stamp—but who would notice that?

Later Ramirez placed the duplicated envelope in box 302, relieved that one more fuss was safely out of the way.

On his way home the name *Emporio* kept recurring in his mind. Wasn't El Emperador, a three-year old—a long shot—running at the track tomorrow?

* * *

That night Mendez came over to Antonio's apartment. The barrel was in a state of excitement.

With a conspiratorial air the barrel placed a photograph on the table in front of Antonio. "Here she is," he said.

Picking his teeth with a matchbook cover Antonio glanced at the photograph. The woman had blond, delicate features.

"That's the one we're looking for," said the barrel, who wore his suit like a potato sack.

Antonio spat out a shred of meat. "It's better than that ink smudge you had before. What's it about?"

"They caught up with Sorge"—almost in a whisper.

"Sorge?" Antonio pursed his lips.

"He was a double agent, I hear."

"And the girl?"

"She was working with him."

"Is she *here?*"

"She could be right under our noses," said the barrel.

Antonio began to study the photograph.

An interesting face, he thought.

Later that night in his apartment he affixed the photograph to the wall in his bedroom, contemplating the features of the face. Still later, on his way out for dinner, his mind unaccountably turned to the woman in sunglasses at the El Aristos. Her image kept recurring to him now.

The next morning when Catherine got Smithy's letter her anxiety was relieved.

She read the message and burnt it in an ashtray in her room. Within twenty minutes she was checked out and on her way to the airport.

On the plane she tried to relax but in a corner of her mind remained a fragment of a memory—the envelope burning. Something had seemed odd about the envelope; she didn't know what, and it left her uneasy. Later her migraine began to tear at her again.

Late that afternoon Antonio approached Ramirez at the desk of the El Aristos.

Antonio was galled by the smirk on the clerk's face. In one afternoon—on a long shot El Emperador—Ramirez, that born loser, had recouped all his losses and more. For the first time in years he had come out ahead.

Leaning confidentially over the desk, Antonio asked Ramirez about the woman in 302. He'd been thinking of her all day, his mind feeling her body in anticipation.

The runt, Ramirez, smiled. "She's gone," he said.

Antonio's face expressed disappointment.

"She packed and left," the clerk emphasized.

"Went home?"

"To Veracruz," said the clerk, hardly suppressing his gloat over Antonio's disappointment.

Antonio walked away, putting on a smile and trying to wipe the runt's smirk from his mind.

Sorge was brought into the interrogation room at 1420 hours. There were welts of crusted blood across his face and neck. Hidden from view by his floppy uniform were the brutalizing lacerations gouged out by the bullwhip that had savaged his body the day before.

Manacled and chained, Sorge was placed in a chair positioned to face the high-intensity spotlight. Sorge bore himself calmly, his eyes still clear. To Dufar, Sorge's stoicism and control seemed unreal. It was as if for Sorge fear or pain or memory did not exist.

Latour was not present at this, the third interrogation. Sickened by the thought of further brutalities against Sorge, the dwarf had begged off continuance of his role as observer.

Dufar now faced Sorge alone, one-to-one. To Dufar, Sorge's calm seemed an affront, an arrogance that had to be broken.

Dufar was ready; he felt a tension.

Dufar began.

"Do you recall the questions put to you yesterday?"

"Yes," Sorge said, expressionless.

"Do you wish to amend any previous statement?"

"No."

"Do you wish to confess?"

"There is nothing to confess."

"Very well then," said Dufar, ringing a buzzer.

Presently one of the meat-rackers, a burly chap wearing the customary black butcher smock, came into the room, sniffling and pulling a trolley on which was a waist-high platform with an anvil affixed to it. The technician, Cluzot, held a thin steel mallet in his hand.

Cluzot placed the trolley in front of Sorge, locking its wheels.

"Are you familiar with the anvil?" Dufar asked the prisoner.

Sorge did not reply.

"The metal flap that you see," the Colonel went on, "clamps one's fingers to the anvil. The steel mallet, which Cluzot holds, is capable of breaking one's fingers bone by bone—one hand then the other. The procedure, I'm told, is quite painful. Do you wish to reconsider your position?"

Sorge remained silent.

Dufar motioned to Cluzot. In turn Cluzot seized Sorge's manacled hands, clamping the right one to the anvil.

Seemingly indifferent and almost pliable, Sorge did not resist Cluzot.

When he was ready, Cluzot stood with mallet poised awaiting Dufar's signal.

Dufar took time to light a cigarette. As he exhaled he nodded almost imperceptibly to Cluzot.

Just then Sorge called out. "Wait!"

Dufar quickly waved Cluzot aside.

"Do you wish to make a statement now?"

"Yes—but alone."

Dufar nodded to Cluzot who began unclamping Sorge's hand. In a while, sniffling and wiping his nose on his sleeve, Cluzot withdrew, rolling the trolley after him like a child's pulltoy.

Sorge sat silently, hands on his lap.

Dufar waited expectantly. "Well?"

"Why isn't Latour here?"

"Why do you ask?"

"I insist on a witness present."

"I'm all the witness you need," Dufar said.

"That won't do."

"Your statement will be on tape."

"Tapes can be altered," said Sorge.

"You're wasting my time," said Dufar sharply. "Perhaps Cluzot—"

Just then the jarring sound of the phone interrupted Dufar in midsentence.

Dufar picked up the receiver—it was Barras on the line.

"Yes," Sorge heard Dufar say. "Yes, right away, sir."

When Dufar hung up, he rang for the guards.

"You and I will settle up later," he told Sorge with a controlled glare.

Shortly then Dufar hurried to the emergency meeting Barras had summoned together in the War Room.

The meeting was already in progress when Dufar got there. Standing near the map, facing the senior officers seated around the oval table, Barras singled out Ligny.

"I know what the consensus is," Barras declared, "but I tell you, it doesn't smell right. This morning again—reconnaissance planes over our airspace. Acosta has to be up to something."

"As we see it," said Ligny, "the Hispaniolans are merely reacting to our own move to Tournée. It was predictable—we discussed that."

"That may be exactly what Acosta wants us to think," Barras said, turning now to Dufar who had just sat down. "Colonel, what's *your* assessment?"

Dufar hesitated. "It's hard to pinpoint," he said, "but in my opinion something *is* happening."

"At least someone doesn't think I'm an idiot," Barras remarked. He addressed himself now again to Ligny. "Tell me, Ligny—Acosta has moved his Tenth to Córdoba—why?"

"It's near Tournée," Ligny pointed out.

"And what are *we* doing?"

"Bisguer is already en route to—"

"I know, I know, but is that enough?"

"For the time being, yes—quite enough. We're watching it closely," Ligny assured him.

Later Barras dismissed Ligny and his senior officers, asking Dufar to remain behind. Barras's eyes, Dufar noted, brooded with a simmering dissatisfaction.

Latour, who had served coffee at the meeting, now poured cognac. Barras came over and put his arm over Dufar's shoulder.

"Ligny's first-rate," said Barras in confidence, "but he hasn't a nose for these things. Something is wrong—I can feel it, Dufar."

"I agree," said the colonel, mindful of Barras's awesome presence. "Ever since Sorge came back—"

"Dufar—listen. I want you to contact your people and get me reports of anything unusual. Establish a command post in my office. You'll work directly with me. Table everything else—everything."

"Including Sorge?"

"Never mind him."

"He seems ready to make a statement," said Dufar.

"Forget Sorge," said Barras. "He'll only lead us around by the nose. He betrayed us once. Do you think you'll get the truth out of him now?"

Setting up a command post in Barras's office, Dufar began to summon aides and issue instructions. In time, as the aides returned with reports, Barras and Dufar questioned them closely, probing and sifting information like hounds on the hunt.

Barras persisted with Dufar hour after hour into the night. There were rumors, opinions, probabilities, but nothing solid turned up. Yet, like a suspicious peasant, Barras did not let up.

At one point, as Dufar questioned an intelligence officer, Barras excused himself, saying, "Stay with it, Dufar. I'll be back. We've a long night ahead of us."

Going down the hall, Barras proceeded to his study. It was a simple room with a desk and military cot, a room he used for solitude.

Presently he put in a call to Latour, whom he had earlier sent to Communication Center.

At Communication Center, the dwarf sat at a desk in a private room, sitting through cables of the last thirty days. He had had instructions from Barras to examine each cable, in or out. With the dwarf's knowledge of affairs, it was Barras's hope that Latour would turn up some clue that M-5 had missed.

The dwarf went through the cables listlessly, his heart not in his work. He reproached himself that he had not come up with a plan, any plan, which would help Sorge. His mind turned this way and that, but in the end he had to concede that security measures within the Fortress doomed in advance any hope of escape. Sorge, he felt, was as good as dead.

The dwarf's bleak thoughts were interrupted by a call from Barras, asking him to come to the study. Laying aside the cables, the dwarf walked down the hall with a heaviness in him.

When he arrived at the study, Barras drew him aside, locking the door behind him. The dwarf was puzzled.

"Latour, there's something you must do for me," Barras said. "It's only between us, you understand."

The dwarf nodded, his eyes curious, wondering.

"Not even Ligny or Dufar must know," Barras said to him. "This is between you and me—and Sorge."

The dwarf's eyes widened with astonishment.

"Sorge has been acting for me," Barras explained. "It involves intelligence of highest priority. We need your help, Latour."

The dwarf's heart pounded, and he wanted to cry out for joy, but he restrained himself in view of the seriousness of the occasion.

"Here is an envelope," Barras said to him. "Inside is my signed authorization for Sorge's release. Now here is what you have to do . . ."

Barras began to instruct him carefully and minutely, and when he was done he said, "Be careful. If word gets out, everything we've done so far goes up in smoke."

"Yes, I understand," said the dwarf, quite aware of his awesome responsibility. Although Barras hadn't divulged the ultimate purpose behind the secrecy, Latour did not question his orders. Barras's trust in him was like a bond joining him to Barras.

As the dwarf began to leave, Barras stayed him momentarily, saying, "When you get back we'll make up for tonight at Mama Sere's."

Barras winked at him but the dwarf did not respond; he had a feeling that he would not be back and that he was looking at Barras for the last time.

As he left the study a certain nervousness began to take hold of him. Much depended on him now and there was little room for mistakes.

At the motor pool he requisitioned Barras's command car.

Barely reaching the pedals he drove alone toward the Fortress, his headlights illuminating the brick-lined roadway.

In the commandant's office he presented the authorization to Captain Derac, who was in charge of the Fortress. Examining the document, Derac asked the dwarf, "Do you have Colonel Dufar's approval?"

The dwarf feigned indignation. "Do you question Barras's signature?"

"No, but procedures require—"

"Confirm it then. Call Dufar—he's with Barras, in his study."

Derac hesitated.

"Use the red phone. Dial one-two-three."

Derac dialed. On the other end of the line a harsh voice responded. "Yes?"

"I'm sorry, sir, but—"

"But what?" Barras's voice rasped out.

"Latour is here with an authorization—"

"What's the problem?"

"I have instructions from Colonel Dufar—"

"Who is this?"

"Captain Derac, sir, of the—"

"Do you recognize my signature, captain?"

"Yes, but—"

"Do you question my authority?"

"No, sir."

"Then carry out my orders. I want Sorge here in fifteen minutes. Is that clear?"

Before the captain could answer, the phone clicked dead.

The captain stared at the phone, hesitant, uncertain.

Latour waited anxiously, moments passing, each moment a nervous heartbeat. Finally, decisively, Derac picked up the phone once more. Ten minutes later Sorge was brought into Derac's office and the dwarf felt relieved and happy to see him. Sorge, he saw wore the same black worsted he had worn on his arrival three days ago. His hair was cropped and his unshaven face bore deep, crusted wounds. There was a stiffness in his walk; each step, Latour could guess, took its toll in pain.

"I'll get an escort," Derac offered.

"It's not necessary," said the dwarf, thinking quickly. "There's an escort waiting for us at the palace."

Shrugging, not insisting, Derac accompanied them to the command car.

On the cobbled roadway, Derac watched the command car drive off. Expecting the car to turn right at the crossroad, the captain observed it turning left, presumably toward Dessalines roadway, which was the long way around. Derac now expected to see the headlights of the command car between the even rows of trees near the barracks, but there was no sign of lights.

The captain ran out toward the crossroad. The command car was gone from sight.

Less than two minutes later the triple alarm sounded and chaos broke loose.

Sorge had allowed four minutes fifteen seconds for the drive past the outskirts, to the marina on the south end of the bay. As Latour drove off, with Sorge in the back seat, Sorge quickly briefed the dwarf, explaining to him what had to be done at the marina. At the same time, unwrapping from its waterproof cover an automatic rifle, Sorge began to assemble it. Glancing back, Latour recognized the heavy cover; and he recalled the canvas-wrapped package he had carried this morning, at Barras's request, to the command car. What had seemed odd to him at the time became clear now. Later, in retrospect, Latour marveled at the careful planning that must have gone into all that he was now witnessing.

As they came near the marina, Latour heard in the distance the pulsing sirens of the triple alert. He became tense; his stomach began to churn.

At the marina Latour got out of the command car and approached the two marines who guarded Barras's launch, the X102.

Sorge remained in the car, lying on the floor in the back.

The guards, recognizing Latour, let him approach.

Latour beckoned to the marines, asking them to come with him to the command car. He had a heavy package, he said, that had to be brought aboard the X102.

The guards began to come with him, but the continuing sounds of the sirens gave them pause.

"What happened?" one of the guards asked the dwarf.

"Some saboteurs—down the coast," Latour improvised. "It's nothing much—only three of them."

"Where did they land?"

"Seven kilometers—south," Latour pointed. "Come, get the package," he urged. "Barras is waiting."

The marines, not moving, stood listening to the sirens, scanning the vicinity, wary and tense.

Finally one of them began to walk toward the command car, the other following at a distance, still observing the parameters of the marina, as if to sniff out potential danger.

The first guard slung his rifle over his shoulder as he came near the rear door of the command car.

The dwarf was in a nervous sweat. The sounds of sirens were growing louder. Time was running short.

The first marine began to look around again along the pier and toward the road from Port-au-Grasse.

"I've got to get back," the dwarf urged him.

With a shrug the marine slowly turned and began to open the back door. As he did so his face froze at the sight of an automatic rifle aimed at his head. Behind the rifle were cold, deadly eyes.

* * *

It was close, with time lost disarming the marines, forcing them to the pier where Latour pushed them, each in turn, into the dark waters of the bay.

The sound of sirens tore closer through the night.

Boarding the launch, Sorge got its engine running as Latour cast off and clambered aboard.

Three jeeps loaded with paratroopers now swung into view.

The launch began to move off, its powerful engine churning. A burst of automatic rifle fire chattered against the metal hull as the launch began to surge out into the bay, toward the moonlit open sea.

Dufar exploded when he heard the news. The impossible had occurred—Sorge, with Latour, had escaped!

In a state of fear Dufar nervously informed Barras of the escape. Dufar was in a sweat.

Barras summoned Ligny to his study and ordered him to dispatch coast guard cutters, helicopters and a naval plane to search out and intercept the X102.

"Find them, Ligny," he cried out. "Find them. Destroy them! I want them dead—both of them!"

Later Barras had Dufar send for Derac, and as Derac began to explain, Barras cut in. "What authorization?"

Derac nervously handed him the document.

Barras glared at it. "Are you blind? Is that my signature?"

"But I spoke to you—you authorized—"

"You spoke to *me?*"

"Yes, I believe so, sir."

"Idiot! There are three connections—it could have been anyone. You had orders, captain, not to move Sorge without Dufar's approval, is that correct?"

"Yes, sir."

"Why did you disobey those orders?"

The captain hesitated, unable to answer.

Barras turned to Dufar. "Place this man under arrest," he ordered. "Hold him incommunicado until further notice."

Afterward, alone with Dufar, Barras became aware of an uneasy expression in the colonel's eyes. Barras recognized that Dufar had by now put it all together and was thinking the unthinkable. Barras had expected as much and was prepared for it.

Opening his desk drawer, Barras drew out a .38 automatic. "You must trust me, Dufar," he said almost with regret. "Whatever I do, trust me."

Dufar stared at the gun, his eyes wide open with disbelief.

Barras rang for the officer of the guard.

"Captain, place Dufar under arrest. The charge—treason against the state."

"But, sir—" Dufar started to protest.

Barras broke in. "If you say one more word, Dufar, you're a dead man. Is that understood?"

Dufar, immobilized by fear, remained silent.

Barras accompanied Dufar and the captain to the Fortress, to the third level, to cell 325X. After Dufar was locked up, Barras took the key from the guard.

As Barras strode away, the captain of the guard stared at him astonished, unable to understand what was happening. It had been an incredible, improbable night so far. What more could happen?

In his villa Fouché was awakened by his aide who had just heard the news about Sorge. Details were skimpy but it was clear that Sorge and Latour had escaped.

Fouché was elated. His evaluations, he felt, had been right on mark, even if somewhat altered. Instead of Sorge getting the dwarf out, it was the other way around—the same result, was it not?

Fouché called up Svensk. "We just got news about Sorge—" he began.

"Yes, I know. I heard about it a half hour ago," said Svensk dryly. "Your people always seem to be a half hour behind."

Ignoring the jibe, Fouché asked, "What do you think?"

"About what?"

"Latour, of course."

"It's still only speculation," said Svensk.

Fouché hung up, angry at the rebuff, angry that he couldn't get past Svensk.

Events, Fouché felt, would prove him right, and neither Svensk nor those time-serving bureaucrats in Moscow could alter that.

Early in the morning at 0322 hours, one of the helicopters sighted the X102 and radioed back. At 0327 hours a naval bomber, almost at sea level, dove in toward the launch, releasing two torpedoes. A huge explosion lit the sky. In that moment the X102 had ceased to exist.

The report was later confirmed by a cutter which surveyed the fragments of wreckage.

When Barras received the confirmation, he dismissed the courier and went to the solitude of his study. It had been a hard day, hard yet satisfying. Everything—all of it—had worked out according to plan.

Barras remained alone until the sun began to rise. By habit he reached to ring for Latour. He paused, reminding himself that the dwarf was gone from him for good. He'd miss Latour, miss that odd shape running his errands. Yet, in truth, the dwarf, like everyone else in Barras's life, was expendable. For Barras, only one constant existed—the nation. The nation alone endured.

Svensk got in touch with Fouché by phone. "Have you heard about Sorge?"

"Yes, I know, he's dead," said the general. "I heard of it an hour ago," he added as a dig at Svensk.

After hanging up, Fouché felt depressed, his temporary hopes of Latour's defection suddenly gone. In one night, gone. It had been that way at Valmy, expectations crushed in one night. Life itself fragile, hanging by a thread. One day suddenly, unexpectedly, the thread is cut.

Late in the day Dempsey received the print by special courier. The print was somewhat fuzzy but clear enough considering it was a blowup of a snapshot taken with a small-lens camera at a distance, probably under covert circumstances. He recognized the face in the photograph of Sorge. It was Smithy's. Sorge and Smithy were one.

He put in a call to Washington but Cunningham was not in his office and could not be reached.

That night as he lay in bed, his mind turning over and over restlessly, he began to feel a presence in his room. A sudden sense, a mood, a shape, an image.

Water, a calm sea. Moonlight. A figure. Two figures. In the sea? On it? The images were unclear.

Two figures. One, a child; the other, out of focus.

No, not a child—a man. A man's face with wrinkles. A man with a misshapen body.

There was more clarity now.

A dwarf in a calm sea—where? A dwarf holding on to something, the other hand reaching out toward him. Subliminally then he became aware of his father's hand, a glimpse of an outstretched hand, and of a small boy shuddering at the sight of it, covered as it was with blood and dreadful meaning—a moment in time that for him was never forgotten, never forgiven.

The next morning, as he was leaving his apartment, Dempsey got a call from Washington.

It was Cunningham, asking about the photograph.

"Yes, I got it," said Dempsey. "Sorge and Smithy—they're the same."

"Are you certain?"

"Identification is positive."

"In that event, I would say you could safely close the book on the matter."

"Why? What's happened?"

"Sorge, I'm informed, is dead."

"Dead? How?"

"He attempted an escape last night—by sea."

"By *sea?*"

"I don't have much to go on."

"How was he killed?"

"Torpedoes."

"Is that confirmed?"

"His boat, I hear, was demolished."

"Was he with someone?"

"What was that?"

"I said, was he with someone?"

"Yes, why?"

"I need it—for my report."

"Yes, of course. Yes, he *was* with someone."

"Anything more?"

"The other man's name was Latour, if that's of interest to your report."

"Latour—was he a small man? I mean, did he happen to be a dwarf?"

There was silence on the other end.

Finally, "Yes, but how—"

"It's just some information I happened to come across."

"I see."

"Were the bodies found?"

"My information doesn't indicate—"

"They may still be alive then."

"It's possible, of course. Anything is possible."

"If the bodies weren't found . . ."

"What are you suggesting?"

"Could your people find out?"

"I could make inquiries, yes."

"It's important," said Dempsey.

"I'll do what I can," Cunningham said, but Dempsey could tell by his tone that Cunningham was tired of the matter. Perhaps he'd make a few casual inquiries. Or perhaps he'd merely make a note in his files and close the matter from his mind. It was hard to say.

When Dempsey hung up he began to wonder—was he beating a dead horse? The images he had seen last night could mean anything—a dream, a distortion, a memory. Yet one thing was sure: dead or alive, he had confirmed the existence of the dwarf. And maybe it was not over yet. Maybe there was a hand yet to be played out.

Two days after the sinking, a seaman on the deck of a freighter saw in the distance some floating object. As the freighter came nearer, the object took on a clearer shape. In time the seaman was able to make out two figures on a collapsible raft. One of them was a dwarf, a being with sad, brooding eyes.

Three days later word came, confirmed by two sources, that fifty-four hours after the X102 had sunk, two survivors of a "shipwrecked fishing boat" were picked up by a Greek freighter, the *Tina*, on its way to Tampico, a port on the east coast of Mexico.

The two men, purportedly the victims of an engine explosion, had kept alive on a collapsible raft. One of the men was described as medium in height, with scars and cropped hair. The other, a dwarf not more than four feet tall. Both carried waterproof packets around their waists.

In Tampico, before customs inspection, the two survivors disappeared from aboard ship. No trace of them was found.

* * *

Dempsey took an early flight to Mexico City where he met with Captain Ortega, whom he knew. Two years earlier Dempsey had dealt with Ortega on a confidential matter. A gruff, bald man with quick eyes, built like a middleweight in prime, Ortega had a surprising command of English.

At Cunningham's suggestion Dempsey now treaded his way carefully with Ortega, omitting all mention of Sorge and limiting his case to its police aspects. Dempsey's case, as he presented it, involved a suspect named Smithy who was wanted for three murders and possible connection with another. He was last seen in the company of a dwarf on a Greek freighter, the *Tina*, in the port of Tampico. Within that framework Dempsey gave Ortega as much detail as he had.

He showed the detective Sorge's photograph. "This is what he looks like."

Ortega studied the print. "Is it important?"

"For me it is."

"It's out of my jurisdiction, you know."

"All it may take is a few phone calls."

Ortega smiled, a used-up cigar between his teeth. "For a friend —why not?"

"It can't be too hard," Dempsey said. "You're looking for someone with a dwarf."

"Unless he's disguised," Ortega grinned. "But how does a dwarf disguise himself?"

By next morning Ortega had put together some interesting facts.

Two days earlier, at 9:30 in the morning, a thin, medium-sized Mexican with several scars, ostensibly a businessman with an attaché case, entered the Tampico airport en route to Mexico City.

A few moments later a legless invalid, a blanket around his lower body, propelled himself by wheelchair to the ticket counter behind the businessman. The invalid, having the dried, worn face of a field worker, nudged the businessman to buy a ticket for him to Mexico City.

The flight tickets disclosed their names to be Hernandez and Orozco. The businessman, Hernandez, according to the ticket clerk, spoke fluent Spanish. Orozco appeared to speak little, and only to Hernandez who had to bend over to listen.

The two, a strange pair, boarded the plane at 9:55. Hernandez assisted the invalid, with his blanket around him, to his seat.

At the airport in Mexico City, using a fictitious address, Hernandez rented a blue Citroën at a car rental agency.

A mechanic reported seeing the pair get into the Citroën with one piece of luggage and the folding wheelchair.

As soon as Ortega had the assembled facts, he put out an alert for the Citroën, circulating its license number and a description of the pair throughout the city and surrounding areas.

Ortega called Dempsey at his hotel, telling him what he had found out. Ortega seemed in a good mood but when Dempsey got to his office he was surprised to find the captain in a bad temper.

"Why didn't you tell me?" Ortega said hotly.

"Tell you what?"

"I'm talking about Sorge."

"Smithy or Sorge—it's the same man."

The veins on Ortega's temples pulsed.

"I don't like being made the fool."

"All I want is to close a case."

"It's not a case. Sorge is a political matter. A hornet's nest."

"Politics is not my business. Murder is."

"That's *your* problem," Ortega shot back.

"What's yours?"

"Sorge is a political refugee."

"He's a killer."

"He's been granted asylum by our government."

"Two of my men are dead."

"It's out of my hands. It's no longer a police matter."

"Who do I have to see?"

"Go through channels," Ortega said. "But as a friend I must tell you, go back, forget it. It's a closed case. Closed."

"I'll do what I have to do."

"It'll take years."

"Not for me," said Dempsey. "Not this one."

He paused a moment.

"I'm sorry I caused you trouble," he said.

Ortega shrugged.

"I'd be angry too," he said, and you could tell he meant it and he'd help if he could.

That evening as he rubbed cologne on his angular face, Antonio reflected on the rumblings that had come to him through Mendez, the barrel. Rumors that Sorge, first thought dead, was alive and here in Mexico City. Rumors that Sorge had already arranged through Fouché to get asylum for himself and the dwarf, Latour. There was talk too of a blood purge in Caribe at the highest levels of M-5, with more to come before the dust settled.

Antonio studied Catherine's photograph which was tacked to the wall. It was a face that stirred the imagination. As he looked at the blond, fragile features he kept thinking of the dark-haired woman in sunglasses who had checked out of the El Aristos.

He kept looking at Catherine and thinking of the woman in sunglasses, their images alternating, sometimes fusing, until suddenly, unexpectedly, his mind exploded with a shock of recognition!

Late Thursday afternoon in an outlying residential section of Mexico City the blue Citroën turned into a driveway adjacent to a white stucco dwelling that had a slanted roof of reddish Mediterranean tiles.

The businessman "Hernandez" got out of the car and went around to the back of the house. With a key retrieved from under a rock he opened the back door. Subsequently Hernandez lugged a large, lumpy laundry bag from the car, dragging the bag along the walk, up the back steps into the kitchen. That done, Hernandez drove the Citroën into the garage and locked the garage door.

When Sorge got back into the house, Latour was already out of the laundry bag, rubbing his back. Latour's face was still covered with his dark, sunburnt "Orozco" makeup.

The window shades throughout the house were drawn down, giving the room a twilight appearance.

Sorge tested the lights and dialed a random number on the phone to confirm that it was in order. Observing the rooms and furniture, Sorge was satisfied that nothing had been touched since he had rented the house several months ago under the name Siqueiros.

Presently Sorge and Latour ate some canned food from the refrigerator, eating at the kitchen table without a word between them, each with his own private thoughts.

Later, washing off his makeup, Latour lay down on his bed without undressing. He was tired and was soon asleep. To Sorge, the dwarf seemed like a child asleep, an old child with a sad, crinkled face. Sorge covered the dwarf with a blanket.

Sorge was at ease with Latour. The dwarf had endured the harrowing ordeal at sea without a murmur. Like a little soldier born to obey, he did without hesitation what he was asked to do. Though kept in the dark as to Sorge's ultimate purpose, not once had the dwarf questioned that purpose.

Presently, in the closet of his own bedroom, Sorge slid aside a false panel behind which were several packets. Sorge examined the contents, making a final check of each item—the several passports for himself and Latour; some makeup and hairpieces; a chest of emergency medical supplies; a brown monk's habit with rosary beads; a flexible diplomatic briefcase with its chain and handcuff; currency in pesos and dollars; a package of plastic explosives; one Walther P–38; and a high-powered automatic rifle—weapons kept ready as a matter of precaution.

Later Sorge poured some Perrier. He was ready now.

Locking the door of his bedroom Sorge dialed Fouché's private number.

Ari answered.

"Get me Fouché," said Sorge in a crisp French.

Ari was startled by the voice. "Sorge?"

"Get me Fouché," Sorge said again.

There was silence.

Sorge quietly sipped his Perrier.

The general came on. "Fouché."

Sorge took his time responding. "There is a matter we must discuss . . ." he began.

"Yes, I understand."

"But first I must know—can you arrange asylum for Latour and me?"

"It's possible, yes."

"Before we proceed, I require a firmer understanding."

"I need some time. Where can I get in touch with you?"

"I'll call you," said Sorge.

"When?"

"When I'm ready."

"And Latour—how is Latour?"

"Well and safe."

"Is he with you?"

"No, but he's available," said Sorge, hanging up without a further word.

Sorge sat on the bed, sipping Perrier and mulling over the general's concern for the dwarf.

Without much being said, Fouché seemed quite cognizant of

what was involved, and eager to come to grips with it. As always Fouché seemed a step ahead. In all probability he had already analyzed the heart of the situation—to a point. You could almost count on that, on Fouché being accurately perceptive to a point. Beyond that, Fouché was blind. Though he seemed a step ahead he was in reality a step behind. Believing only in himself, his perceptions were inevitably distorted by vanity. It was that distortion, in truth, that had prefigured his debacle at Valmy. In the end, to be sure, it would be his ruin.

Sorge began to work his muscles, testing their responses. Considering his ordeal in Caribe, his reactions were reasonably what he could expect, and quite enough for the demands of the situation.

Afterward he lay on the floor, relaxing, withdrawing into his cool center, away from feeling and perception. He awoke in an hour by his own internal timing, refreshed and ready for the last phase of his plan.

He was close, very close now, and with luck . . .

Later, as Siqueiros, he left the house and walked some distance to a bowling alley in the business section. He did not use the Citroën he had rented. It was unlikely that his irregular entry into Tampico had been traced here; nevertheless, since the possibility existed, he had to consider the Citroën unusable. It was not a crucial factor, though; elsewhere he had two other vehicles available and ready.

In the bowling alley he had to wait a long time before his call to Cathy was put through to the Hotel Emporio.

Finally she came on line.

"Lizabeth?"

"Smithy?"

"Everything all right?"

"Where are you?" she asked.

"Any problems?"

"I'm all right," she said.

"You sure?"

"Yes, but when will I see you?"

"It won't be long. Wait for me."

There was a pause.

"Lizabeth?"

"Yes?"

"I miss you," he said. "I miss you very much."

After he hung up he sat in the booth, thinking of her. She was in Veracruz, away from Mexico City—perhaps safe, but there was no certainty she hadn't been traced. A possibility existed that she was under surveillance, unaware of it. All in all she had become a risk for him. From the time she had become a suspect with him she had to be considered "contaminated."

He kept thinking of the situation, coming to no conclusion. There was time enough later, he thought.

Two days later, in his room, at 2130 hours, Sorge put in another call. Fouché responded after the second ring.

"Did you handle the matter?" Sorge asked.

"Yes, it was settled. Yesterday."

"For both of us? Any conditions?"

"None. The asylum is unconditional."

"At what level?"

"The highest. Is Latour with you?"

"No."

"May I speak with him?"

"Later," Sorge said. "The price is a quarter of a million. Can you handle it?"

"Yes, but I need more specifics."

"Where can we meet?"

"As before, you'll deal with Ari."

"That'd be a waste of time," Sorge said. "Ari has to clear

through you. No, I'll meet with *you*. We'll settle everything in one evening—tomorrow."

Fouché was silent.

Sorge said, "Bring as many guards as you feel you need. I won't be armed."

"That's not acceptable."

"In that case I'll deal with Svensk."

"Svensk?"

"At least he's not afraid to meet me," Sorge said.

Fouché didn't respond at once.

Finally he said, "Come to the villa then."

"That's too much of a risk," Sorge countered. "Dufar's people will be watching for me at the villa. I'd be dead before I got to the front gate."

"I can arrange protection," Fouché suggested.

Sorge did not respond.

"Well?" said the general.

"All right, I accept," Sorge told him. "I'll call you later to work out timing and security."

Sorge hung up then.

It was done, he thought. The final phase was in motion but he felt no elation. A deadness was in him.

A quarter of a million was waiting for him. Alternatively, he knew he could be dead before tomorrow was over. But neither the money nor death mattered much without Cathy. Without her he existed, as always, at the dead center of nothingness.

It was 2117 hours.

The general sat with Ari in the windowless study. There was not a sound from outside to disturb the silence of the room.

Ari wiped his bull neck with a colored handkerchief. He looked at his wristwatch.

"Thirteen more minutes," he commented.

216

"Be patient," said Fouché, smoking a cigarette, his eyes intense behind steel-rimmed glasses, his goatee at a tilt.

"I don't trust Sorge," said Ari.

"Nor do I, but we have no choice, do we?"

"I don't like the idea of him coming here."

"It was either that or Sorge dealing with Svensk," said the general dryly.

For the general, the thought of Sorge dealing with Svensk had been intolerable. It would have given Svensk another opening. It would have put more doubt in the minds of those bureaucrats in Moscow. Fouché could almost imagine the armchair comments—"Can't that Fouché handle anything himself?"

Under the circumstances Fouché knew he had no choice but to deal with Sorge initially. Later, of course, Svensk could come in for the money arrangements, but not before the essentials were agreed on.

Fouché asked, "Is security in order?"

"There are roadblocks on every approach," Ari said.

"And internally?"

"Tight as a drum," said Ari.

"Nothing must happen to Sorge until Latour is in our hands," said the general. "After that, let the wolves have him."

"Or Dufar's Special Unit."

"It's the same thing," the general said.

A cowled monk, limping somewhat, came into view, crossing the street toward the whitewashed walls of the villa rising into the clear night.

At the heavy iron gate the monk paused to look behind him. The monk rang the bell at the entrance.

In an unmarked police car, Ortega spoke briefly into a handset. "He's at the gate now."

Ortega looked around. Nothing moved along the avenue. Every approach to the villa had been sealed off by roadblocks.

Ari, waiting for Sorge's signal—two long rings and a short one—opened a peephole in the gate. Recognizing Sorge's face beneath the cowl, Ari opened the gate. "Come in," he said.

Two guards directed Sorge down a path into a concrete, bunkerlike room adjoining the villa. The "decompression chamber," as it was known, was a bare, windowless room with a Judas hole in the wall facing the villa.

Sorge was alone with Ari in the room.

"Our usual precaution," said Ari.

"Yes, I know."

"Take off your clothes—everything."

"Is it necessary?"

"It's required," said Ari.

Sorge shrugged. Without a word more he stripped naked, bending the pliable attaché case through the broad sleeve of his robe. His body was crusted with scars.

Ari pointed to the briefcase which was attached by chain and handcuff to Sorge's wrist.

"What's that?"

"My papers."

"Remove the briefcase," Ari ordered.

"I haven't the key to the handcuff."

"You can't take it inside," Ari insisted.

Sorge considered the matter.

"Cut the chain off," he said.

"Cut it off?"

"With a hacksaw—or a bullet," Sorge suggested.

Observing Sorge through the Judas hole, Fouché was somewhat awed by the scarred vestiges covering Sorge's body, those remnants of brutality that had been inflicted in the Fortress.

* * *

When the inspection was finished, Ari returned the monk's habit to Sorge.

Sorge's briefcase lay on the floor, Ari having severed it from its chain with a single shot from his automatic.

As Sorge put on his habit, Ari said, "We can go in now."

"Take the papers from the briefcase," Sorge said. "The general will need them."

Ari tried the latch.

"It's locked," he said.

Sorge quietly retrieved the key from under his tongue.

Chagrined, Ari examined Sorge's mouth carefully but found nothing more.

Removing the papers from the briefcase, Ari went to the door and knocked three times.

Two armed guards opened the door from the outside.

"Clean" now, Sorge went out first, Ari behind him. From Sorge's wrist hung the stub of a chain still attached to the handcuff on his wrist.

Sorge put the cowl over his head. As he walked limping, he had the appearance of a penitent in prayer.

On the path leading to the side entrance of the villa, Sorge paused unsteadily.

"What's wrong?" Ari asked him.

"A concussion," Sorge said.

"Do you need to rest?"

"It's only a dizziness," Sorge said, waving him aside.

At the desk in his study, the general sat now observing Sorge, who was seated on a wicker chair, his cowl thrown back.

The door to the study, like that of the "decompression chamber," was locked from without.

Ari stood warily to the side, his gun in readiness, a mistrust in his eyes.

The general glanced at Sorge's papers on his desk.

"You've come a long way," he said to Sorge, his foe for many years.

Sorge nodded.

"We thought you were dead," Fouché said.

"As you see, I'm here."

"And Latour—where is Latour?"

Sorge didn't answer. His eyes were closed, his head bent forward.

"Anything wrong?" Fouché asked.

The general glanced at Ari.

"A slight concussion," Ari explained.

Sorge gradually opened his eyes.

"I'm sorry," he said. "I don't mean to waste your time."

"Do you need a drink?"

"I'll be all right," said Sorge.

Fouché glanced at the typewritten papers Sorge had brought with him.

"Are these your terms and conditions?"

"Yes, as a basis for our negotiation."

The general began to read the first of eleven pages. Reading quickly, the general turned a page.

"You're quite thorough," Fouché remarked without looking up.

Sorge said to him, "As you read, you will note my conditions relating to security."

The general nodded, scanning the second page.

Sorge said, "It may seem I'm overly anxious for the safety of Latour and myself, but under the circum—"

Sorge did not finish. His head dropped and suddenly he fell forward from the chair, sprawling face down on the floor.

He lay there unmoving.

* * *

That same evening McClosky picked up Dempsey in a Plymouth just off Avenida Juárez. Dempsey had no idea what McClosky wanted; Cunningham had called to suggest the meeting.

McClosky drove around the busy, lighted downtown section. He was a compact, pug-nosed man with hard blue eyes and curly hair; he wore a tight, salt-and-pepper suit.

Dempsey asked him, "Where are we going?"

"Nowhere." McClosky's voice was cold.

"What did Cunningham tell you?"

"To tell you to go home."

"Who do you work for?"

"I just give advice."

"I'm here to get Smithy."

"Sorge is no concern of yours."

"He's killed two of my men."

McClosky shrugged. "Sorge has been given asylum here."

"How does a killer get asylum?"

"Connections. That's how."

"Who's the connection?"

"A general. Name's Fouché. Know him?"

"I was told to stay clear of him."

"You do that," McClosky said. "He's a real troublemaker."

McClosky was chewing some gum, mulling.

He was saying, "That Fouché's got nine lives, I swear."

"I know. I heard about that."

"By last count he's survived six assassination attempts. *Six.*"

"Were *we* involved?"

McClosky shook his head. "No, but you won't find me crying at his funeral either."

"The government here know what Fouché's up to?"

"Sure, but they look the other way. Fouché's here under asylum. Gives the government a humanitarian posture. Know what I mean? If we make a fuss we'd be accused of interfering in their sovereignty—and that's why *you're* going home."

"Just like that?"

"If you try to interfere, wires will burn from here to Washington—"

"What's so important about Sorge?"

"He's a defector—he and that dwarf he's with," McClosky said. "They're heading right into Fouché's arms, and that suits government policy here. There's heavy security right now around Fouché's villa, and if I had to guess, Sorge will be there tonight selling out the Barras regime. He could be there right now, you know."

"And we can't touch him?"

"No, we can't touch him."

"He's killed three, possibly four men. Maybe more."

"It'll be passed off as political necessity."

"Tell me about Sorge."

"What difference does it make?"

"I want to know what I'm dealing with."

"There's not much to tell."

"Then it won't take long, will it?"

McClosky shrugged. Loosening a bit, he said, "Sorge has been cozy with Barras, maybe five years or more. From what I hear, Sorge was one of the best."

"Best at what?"

"Dirty laundry—that sort of thing. You know."

"And before Barras?"

"Sorge operated in North Africa, Southeast Asia—"

"As what?"

"As a mercenary, a professional killer."

"An assassin?"

McClosky almost smiled. "It's funny, you know."

"What is?"

"Sorge and Fouché. Working together, I mean. For years we had it figured that if anyone could get past the general's security and chop him down it'd be Sorge."

"Say that again."

"I said, if anyone could have gotten into the villa—"

"Into the villa? That's exactly where Sorge may be right now. *In* the villa."

McClosky turned, saying nothing, but you could see his thoughts spinning.

"It's possible, isn't it?" Dempsey said.

"If you're right, do you have any idea what had to be involved? It would boggle your mind."

"Mine or Fouché's."

"It's hard to believe."

"That's exactly why it may work."

McClosky thought about it. "Let it drop," he said.

"We ought to tell someone."

"If you're wrong we'd be accused of meddling."

"You don't give a damn?"

"About Fouché? If he succeeds, you know the cost? Even if he doesn't, you know how many bodies will pile up before he's through? And you want me to worry about *him?*"

Dempsey remained silent.

McClosky went on. "If Fouché were here where you are, you think he'd give it a second thought? Or his backers, the KGB—can you imagine *them* worrying or pausing a moment?"

"All I know is two of my men were killed."

"Maybe Sorge had to do it to get where he is tonight."

"It crossed my mind, and it doesn't wash."

"Let's stop and have a drink," McClosky suggested. "Let's wait it out and see what happens."

"No. No, stop the car."

"Why?"

"I'm going out there—to the villa."

"For what?"

"To get Smithy."

"You're staying right where you are."

"Is that an order?"

"It's an order."

"You'd have to use your gun," Dempsey said evenly, "and I'd have to kill you."

McClosky glanced at him.

Dempsey asked, "It's not worth that much to you, is it?"

McClosky thought about it. He said, "You're heading for trouble, you know."

"I want Smithy," Dempsey said. "The rest doesn't matter."

"You can't win this one."

"Maybe not but I mean to try."

Lying face down on the floor of the study, Sorge heard Fouché's nasal voice. "Is he dead?"

"I don't know," said the general's aide.

Sorge's arms lay under him. With his left hand, he quietly unlatched the handcuff. Opened now, it became a deadly pointed weapon. Sorge was aware of Ari approaching closer, closer. Suddenly, Sorge shot his left arm forward around Ari's heel, pulling back and toppling Ari to the floor.

Sorge sprang up toward Fouché. The general, retreating, was unable to evade him. Fouché's eyes bulged with fright. Sorge wrapped an arm around the general's neck, pressing the lethal point of the open handcuff against Fouché's jugular, drawing a trickle of blood.

"Put the gun on the desk," Sorge ordered Ari.

Ari spat out a vulgarity in Greek; he rose up.

"On the desk," Sorge repeated, pressing deeper.

"Do as he says," Fouché cried out.

Ari obeyed the general.

"Now move back to the wall."

As Ari moved away, Sorge picked up the gun. He held it casually at his side.

He said to Ari, "Listen carefully. I won't repeat myself."

Ari listened, his jaw tight.

"Get the general's sedan. Drive it to the front gate, facing right. The general and I will leave together. If anything occurs, even by mishap, consider the general dead. Someone may shoot me from behind but don't count on it that I won't be able to get off at least one shot. Is that clear?"

Ari nodded, and Sorge turned to Fouché.

"I'm sorry it has to be this way, General," he said in a calm tone. "Unfortunately Latour has disappeared. Perhaps he's had second thoughts—I don't know. In any event I still want my money. To be fair, I'll accept less. Your ransom, General, is one hundred thousand."

Fouché took off his glasses, wiping them with a handkerchief.

Sorge said, "I've no intention of harming you, General. One day you'll be back in power in Caribe. I suggest neither of you jeopardize that future."

Fouché put on his glasses, somewhat relieved, having feared worse.

The money, he knew, could be raised, but that was the least of it. Harder to swallow was the embarrassment of facing Svensk later in a deteriorated position.

Resigning himself to the situation, Fouché faced his aide in a frame of command once more.

"Do as he says," Fouché ordered.

"Yes, General."

It was past ten at night when Dempsey got to the vicinity of Fouché's villa. His cab was stopped at a roadblock there.

He got out of the cab and flashed his identification to one of the plainclothesmen in the area.

The detective seemed not to understand.

"The *comandante,*" Dempsey said.

"Ah, *el comandante!*"

Another detective came over and Dempsey spoke to him. "Wait here," said the second detective in English.

When the detective returned he said, "Come with me."

Dempsey walked with him toward the villa. Dempsey saw it for the first time, the whitewashed walls, the iron gate.

They came to an unmarked car with two men in it. Dempsey recognized Ortega sitting next to the driver, his window open.

Ortega said, "Get in the back."

Dempsey got into the back seat.

Ortega did not turn around. His eyes were on the villa. In front of the villa was a black Buick facing in the same direction as Ortega's car.

Dempsey asked, "Anything happening?"

"Why did you come?"

Dempsey saw a green light flash over the gate—three times.

"What's that?"

"I told you—go home."

The gate was opening.

Dempsey saw a man in a white suit emerge, accompanied by a monk.

"Is that Fouché?"

Ortega didn't answer.

"Who's that with him? Sorge?"

"I told you, keep out of it."

Ortega kept observing the pair as they entered the Buick, with Fouché in the driver's seat.

"Now he'll have his chance," Dempsey said.

"Chance? For what?"

."An assassination."

Ortega glanced back quickly.

"What do you mean?"

The Buick began to drive away. Ortega signaled his driver to follow and picked up his handset.

Ortega's car followed at a distance of seventy-five yards. There was a roadblock two streets down.

Dempsey felt constrained; he had to let events take their course.

Ortega asked, "What have you heard?"

"It's your problem, Ortega. You handle it."

Ortega was at the speaker again. Dempsey could make out some of the words. The word *asesino* did not elude him.

Sitting alongside Fouché, Sorge was minutely aware of his surroundings, of the roadblock ahead and of the car behind moving in closer. He noticed a quickening of activity at the roadblock.

"Go slowly, don't hurry," he said to Fouché. "Turn right at the corner."

In Ortega's car Dempsey watched it happening. He saw the Buick turn right. He saw it next going up a driveway out of view. The next thing he saw and heard was a violent explosion that shot up into the night.

Police cars were now converging from all directions toward the explosion. For a time no one could get close to the intense flames.

Afterward the police found a body charred and fragmented almost beyond recognition. The body was later identified as that of Fouché.

Sorge was nowhere to be found; once again he had made a clean escape.

In retrospect, as it was all reconstructed, Dempsey was amazed at the planning that must have been involved, and of the audacity of it—an assassination within a cordon of police. It was, he had to concede, a feat almost beyond the imagination.

Later, as he drove back to his hotel, Dempsey was aware of the calm he felt. Sorge's escape had not mattered to him; for he considered that Sorge was *his* and that nothing outside them would intervene. In the end it would be settled between them, between them alone.

He was convinced he could get at Sorge through Catherine. He could guess that Sorge was on his way to meet her. She was the link to him, his vulnerability. If you found her you'd find Sorge.

Suddenly now again he was thinking of the dwarf, of the image that had come to him in his room in the stillness of night—a dwarf with sad eyes and hand outstretched, reaching out toward him as if for help. In the end there remained in his mind only an image of a beseeching hand; it remained in him like an elusive tremor.

Late that night Barras ordered Dufar's release. When the colonel was brought to him, and they were alone in the study, Barras said, "Sit down, Dufar."

Unshaven and shabby, Dufar sat down uneasily.

"It's time you know," said Barras. "Fouché is dead."

"Dead? But how?"

"It was done by Sorge."

Dufar's expression changed from surprise to a sudden, if incomplete, recognition of what had been involved.

"My only regret, sir—" he began.

"Not even Ligny knew. If something had gone wrong, even if by accident—no, I didn't want those suspicions. You and Ligny are the nation's future."

Dufar was elated that his name had been linked with Ligny's yet he was puzzled by the omission of Sorge's name.

"Where is Sorge now?" he asked.

"He's not coming back. What he did he did for money, a quarter of a million. A man who's had a taste for that kind of money cannot be trusted."

"I see."

"If word gets out we were behind this, it would embarrass us before the world. Sorge could use this. He may become greedy—"

Barras rose and walked toward the window.

"I want him dead," he said flatly.

Dufar nodded.

Barras went on. "There's something else. Sorge brought a woman into the plan; he broke the chain of secrecy—"

"Yes, I know about her."

"She's in Veracruz. Your people know where she is," Barras said. "As for Sorge, it won't be hard to get at him. He'll be off guard when he goes for his money."

Barras brought out a map from his desk. "Here," he said, indicating a point somewhat south of Mexico City.

"And the woman?"

"Keep her under surveillance until Sorge is dead. Then do what has to be done, but do it quietly."

"And Latour?"

"I want no traces. All that the world will know is that Sorge, a defector, was involved in a ransom plot. It is all anyone will know, except you and me."

Barras and Dufar then discussed the drawing together of all the loose ends of Operation Bluebird.

At one point, Dufar had to ask, "Why did he undergo such risk and torture? For money?"

"Why? Because he is Sorge, and because it was impossible."

"At such a cost?"

"The pain?" Barras shrugged. "He can withdraw his mind from pain. It's one of his little secrets, you know."

Afterward Barras said, "Don't take pleasure in what you have to do. Remember, Sorge was with us at Valmy. Kill him, but do it with honor. When he's dead, there'll be a brigadier's star for you, Colonel."

Barras next summoned Ligny and informed him that Fouché was dead.

"I've heard," said Ligny, wasting no words.

"It's time to settle accounts," said Barras. "With Fouché dead, supplies will dry up. How much time do you need to clear that rabble from the hills?"

"A year—at a minimum."

"Then do it. We've been bled enough. Burn the hills if you have to, but root them out."

Ligny nodded and rose to set in motion the hammer of war.

Later, Barras sat back to mull over the situation. There would be heavy losses, he knew, in breaking the back of that rabble, perhaps more than Ligny would admit. Yet in time those losses could be made up. In time too the nation would be cleansed and ready for the blow against Acosta—Ligny's armor avenging the infamy of Massacre River. It was a dream that consumed him, and for that dream all was expendable. The nation alone had meaning for him. He and the nation were one body and one soul.

The small pickup truck with canvas cover proceeded along a dusty road through farm country. In back of the truck were cases of produce and a potato sack. The truck turned left toward an abandoned barn.

Wearing a straw hat and denims, Sorge got out of the truck; he had a dark, sun-weathered look. The sun was high in the motionless sky. He began walking toward the barn to get the money that was arranged to be there in a sealed box. He was unarmed; his P–38 lay on the front seat of the truck, under rags.

As Sorge came closer he noticed varieties of footprints. Without changing his pace, Sorge walked past the closed barn door and around. When he sighted his truck he began to run toward it. As he ran, three men emerged from the barn with automatic rifles, firing as they came. A bullet ripped into Sorge's shoulder as he dove behind the pickup. Sorge grabbed his gun from the front seat.

Flattening himself to the ground, Sorge rolled beneath the truck, getting off a clean shot, cutting down one of the men. Bullets splattered around him as he slid toward the back of the truck where he ripped off a shot at the pelvis of another of the gunmen. The man crumbled with a hideous scream.

The remaining man, suddenly alone now, crouched down, using the front of the truck as cover.

Sorge got up from under the back of the truck and waited. At one point the third gunman raised his head slightly, momentarily, above the hood. In that moment a bullet tore through the top of his skull.

Sorge now approached the second gunman, who was holding his groin, lying on the ground, screaming with pain. The gunman looked up with terror as Sorge drilled him between the eyes.

Sorge now surveyed the scene. Three corpses, four bullets, one wasted. The men, Sorge recognized, were part of the Special Unit that had been formed against Fouché.

By now Latour was out of his potato sack in back of the truck, bewildered by the havoc around him. He saw Sorge holding a handkerchief to his wounded shoulder.

The dwarf looked around at the dead men.

"Who are they?"

"Dufar's men."

"Dufar?"

"Barras wants us dead."

The dwarf was stunned.

Reflecting on the situation, Sorge now recognized the flaw in his plan. He hadn't gauged the peasant logic in Barras's harsh,

suspicious mind. It was a flaw, of course, that was obvious only i
retrospect.

Later that night, just off a side road, as they ate out of tin
Sorge thought about what had been. At a dozen points, he reco
nized, his plan could have gone wrong. Except for a run of luck the
had been no reason why his plan had turned out with such flawle
perfection.

He had accepted the risks because of Cathy. With the mone
he was to get, he had planned to go away with her, to chang
identities and resume what they had once had together. Of cours
all along he had known that it could never be the same aga
between them. The love she had once had for him was only a drea
now; yet for that dream he had gone ahead with a plan that, by i
nature, was almost suicidal. Had that been the point of it all? I
didn't know and, perhaps, never would.

He felt empty now, disembodied.

There was only Cathy left; she and the memory of a drean

A day after Smithy's call, Cathy had gotten a letter from hi
postmarked Mexico City, instructing her to go to the Posada del S
a small hotel on an island near Veracruz. Following his direction
she went by bus along the coast to a landing, where she took
motorboat that made the trip to the island three times daily.

The island itself, a half mile long, was a sliver of sand in t
Gulf. It had thick, tropical growth. At one end was a cleared ar
with a hotel, some cottages, a cantina and a pier for fishing boa

The hotel, two stories in height, had peeled walls that fade
into a decayed pink. Wearing her sunglasses, she registered at t
hotel, taking an upstairs room, one of eight in the hotel. She w
greeted by a slender, graying woman, Señora Mercador, who ran t
hotel with the help of a young girl and an old man.

There were two other occupants in the hotel, both pensione
Of the cottages, one was occupied by a tourist couple from Bosto

another by an elderly gentleman from England who went out each day to fish and sleep.

Waiting for Smithy, Catherine sat under shade on the beach, but more often stayed in her room. In the evening she went to the cantina, which was run by an old man who did casual labor around the grounds and who had a working knowledge of the erratic juke-box, the sole source of entertainment at the cantina.

Catherine continued to suffer from cramps and migraines, feeling depressed and isolated. She knew she'd have to see a doctor soon before it was too late.

The day after she arrived, two Mexicans registered at the hotel. One of them, a man of about thirty, wore a flashy sport jacket; the other had a pocked face. That night at the cantina she became aware that the two men, who had come there, were staring at her. Feeling uneasy, she got up and left, but her uneasiness remained. Were the men part of the organization Smithy had told her about? Were they killers too, like Robert? She kept wondering about the men and could not sleep until the early hours of morning.

The next day the two men left the island, taking the morning boat. Catherine was relieved to find them gone.

The next morning in the lobby Catherine saw the newspaper that had come in from Veracruz. She recognized the photograph on the front page—Smithy! The headline read: EL ASESINO!

With the paper and a Spanish-English dictionary she'd gotten from the proprietress, Catherine went to her room, locking the door. She began to translate the text, and with an effort she was able to make out that Smithy, referred to as Sorge, was the object of a manhunt for an assassin.

She was stunned. Smithy, she realized, had used her. He had played on her fears to get her out of the city, moving her from place to place so that he could meet her here. It had been a hoax, all of it.

Her first impulse, out of anger, was to pack and leave the island yet she couldn't bring herself to do it. Smithy was in trouble; she couldn't run out on him, not now. When she had needed someone it was Smithy who came, Smithy who had loved her. He had hurt her but he had loved her too; and in his way he always would.

She began to think of Robert. She wanted to call him, to hear his voice again, but what could she say to him that wouldn't involve Smithy?

Later, on the extension phone in an alcove of the lobby, she put through a long distance call. As she waited for the connection she began to feel cramps. The pain intensified, and the receiver dropped from her hand, and she was suddenly thinking—maybe that part of it wasn't a hoax. Maybe it was real. Maybe Robert *was* one of them.

She was uncertain and in pain, and she almost vomited. In a while she hung up the receiver and began to cry. She was like a child crying.

That night, in her sleep, her nightmares began again. She heard sounds of crying, like pains piercing her, and she could not shut them out. Where was Smithy? Why was he gone so long? He had gone to get milk, he had said. Where was he? Oh, God, where was he?

Dempsey remained in Mexico City waiting for events to break. A massive manhunt for Sorge was being directed by the Mexican secret service. Dempsey had little contact with the search; he was closed off from it as he was from Ortega. His numerous phone calls to Ortega remained unanswered or shunted aside. His only link to the case was Martin, and Dempsey kept in close touch with him by phone.

Flight lists to Mexico City out of JFK and outlying airports had been sifted through. Three names out of JFK were still unaccounted for, Martin had informed him.

"We're still checking," Martin told him.

It was by no means certain Catherine had taken a plane to Mexico, or to Mexico City itself, but it had to be checked out. It was possible, of course, that she was traveling with a lost, stolen or forged passport. It was a possibility too that she had remained under cover in New York. Whatever the possibilities, there were at the moment three names that hung like loose threads. Cissy Bentley, Elizabeth Calder and Sarah Valli—three names not satisfactorily traced to a known address.

For the record, Dempsey put in a call to Ortega to tell him of the three names. As he had expected, Dempsey was shunted off to an aide who was cool, polite but uninformative about Ortega's whereabouts.

That done, Dempsey began making the rounds of likely tourist hotels in Mexico City, working at random.

At about eight that evening he entered the lobby of the El Aristos, number twelve on his list. Identifying himself to one of the desk clerks, he showed the man a photograph of Catherine. The clerk, a lean, gaunt man who spoke fluent English, was unable to recognize the photograph. In the hotel records, however, the clerk did come upon the name, Elizabeth Calder.

Dempsey focused on the card; it was a piece of luck he had not counted on.

The card indicated that Elizabeth Calder had checked out three days ago.

"Is there a forwarding address?" he asked.

The clerk shook his head, his sallow face like an El Greco.

"Could you check your files?"

The clerk hesitated; he wasn't sure of Dempsey's authority nor of his own position in the matter.

Dempsey put his badge and identification on the counter. "I need the address," he insisted.

The clerk then picked up a phone, dialed, spoke in Spanish to someone, waited, listened, hung up.

"I'm sorry." A gesture of regret. "We have no address."

"Who checked her out?"

El Greco scanned the card.

"Ah, Ramirez. Yes, Ramirez."

"Where is he?

A hesitation.

"Is he off duty?"

"Yes."

"Do you have his phone number?"

Further hesitation.

"His phone number," Dempsey repeated.

More resistance.

El Greco was reaching for the phone on the desk. "Perhaps the manager—"

"That won't be necessary," Dempsey said, jotting a number on a pad. "Call this number. Ask for Ortega. Captain Ortega."

The clerk began to dial, and Dempsey knew that his private investigation had come to an end. He had gone as far as he could for the moment.

Dempsey waited for Ortega in a booth at the bar in the El Aristos. The room was crowded and smoky. Dempsey knew he'd have to deal now with Ortega. There was no getting around that for the moment.

Not more than fifteen minutes later Ortega came in and sat down opposite Dempsey. He had come in with two men but they stood aside near the entrance, their faces masks of studied indifference.

Ortega himself was unsmiling.

"What's it about?" he demanded. "Who is this Elizabeth Calder?" It was obvious he had already questioned the desk clerk, if only briefly.

"She's a name that came up."

"Yes?"—coldly.

"She's a lead—to Sorge."

Ortega's eyes stirred.

"Tell me about it."

Dempsey began to brief him, and when he was done Ortega said, "You should have called me before this."

"I did. You weren't in."

Ortega was examining his stubby fingernails. He said, "You should have *insisted* on getting me."

Dempsey was holding an empty shot glass. He moved it now like a chess piece toward Ortega, saying to him, "Next time pick up the phone."

Ortega moved back the shot glass. "What else do you know?" he asked.

"You have it all. It's all on the table."

"Everything?"

"Yes, everything."

Ortega rose; he knew he'd get nothing further from Dempsey. Without a word more he moved with powerful strides toward the entrance, his two men following in his wake, and Dempsey wondered whether he would hear from Ortega again.

Dempsey was somewhat surprised to get a call from him late the next morning asking him to come to headquarters for a meeting. That had to mean, Dempsey guessed, that Elizabeth Calder's tracks had gone cold.

When he got to Ortega's office he found that his hunch had been on the mark. So far, the only tangible result was the identification of Elizabeth Calder as Catherine. A waiter, a bus boy and the cab driver who had taken her to the airport had each made an identification from Catherine's photograph.

Dempsey sat to the side of Ortega's cluttered desk.

He asked, "What about the clerk? The one who checked her out?"

"Ramirez? We talked to him. Twice. He didn't remember her at all."

"Did he check her out?"

"Yes, but he couldn't identify the photograph," said Ortega, shrugging. "It doesn't matter. We have three—*three* positive identifications. Another won't bind it more."

Dempsey noted that in his mind.

"What else?" he asked.

"As far as we know she's still in Mexico."

"Any tracks at the airport?"

"We have two teams there. On the day she left, eight planes were backed up—a lot of confusion."

"She may have used another name."

"We're checking—everything."

Dempsey shifted back.

"How positive were the identifications?"

"We're satisfied."

"Any changes in appearance?"

"Yes, the hair. Dyed black."

"Anything else?"

"Yes, she wore sunglasses most of the time."

"Was she identified *with* sunglasses?"

"No, without. From time to time she took them off to clean them," said Ortega. "The waiter saw her twice without glasses. He's very positive it was her."

"Why *very?*"

Ortega smiled. "She is a very pretty woman, no?"

Dempsey nodded.

"By the way . . ." said Ortega.

"Yes?"

"If you hear anything more . . ."

"Of course."

"One hand washes the other, no?"

Dempsey nodded in agreement.

"Keep in mind," said Ortega, "we want Sorge as much as you do."

Dempsey understood. Fouché had been assassinated less that seventy-five yards from Ortega and a cordon of his men, and he'd be a long time living that down, unless of course he could break the case open. You understood how he felt, and you could almost feel sorry for him.

Later Dempsey went to the El Aristos, where he bought a newspaper. In answer to his inquiry the woman in the shop pointed out Ramirez, the desk clerk.

Presently, from an armchair in the lobby, Dempsey began his observations of Ramirez.

Ramirez, he noticed, was a thin runt of a fellow with an uncertain smile. Sometimes harassed, often nervous and fumbling, Ramirez managed to function.

Dempsey kept watching, carefully observing, noting the small matters in the life of a clerk.

He saw Ramirez glancing at the clock behind him. A hasty look at a racing form. A nod to someone; a quick chat, an interruption. Ramirez scratching his nose.

Later, Ramirez watching out of the corner of his eye the sinuous walk of a young woman.

Dempsey folded his newspaper and got up to leave. He had seen enough.

It was late afternoon when Ramirez emerged from the El Aristos. Dempsey caught up with him near the corner.

"Ramirez?"

The clerk turned.

"I'd like to talk with you."

The clerk's expression froze.

"Could we have a drink somewhere?" Dempsey said.

"No, I must—"

"It's about a friend."

"A friend?"

"Elizabeth Calder."

Ramirez did not move.

"Are you from the police?"

"No, but I think we ought to talk."

Ramirez thought about it for a time. "Where?" he asked.

"Wherever you say."

Ramirez suggested a nearby bus terminal and they went there. They sat on a bench near the back.

Dempsey showed Ramirez the photograph.

"Do you recognize her?"

A pause.

"I told the police—" Ramirez began.

"I'm not with the police. I'm a friend."

Ramirez stared at the photograph.

Again: "Do you recognize her?"

A hesitation. Lips tightening.

"I told them—"

"It's important, Ramirez."

"If I could help . . ." a helpless shrug.

He was handing the photograph back to Dempsey, but Dempsey made no move to take it back.

"What do you think?" Dempsey asked.

"Think? About what?"

"She's attractive, don't you think?"

"She *is* attractive," admitted Ramirez, loosening a bit and remembering.

"She and I were close—very close . . ."

Ramirez was looking once more at the photograph.

"She had a way of walking . . ." said Dempsey.

"Yes, I know. She—" Ramirez caught himself.

Dempsey said nothing.

Ramirez began to stare at the floor.

Finally he said, "What do you want?"

"You checked her out. Where did she go?"

"She didn't say."

"Why did you lie to the police?"

Ramirez shrugged.

"Did you lie because **you thought** she was in trouble?"

Ramirez looked up at Dempsey.

"She *is* in danger, you know," said Dempsey.

"Danger?"

Ramirez was wavering.

For a time he searched Dempsey's eyes.

"You can help her," said Dempsey.

Ramirez's lips tightened again. Finally, leaning over, he said in a whisper, "El Emporio."

"Where?"

"Veracruz," said Ramirez almost inaudibly, as if to say the name yet not say it. His eyes still searched for reassurance.

"It's just between us—you and me," said Dempsey.

Ramirez managed a wan smile.

Later, Dempsey reflected on the way he had gulled Ramirez. It had to be done, he knew; yet he felt badly about it. Ramirez had deserved better. He was inept and gullible, but he had a sweetness of heart you seldom came upon. The poor dumb bastard—you wanted to tell him it would all come out right, and you could almost wish it that way for his sake alone.

After he had packed the few belongings in his room Dempsey put in a call to Martin to let him know he was checking out.

Martin was surprised. "Are you coming back?"

"No, I'm on a lead."

"You working it alone?"

"Yes, alone."

"Sure you don't need help?"

"I can handle it."

Martin said nothing.

"I'll keep in touch," said Dempsey.

"Dempsey."

"What?"

"I want Smithy—*alive.*"

Dempsey did not respond.

"Dempsey?"

Martin heard the phone go dead.

Changing directions twice to make sure he wasn't followed, Dempsey made his way by rented car toward Veracruz. En route he used a bus for a time to break his trail.

He tracked Catherine to the hotel in Veracruz, and within a day was able to trace her through a bus driver to a landing which was the terminus for a small island to the northeast on the Gulf.

It was late at night, past midnight, when he got to the landing. His luck so far was holding, yet how much longer would it hold? He was beginning to feel again the trajectory of a momentum rising up in him.

The landing, he saw, was isolated and deserted, and he wondered how to get to the island at this time of night.

Presently he began to hear the sound of a motorboat coming in toward the landing. He waited under lights that were hung between poles. As the boat came in and tied up, he saw the owner, a wiry old man in a white captain's cap, helping a man out of the boat. The man, carrying a doctor's bag, thanked the owner and went off to his car parked nearby.

Dempsey spoke now to the owner, who resisted his request to make one more trip to the island. The owner explained in manageable English that he had already made a late emergency trip there with the doctor.

Dempsey glanced around and saw the doctor already on the road, driving off.

"What happened?" he asked the owner.

"A sick woman—"

"American?"

The owner nodded.

"I have to see her," Dempsey insisted, taking some bills from his pocket.

The owner, counting the money, seemed satisfied.

"Vámonos," he said with a gesture.

The trip to the island, under a clear moon, did not take long. The captain left Dempsey off at the pier, and, pointing out the hotel, headed back to the mainland.

In the small lobby of the hotel Dempsey came upon Señora Mercador, sitting in a wicker rocking chair, almost dozing off to sleep. She had a kind face and wore a black dress with lace collar that was reminiscent of bygone years. Behind her, two potted plants rose woefully toward the ceiling.

As he approached she opened her eyes.

"I'm Robert Dempsey," he said to her.

"Ah, so you are Roberto," she said graciously.

He came closer, surprised that she knew him.

"I saw the doctor on the landing," he said.

"Yes, I had to call him." She nodded toward the rooms upstairs. "She's asleep now."

"What happened?"

"You don't know?" Señora Mercador gestured with delicacy toward her womb. "You didn't know?"

"No, I didn't know."

"She became sick," she told him. "I had to call the doctor."

He waited for her to continue.

She went on. "When he came she wanted him to—" She began to grope for words. Then with a gesture she said, "You understand, no?"

"An abortion?"

"She begged him but he had to refuse her," she explained. "She begged and she cried, but what could he do?"

"He gave her sedatives?"

Señora Mercador nodded.

"Which room is she in?"

She pointed. "That one, to the right."

Dempsey went toward the staircase.

"She needs you," said the woman.

Dempsey paused.

"In her sleep she keeps calling your name."

He went a step further.

"Be gentle with her," the woman said. "She needs you; she needs you very much."

By moonlight, which came through the window, he saw Catherine in bed, asleep. She was calm now, a softness in her; and he remembered, as he had many times, how it had been between them. He remembered her words and the intimacy he had felt with her; yet at the time, at each moment of it, she had been carrying Smithy's child.

Catherine woke late in the morning. Her mind was unclear, unsure, and when she saw him she sat up with a sudden fear. Her breasts were naked and she covered them with the sheet.

She heard him say, "It's time to go home," and there was no warmth in his eyes.

Home? What did he mean?

He was saying, "There's a warrant for your arrest."

"Are you with the—?"

She stared up at him with an expression he did not understand.

She began looking at the wall for a time, away from him, then at him, saying, "I didn't *do* anything. I mean—"

"We know the call you made to Krone."

"Krone?" She searched her mind. "I don't know any—" but then she remembered the call she had made for Smithy.

She rose and put on a robe. Standing near the window, she could see the shimmering Gulf. She was trying to clear her head; she lit a cigarette.

She heard him ask, "Why are you here?"

"Smithy told me . ."

"Told you what?"

"That some people were out to kill him and . . ."

"And what?"

"And me," she said.

Her back was toward him, and he could not tell whether she was lying or not.

"What people?"

"He told me you were one of them," she said to him. "I wasn't sure."

She turned to him now, wondering what he was thinking.

"I wasn't sure," she said again.

"Tell me about it."

She was holding her arms around her body as if to hold herself together.

She began to speak. Her words came awkwardly, disjointedly, and once she paused for another cigarette, inhaling it deeply. Bit by bit she told him about the call, her fears, of her flight to Mexico City, to Veracruz and here. It all sounded so crazy as she told it, she was sure he didn't believe her.

When she was done he just stood there not saying a word.

Her mind was clearer now.

She asked, "Who's Krone?"

"He's dead," he said, and it sounded that way, *dead*.

"I didn't know him," she said, wanting him to know that, even if he didn't believe it.

245

"Has Smithy called you here?" he asked.

She shook her head.

"Why did you go back to him?"

She didn't respond.

"When will he be here?"

"I don't know. He hasn't called."

"I'm taking you back to the mainland," he said. "Someone will take you to New York. You can get help there if you need it."

"Help?"

"If you're sick . . ."

She looked away.

He said, "I saw the doctor last night."

She remembered the doctor now and became wary.

"What did he say?"

"It's Smithy's, isn't it?" he was asking. It wasn't a question, it was more an accusation.

She didn't answer at once and when she did, it was only a nod; she couldn't say the words.

"Where's Smithy?" he was asking.

"I don't know," she said, and it was true but it sounded like a lie in her mouth.

"When he shows up I'll be here," he said.

"He won't come," she said. "If I'm not here, he won't come."

"Then I'll have to find him."

"Why does he matter so much to you?"

"He's killed two of my men."

"Is that why you're angry?"

"Better start packing," he said.

"Are you angry because of me? Is that why—because of *me*?" He didn't respond.

She washed up and then began to pack.

She paused once, looking up from her suitcase on the bed.

"You won't find him," she said to him, her tone almost defiant. "You'll never find him."

"I'll find him."

"And kill him? Are you that angry at me?"

She continued to pack.

Once later she paused again and said, "How did it come to this?"

"Lie by lie."

"I loved you," she said. "I *did* love you."

"It doesn't matter now, does it?"

"It matters to me."

"And Smithy? Does he matter too?"

"It's been over between us—for years."

"You're carrying his child."

"I didn't want it," she said. "It just happened. I didn't want it."

"Why were you waiting for him?"

"I had to wait," she said.

"He's a murderer."

"I didn't know it."

"You know it now, and you'd still wait for him, wouldn't you?"

She looked away and began to smooth out a blouse in her suitcase. Without looking up she said to him, "I didn't mean it to come to this."

"Why were you waiting for him?"

"Because he needed me."

"That's not an answer."

"He's all I could count on."

"What else?"

"We're all that's left—just Smithy and me."

"I don't understand."

She continued packing.

"He's all the family I've got," she said. Her voice was cracking.

"What are you telling me?"

"You wouldn't understand."

"Try me."

"He's my—"

"He's your what?"—explosively.

"He's my brother," she said suddenly, almost defiantly. He had wrested it from her, her dirty little secret. He had left her naked; but it was out now and she was free of it.

She kept arranging her suitcase, unable to look up at him. She waited for a word, any word, but he said nothing; and she felt the coldness of his silence.

Not a word, except once, when he said to her, "I'll take that passport." That was all he said, and it was as if he had never known her.

She threw the passport on the bed and closed her suitcase now and he could see her tears as she tried to hold herself together.

In the lobby Dempsey waited with Cathy at the desk while Señora Mercador prepared the accounts. Upstairs Cathy had taken some capsules to calm herself, and now she stood quietly apart from him without a word passing between them. Señora Mercador glanced up at them once with concern for Cathy and with reproach for him. He was reminded of the woman's words last night—"She needs you. She needs you very much."

He wanted to reach out to Cathy. He softly said her name but she did not turn to him. She was apart from him, and each moment that passed seemed to widen the distance between them. She was staring blankly at a lithograph on the wall, and only the trembling of her eyelids showed the hurt she felt. She was isolated, fragile, vulnerable.

Once later he reached out and took her hand in his, saying her name. She turned, looking up at him expectantly, her eyes shimmering at the edge of tears. "It'll be all right," he said to her, wanting her to know.

At that moment two men with sailing jackets and masks burst into the lobby.

One of them, a big man with arms like sides of beef, held an automatic rifle. His mask was like a child's mask of a Halloween pumpkin. The other man, thinner and taller, wore the mask of a clown made of papier-mâché.

In English, the clown mask said to Cathy, "Go to your room and stay there. We'll tell you when to leave."

She looked toward Dempsey.

He said to her quietly, "Do as he says."

Reluctantly she began to go upstairs. On the landing she looked down at Dempsey.

He said to her again, "Do as he says."

Presently the clown began to search Dempsey, taking his .38 and his identification papers, examining the papers carefully.

"Sit there," he said to Dempsey. "We'll get to you later."

Dempsey went toward a frayed wicker chair in the corner of the lobby. As he passed the window he observed three men near the cantina, each casually dressed and armed with a rifle, each wearing a mask.

The clown now said to Señora Mercador, "Go to your room. Stay there. We'll answer the phone."

"What is it you want?" she asked with dignity.

"We're waiting for a friend. When he comes, we'll go. We're not here to make trouble."

Through the window Dempsey could see other armed men. There were at least eight in all. He had no idea who they were but he could guess they were waiting for Sorge.

He was still in the lobby, under guard, when the call came; it was 2235 hours.

Cathy was brought down to the lobby. She seemed calm; from the expression in her eyes he knew she must have taken more capsules.

Holding his hand over the receiver, the clown said to her, "Remember, act as normal. If you make one mistake, or he doesn't come, you're dead."

Cathy took the receiver. Another of the men, in a tiger mask, got on the open extension in the alcove. Dempsey could tell from the way the others deferred to him that the tiger mask was in charge.

Dempsey, bound to the wicker chair, was guarded by a sun mask, who kept an automatic aimed at his skull.

Cathy was looking at Dempsey as she held the phone; she hesitated some moments before she spoke.

"Hello," she said into the speaker, a slight quaver in her voice.

She heard Smithy's voice, "Lizabeth?"

"Yes, are you all right?"

"Any problem?" he asked.

"No, just boredom," she said. "I miss you, love, I miss you very much."

"I miss you too," Smithy said. "It won't be long now. Wait for me. I'll be there soon."

"When Cathy hung up, the clown exclaimed, "That's it! He's around nearby. He'll probably come tonight. Better pray for it. All we want is him. So pray, love," he said, imitating her expression to Smithy.

Cathy kept looking at Dempsey with an uncertain expression.

The clown then conversed aside in low tones with the tiger mask. When he was done he said to Cathy, "Go upstairs. We'll have to tie you again. Sorry, love. Orders."

She went toward the steps, paused, then began to approach Dempsey. "I'm sorry," she said to him. She came closer but the pumpkin mask prodded her with his rifle. She began to walk upstairs, the pumpkin mask with her. On the landing upstairs she turned, and Dempsey could see her lips moving, and she was silently saying, "I love you. I love you."

He recognized what she had done. By a word or a phrase she had warned off Smithy. Her words now, spoken as last words, lingered in his mind after she was gone from view. It meant, of course, she had little hope either of them would survive.

The clown sat down behind the desk and laid on it a rifle of Czech manufacture.

"Pray," he said to Dempsey. "Pray that Sorge comes."

The clown waited; the sweat of waiting had begun.

In a while two guards came in. At the tiger's direction they took Dempsey to one of the cottages and tied him up with strong cordage.

As he lay in the darkness, bound to the bed in the room, he kept thinking of Cathy, wondering how long she could hold herself together with pills. How long before she cracked?

He kept thinking, wanting her to know he cared for her and she was not alone. Whatever she was and whatever had been, he still cared for her. Out of a lifetime she was all he had; the only feeling of love that remained in him.

Afterward he began considering possibilities. Cathy had warned Smithy; he was sure of that. Had she hoped that Smithy, forewarned, would still come for her? Maybe—he wasn't sure; but one thing was certain—Smithy was out there somewhere like a loose wild card. Yet he couldn't count on that.

The masks, he knew, weren't likely to leave witnesses around, least of all him, a detective. He didn't know how much time he had but he knew he'd have to make his move, and make it soon.

Sorge kept thinking of the phrase Cathy had used—"I miss you, love." She had never used that expression before. He sat near the phone. He wore the uniform of an air force navigator, ostensibly on leave in a motel ten kilometers south of the landing. There was a pulse of pain in his shoulder.

He could guess Cathy was being held as bait by Dufar's local men; and he had to assume it was only a matter of how and when they'd get rid of her. To go to the island was a high risk, yet it was unthinkable to abandon her. She was at the core of his existence, and if it had to end for him, as some day it would, let it be now, he thought. Without her, what did it matter, now or later?

He went to the bedroom where the dwarf was resting on the bed. The dwarf wore a loose shirt and denims.

"We've come to an end," Sorge said to him.

The dwarf sat up. He was not surprised. "I've been a burden, I know," he said.

"We've managed up to now."

"You could have gotten rid of me before. Why now?"

Sorge shrugged.

"Along the way, at any turn, you could have abandoned me," said the dwarf.

"It wasn't necessary," Sorge said. "Besides, we've been through a lot together, you and me."

The dwarf understood, and he said, "Whatever has come up, perhaps I could help."

"No. No, it's something I must do alone. You can have whatever money is left."

"I wouldn't get in your way," the dwarf persisted.

"There'd be risk if you came with me."

"What's one more risk?"

"Why would you take it?"

"In my whole life you're the only one to care—"

"Care?"

"—whether I lived or died," said the dwarf, and there was a sadness in the way he said it.

In his way Sorge could understand that sadness and the terrible loneliness of it. He began to reconsider, and gradually a plan formed in his mind.

"Can you handle plastic explosives?" he asked.

"You could show me."

"How far can you swim?"

"From here to the island, if that's what you mean."

"The island?"

"You called there, did you not?"

Sorge smiled. He and the dwarf—why not? Yes, why not?

Later Sorge left the motel, telling Latour to wait for him. Alone now, the dwarf began to prepare himself for what was to come. His time was near, he knew; his death was close at hand. He had had visions of the island to which they were to go. He had never been there but he knew its shape and textures. On that island waited his salvation; and he knew it with his whole being. Out of his hope had come belief; and out of belief had come clarity and certitude.

He was full with the wonder and simplicity of it all. Belief was like an open door, always there, always open. One had but to pass through. For years he had existed with reason and doubt. Now suddenly, with belief, irrational belief, he knew what he had never known before, that he could walk through that door which was always open.

In time, though, the dwarf began to feel uneasy; for he became aware again, as he had before, that his salvation must come through another. Someone—someone unknown to him—had been damned, as he had been, with an unspeakable curse. Out of someone's pain was to come his own peace.

Over and over, as he thought of it, an impulse began to rise in him, to warn the unknown stranger of his impending doom, to cry out: *Go back, go back, go back!* And much as he wanted to, he could not cast the impulse from his heart.

In the end he closed his eyes and waited for what was to be.

His expectations had turned sour in him. His belief began to waver and his stomach began to quiver.

When Sorge returned he put in another call.

A nasal voice answered.

"You know who I am?" Sorge asked.

There was silence.

Sorge asked, "Do you have authority to negotiate for the hostage you're holding?"

Silence.

Someone else got on line. Sorge recognized the voice. It was Escobedo, head of Dufar's Special Unit.

"I want to give myself up," Sorge declared.

A pause.

"On what terms?"

"Release the hostage. She knows nothing. She's of no use to you." Sorge waited for a reply.

"We want Latour too."

"When the hostage is safe you'll have him."

"He must come with you."

"You have my terms."

"What assurance do I have you'll turn him over?"

"You'll have me as surety."

Sorge waited again.

Finally Escobedo spoke.

"Come alone then—unarmed."

"I'll be there."

"When?"

"Soon," Sorge said. "Soon."

He hung up, his eyes cold.

Maneuvering the *Maria* out of a small inlet, Sorge proceeded north by east toward the island. The *Maria,* a gray eighteen-footer, merged into the water and the moonlit night. It was 0320 in the morning.

The dwarf lay concealed, flattened out on the bottom of the craft. Tied around his waist was a waterproof packet.

Steering toward the far side of the island, Sorge headed north along its length toward the bulging tip. He held the craft to a steady ten knots. As he rounded the bulge he sighted the lights of the hotel through the tropical trees and foliage.

"Ready now," he said, preparing Latour.

The dwarf rose in a crouch.

Fifty meters more, and Sorge whispered sharply, *"Now."*

The dwarf rolled over the far side of the boat, splashing into the water, the churn of the motor muffling the sound. In the darkness he began to swim toward an isolated stretch of beach.

Sorge went past the pier, circling offshore at five knots. The island was as he remembered it. The hotel in the clearing. Behind it, six cottages, the generator shack and the cantina, now closed. At the pier were two small outboard craft and a launch, a fifty-footer, with its name painted over.

Escobedo, the tiger mask, was on the veranda, watching the *Maria* moving past the pier, making a wide turn and circling.

Escobedo turned to the clown. "Are the men dispersed?"

"They're in position."

Escobedo felt a nervous tension. On instructions from Caribe, urging maximum effort, he had gathered twelve men. Counting himself it was thirteen to one, safe enough odds except that the one was Sorge, and that made a difference.

The *Maria* circled again.

"What's he up to?" Escobedo asked with irritation. "Go down there. We'll cover you."

With a rifle and a walkie-talkie slung over his shoulder, the clown hurried down to the pier, where Sorge was now feathering in his craft. The clown raised his walkie-talkie.

"He's tying up now," he reported.

In his lieutenant's uniform, Sorge climbed the ladder to the pier. As he began to walk toward the hotel, every rifle within range, and every nerve, was zeroed in on him. Halfway to the hotel he was stopped and searched. Found clean, he was brought to the lobby of the hotel, where four armed men in masks surrounded him.

Sorge recognized two of the men. The tiger mask was Escobedo, a former army officer. The pumpkin, a fugitive from Argentina. The other two masks were probably killers, recruited from the sewage of Mexico City. Counting the men in the lobby, there were eight, possibly ten men. Manageable odds, he thought.

He singled out Escobedo. "Is it *el tigre* now?" he asked in a mocking tone.

"Let's get on with it," Escobedo said in a raspy voice. "Now about the hostage—"

"She is to leave alone and unmolested. When I have proof she is safe at the American embassy you'll have Latour."

"Where is he?"

"Waiting for me."

"How long will he wait?"

"Long enough. Where's the hostage?"

"Safe."

"I want to speak to her."

Escobedo shook his head. "We can't allow verbal contact."

"I won't argue the point," Sorge said. "We've more important matters to discuss."

Later, after all details of the exchange had been settled, Escobedo said, "Can the hostage handle the boat alone at night?"

"She's handled larger craft."

"If necessary, one of our men could—"

"It's not necessary," Sorge interrupted.

"Good," said Escobedo. "As for us, we'll all leave by the launch. We'll be met by helicopters. Before the morning is over we'll be in Caribe. You'll meet old friends there."

Sorge was relieved that Escobedo hadn't made an issue of having someone accompany Cathy. He surmised that Escobedo had instructions to bring all his men back to Caribe, probably on a pretext of security. Barras, you could guess, wanted all traces wiped out. The masks, all of them, were marked for execution. In one way or another, the masks were walking dead men.

After the call from Smithy, Cathy had been brought to her room. One of the masks, the bear mask, was with her, and she had asked him if she could have some pills that were on her bedside table. The bear mask shrugged, as if he didn't care one way or another, and she could guess that her life now was of no account to him or the other masks. Whatever use she was to them was over with.

There hadn't been many pills left, and she took them all, whatever was left, to help her pass the night. She had been aware of the bear mask tying her up but she couldn't remember anything after that.

It was still dark when the clown mask began to untie her. Her mind was unclear, and at the edge of her consciousness were fragments of the dreams she had had, always the same recurring dreams—a child crying, a bassinet, Smithy going for milk in the village, and the *sea*. She remembered the sea, but what else was there? There seemed to be more, but it was just off the edge of her mind.

The clown mask was explaining to her what she had to do, and she understood what he was saying, but it seemed to relate to someone outside her.

Several times he asked her, "Do you understand?"

Each time, in response to him, she had nodded. Yes, she understood, but where was Smithy? she thought. Why was he away so long?

The clown mask, she saw, was packing a few things in her suitcase. Finally she heard him say, "Let's go."

Go? Go where? she thought, but she went with him, following him down a side stairway. As she went she remembered to put on her sunglasses. There was a reason for the glasses but she'd forgotten what it was.

At the pier, where they went, the clown mask asked her again, "Do you understand?"

She began to feel a splitting headache, and she was sick to her stomach, and she wondered, Why did he keep asking her that? Why was he making her do these things?

The clown now had her climb down the ladder to the boat, and he followed her. He began to explain the mechanism of the boat. He started up the motor. He was standing behind her now, and she felt his hands on her thighs, and it didn't seem to matter. Then he was gone, climbing up the ladder. From somewhere up above he was saying to her, "The landing is in that direction. You can't miss it. You'll see the lights."

She stood there, immobilized with uncertainty.

"Move off," he said in a hard way.

The roughness of his voice startled her, and she touched the lever he had shown her.

The *Maria* began to move off into the dark sea.

The sea.

The sea had been in her dream, she remembered, and she was searching her mind, trying to gather the elusive threads there.

As she entered the darkness of the sea she began to tremble.

In the darkness, in cottage four, Dempsey had been bound spread-eagled to the bed, his wrists and ankles tied tightly to the iron bedposts. Gradually, with his right hand, he had managed to get a purchase on the cordage and had begun to work and twist the rope against the serrated bed knob.

The guard, who had entered the cottage now and then with a flashlight to make a casual inspection, failed to notice the fraying of the cordage.

Dempsey's sweat was running.

When the clown returned to the hotel lobby he made no mention of Cathy's odd behavior. It was his guess she had taken too many pills, but she could manage, he felt. What she had to do was simple enough. She was on her way and it made no sense worrying about it now or upsetting Escobedo who had a quick anger. No, better to let the matter rest, the clown concluded.

He glanced around the lobby.

Escobedo was nodding to the bear mask and saying, "Cottage four. Finish it off. *Now.*"

Cottage four. Dempsey.

The bear mask responded, moving out with a rifle slung over his shoulder.

Escobedo now pointed to Sorge.

"Tie him up," he ordered two of the masks.

Sorge moved back a step.

"You'll have to kill me first," he said.

"Tie him up," Escobedo repeated in a harsher voice.

"I won't be bound like an animal."

The two masks moved in closer.

Escobedo's attention was suddenly diverted by the sound of a motorboat approaching the island.

"What's that?"

The clown shook his head.

Escobedo quickly went to the window. He was startled to see the *Maria* returning to the pier. Flashlights from the shore illuminated its shape.

"I thought she left," Escobedo said with quick anger. He ges
tured to the clown. "Find out what's wrong."

The clown hurried out to the pier; he was worried.

Sorge was dismayed by the event. He had considered Cathy
safely out of the way. Her return was an irrationality he hadn'
counted on.

Sorge was thinking now, as if to will the act: *Go. Cathy, go. G
back!*

Seconds were clicking by now, dangerous seconds. Sorg
wanted to cry out, to warn her.

Cathy had left the *Maria* and had begun to climb up the ladde
When she got up on the pier she saw the clown mask coming towar
her, and he was shouting at her angrily, "Get back in the boat!"

"No!" she shrieked. "No!"

She was shaking uncontrollably.

The clown, she knew, was wanting her to go back, back int
the darkness; but out there was the child. She had seen it. It wasn'
crying any more; it was dead. She had seen its face in twiste
strangulation. The horror was there to see and know.

The clown was grabbing her hand. She collapsed to her knee
She cried out to him, "I didn't do it. Smithy, I didn't do it!"

Her screams came wilder. The clown slapped her across th
face.

Out of her depths, out of tormented anguish, she cried ou
"God, God, I didn't do it! I didn't do it!"

She was huddled within herself, shaking, crying over and ove
"God, no, no, *no!*"

The clown stepped back, unable to cope with the pitiful figur
at his feet; what he witnessed was beyond his understanding.

The dwarf had crawled away from the shack. He had taped th
plastic explosives to the generator and had set off the timer at th
moment he had heard the *Maria* take off toward the mainland.

He lay flat in the undergrowth. Earlier he had crawled unob-
served from the beach, past the cantina and around to the generator
shack which adjoined the hotel. At the time, everyone's eyes had
been diverted by Sorge maneuvering the *Maria* back and forth just
offshore.

Holding his ears the dwarf waited moment by moment for the
explosion.

He had his instructions. He was to make his way toward a
desolate stretch of beach, and the rest would be an easy swim to a
point south of the landing where Sorge was to join him if all went
well. The dwarf knew, though, that the rendezvous was not meant
to be. The end for him was to be here on the island. He had to die
here, he thought—God, *God,* let me die!

The blast, when it came, shook the ground with great force,
shattering the generator, exploding chunks of metal into the air. The
shack itself caught fire and flared up furiously.

As the dwarf rose now, a blast of rifle fire caught him from
behind. He fell over, his back ripped open. He crawled a few moments, then lay still. He felt no pain; he was at peace now, waiting
to die.

The explosion shook through the hotel, cracking its walls,
splintering the windows. The lights went dead.

When the blast came, Sorge was ready for it. In the darkness
he hurled himself through the window, his movements calculated
beforehand. A burst of rifle fire swept past him. He landed on the
ground; he was on balance. He ran in a crouch, zigzagging toward
the undergrowth on the mainland side of the island. Two bullets
tore into him, one gouging the flesh of his thigh, the other creasing
an upper rib. He kept going, moving into the darkness until he was
out of sight.

The bear mask had paused to borrow a cigarette and chat a
moment with one of the men patrolling near the cottages. Later,

when he had put out his cigarette and had begun to move in toward
cottage four, a tremendous explosion ripped into the sky.

The bear instinctively crouched down; he waited. Cautiously
then he began to look around. He saw the other men running
toward the hotel. The generator shack was in flames and there was
confusion all around as the flames spread to the hotel itself.

When the explosion came, Cathy felt a shock shiver through
her. She saw the clown running toward the hotel; fearfully she rose
and began to run from the pier.

The bear mask saw her run. At a distance he raised his rifle,
shouting to her to halt.

She did not hear him.

The bear mask pulled his trigger.

Cathy was still running when she felt the impact. She stum-
bled, twisted and fell, and she lay where she fell, a bullet in her
spine.

The bear mask moved on, pleased with himself. It had been a
good shot, considering the distance.

Dempsey had managed to free himself. His wrists were raw as
the last strands gave way. Rising quickly he began to rub his arms
and legs to get circulation going, at the same time observing from
the windows. He was sure he could make his way into the undergrowth around to the back of the hotel, but getting to Cathy was
another matter.

He was waiting now to make his move and wondering how
Cathy was holding up.

He'd make it up to her, he thought.

From a window he saw the bear mask approaching. He saw the
bear mask pause for a cigarette with one of the guards.

Dempsey now went to the other side of the cottage where he

had a view, a fragmented view, of the pier. One mask stood guard there.

Dempsey heard the sound of a motorboat coming in close to the pier. Later he saw her—Cathy! The clown mask was coming toward her, and she was shrieking. Dempsey saw her collapse to her knees. He could hear her screaming but could not make out her words.

She was still there, on her knees, when the explosion ripped open the sky, illuminating the night.

He saw her run, and he saw her body stiffen suddenly from a shot in her back. He saw her begin to fall, turn and crumple to the ground.

The rifle shot he had heard was like an explosion in his mind.

The bear mask, gripping his rifle, kicked open the door with his heel. Inside the cottage, to the side of the door, Dempsey waited.

The bear mask stepped into the room and began to spray the darkened bed with random shots until his clip was empty.

Dempsey lunged, seized the rifle and swung around in an arc. Still gripping the barrel, the bear was thrown off balance against the wall. The rifle fell from his grasp, clattering on the floor.

Recovering his balance, the bear hurled his massive body forward with guttural anger.

Dempsey met him head on.

He deflected the bear's fist and moved in with a short, explosive blow to the abdomen. The bear was stunned but did not fall.

Dempsey bore in now with overpowering rage, with hammer blows that cracked the bear's jaw. He tore in at close quarters, pounding without pause. He ripped open flesh with a shattering force and did not let up until the bear had fallen in a broken heap.

As Dempsey stood over him, the bear bled internally, and in less than a minute his life drained out of him.

Breathing hard, Dempsey picked up the bear's rifle and got

cartridge clips from the bear's jacket. When he was ready he moved out of the cottage, his momentum on a trajectory, his body and mind fused into an instrument of death.

Escobedo and the clown stood in the darkened doorway of the cantina, which they now used as a command post.

In the distance the hotel crackled with flames, its walls being consumed. To the left were the cottages. Nearby, to the right, stood the pier. Straight ahead in the distance lay the tropical darkness into which Sorge had fled.

The clown was listening on his walkie-talkie.

"They've sighted Sorge," he said to Escobedo. "He's boxed in."

Escobedo nodded.

"Where's the bear?" he asked.

"I haven't seen him."

"He should be back by now."

"Maybe the explosion—"

"Find him," Escobedo ordered. "And get Punchinello. I want the launch ready. They must have heard the explosion on the mainland. We don't have much time."

The clown left, and when he returned he was silent.

Escobedo prodded him.

"Well?"

"The bear's dead."

"Where?"

"In cottage four."

"How was he killed?"

"He was beaten. His face is . . ."

"His face is what?"

"It's—it's like *pulp.*"

Escobedo thought about it.

"Where's Dempsey?"

"He's gone—with the bear's rifle."

Escobedo was irritated. "We should have gotten rid of him at once."

"You ordered us to hold him in case—"

Escobedo cut in. "Where's Punchinello?"

"He should be at the launch by now."

Escobedo growled. "What's taking him so long?"

The clown went to the side of the cantina where he had a view of the pier.

"There he is," he said quickly.

Escobedo joined him at the window, and he could see Punchinello approaching the launch.

He heard a single shot then.

Punchinello was reaching up toward his skull, he began to totter, then fell lifeless to the ground.

Escobedo was stunned.

The shot, he calculated, must have come from somewhere within the clump of trees behind the cantina. An incredible shot at long distance through a screen of trees at a moving target.

It had to be Dempsey, he thought angrily.

He ordered the clown to get three men. When they arrived he instructed them to fan out behind the trees, to search out and destroy whoever was there.

When the three men had gone Escobedo waited, sweating. The clown stood near the entrance.

He heard a single shot. Then a burst, and another shot.

Silence now.

Another fusillade, and silence.

A single shot. Waiting again.

The clown began to see someone crawling toward the cantina. He crouched down. In time he was able to distinguish the sun mask.

The clown crept out and helped the sun mask into the cantina. By flashlight he saw the sun mask's jacket. It was blotched with blood.

"Near the cottages," the sun mask managed to say.

Escobedo knelt down.

"The others, where are they?"

"Dead."

"Both of them?"

The sun mask nodded, and his head fell limp.

Escobedo was stunned. Five men already dead and Sorge was still loose. Worse yet, out there was the detective, Dempsey, a killer deadlier than Sorge.

Escobedo pulled his thoughts together.

"Get the rest of the men back," he ordered.

"What about Sorge?"

"Forget him. Leave two men to track him. He's wounded, he can't go far. If we don't get Dempsey we'll all be dead, one by one."

Escobedo wiped the sweat from his neck.

For a time Dempsey heard sporadic gunfire on the mainland side of the island; now there was silence.

The masks, he guessed, were regrouping.

He heard movement now to the side of him.

He moved toward the cottages, gripping his rifle. In his hand it was a weapon of rage.

The fanged mask crept along the ground, lugging a five-gallon tin of gasoline. He and three other masks had orders to set fire to the cottages, to destroy the cover there.

Entering cottage two, the fanged mask began to spill gasoline on the floor and furniture and over the bodies of the two old pensioners who were bound up together in a corner.

Stepping outside the door, the mask sprayed rifle fire inside the cottage. The floor ignited with sudden flame.

As the fanged mask dove to the ground for cover, his forward motion was deflected by a single bullet piercing his throat. With a cry of pain he spun around and fell over dead.

In the cottage the two old men, bound and helpless, saw the terror engulfing them. In a few moments their bodies became part of the conflagration.

The demon mask crept into cottage six with a tin of gasoline. As he rose, two powerful arms reached out toward him in the darkness.

The demon mask screamed out with fright as the arms locked around his neck. The mask struggled and writhed with frantic movement until suddenly the bones of his neck cracked and his body went limp.

At a distance, the two other masks remained in the undergrowth, paralyzed with fear. They had seen the fanged mask cut down and had heard the terrified outcry of the demon mask in cottage six.

The two masks began to crawl away from the terror that moved in the darkness like death itself.

When cottage two had flared up in flames, Escobedo judged it time to flee the island. He ran in a half-crouch toward the launch, the clown behind him, covering him.

Escobedo boarded the launch and started the engine up.

A wind began to stir

The clown was on the pier.

"What about the men?" he called out.

"Cast off," Escobedo shouted.

The clown hesitated.

Just then a flurry of bullets caught him in the stomach. His body wavered, then toppled over into the dark waters, his mask floating, smiling its smile.

Sorge appeared out of nowhere.

A concentrated burst of automatic rifle fire ripped across Escobedo's head. One eye was ground into his skull and globs of brain matter spurted from his head.

Sorge reloaded.

The two men who had retreated from the cottages were uneasy. They had heard the bursts of fire near the pier.

They crept closer.

From their cover they could observe the launch, its engine idling. No one was in sight.

Cautiously they crept toward the cantina.

Suddenly from within the cantina a fury reached out toward them. Bullets chopped down across their bodies. Their bodies jerked grotesquely, then settled down, dead.

Sorge emerged from the cantina. His face was without emotion. He limped somewhat as he began his search for Cathy.

It began to rain somewhat.

The dwarf lay on his back, grievously wounded and in pain now. He could not die, he thought. Had he yet to wait? Would the end never come? he cried out in his heart.

The rain began to fall gently through the leaves and upon his face.

Dempsey was moving toward the ruins of the generator shack. He had avoided the pier, dreading to see Cathy there, lying dead.

Suddenly, unexpectedly, he came upon the dwarf and recognized him. There was blood on the ground around the dwarf.

The dwarf, seeing him, reached out his hand and cried out, "Is it *you?*"

Dempsey came closer; and it was as if he had known this moment before.

"I've waited a long time—" The dwarf's face suddenly became twisted with pain.

Dempsey knelt down, and he was aware there was not much he could do for the dwarf.

"I'm sorry," the dwarf said. "I'm sorry it had to be you."

The dwarf's upraised hand was covered with blood, and there came to Dempsey the remembrance of a time long gone, of his father's outstretched hand begging forgiveness.

Dempsey reached out to take the dwarf's hand, but the dwarf drew back.

"No, no, don't touch me," he cried out.

"It'll be over soon," said Dempsey quietly.

"Do you know me—you know who I am?"

"Yes, I know."

"And you would take my hand?"

"Yes," he said, and he took the dwarf's small hand into his own, enfolding it.

"You do this—for *me?*"

"I do it for him."

The dwarf did not understand.

"I've waited many years . . ." he began.

"Rest now," Dempsey said. And he stayed with the dwarf, watching over him. Presently the dwarf's eyes closed and peace came into him.

Afterward Dempsey washed the blood from the lifeless hand; and it was the hand of his father that he washed. Gently then he wiped the droplets from his father's face and brushed back the matted hair.

"Forgive me," he said.

He laid one lifeless hand with the other, one on one, across his father's body.

"Forgive me my anger," he cried out in his heart, and he felt all the years spilling out of him like tears washing over him.

Later the rain ceased, and he kissed his father's hand, saying in his heart, "Rest now. Rest."

Afterward he put leaves over his father's eyes, as a memory and sacrament.

He rose now, and as he rose he knew that it was not yet over for him.

As Dempsey approached the pier he saw Smithy in the distance kneeling by Cathy. She was lying face down, her head to the side.

Dempsey came quietly closer.

Sensing his presence Smithy turned with a quick, fluid movement. In his hand was an automatic weapon but he did not raise it against the rifle Dempsey carried at his side.

Smithy was observing him warily.

Dempsey came nearer. Cathy, he saw, was unconscious, but alive. At least there was that, and it was enough for the moment.

Smithy nodded toward Punchinello, who lay dead nearby, a bullet in his skull.

"Was it you?" he asked.

Dempsey nodded.

"I put away six," said Smithy. "How many were there?"

"Thirteen."

"Nice piece of work," said Smithy with the appreciation of one professional for another.

Dempsey glanced down at Cathy.

"It's in the spine," said Smithy.

"Help should come soon."

"I'll be gone by then."

"You're not going anywhere."

"It's not the way *I* see it."

"You killed two of my men," said Dempsey.

"Turner? Was he one of yours?"

"He was just a kid."

"I'm sorry about the kid," said Smithy, "but I had to do it, you know."

"And Cathy? You sorry about her too?"

"I didn't know it would come to this."

"You used her."

Smithy shrugged.

"I never meant to hurt her," he said.

"I'm taking you in, Smithy."

Casually and slowly now Smithy began to rise, being careful for the moment not to challenge the authority of Dempsey's rifle. He was weighing the balances. The odds, he knew, given the angles of the weapons, were slightly in his favor, but only by a hair. Dempsey, he could tell, had given him an edge.

Smithy was feeling his trigger and gauging the outcome; an outcome that could end one way or another only in sudden death.

A few moments passed and Smithy suddenly felt the tension go out of him.

"Drop your weapon," said Dempsey. "Use it or drop it."

Smithy shrugged but did not drop his rifle.

"Maybe next time—" he began to say.

"There won't be a next time."

Smithy bent down now to kiss Cathy, saying to her, "I'll be back."

He rose again and began to limp toward the *Maria*, carrying his automatic rifle.

"Stay where you are," said Dempsey.

Smithy turned.

"I'm leaving," he said. "I'm sorry about the kid, but if you want to take me in you'd have to kill me first."

Dempsey lowered his rifle.

"You wouldn't shoot in cold blood, would you?" said Smithy. "No, I didn't think so." He smiled knowingly and began to limp once more toward the *Maria*.

Dempsey made no move. He had come a long way for this moment, but, now that it was here, it didn't seem to matter. The anger had been drained from him.

He heard the sound of boats from the mainland.

"Take care of her," Smithy called back to him. "If she doesn't make it . . ."

Smithy's voice began to waver. He was thinking of Jenny, his younger sister, and of how she was buried. She was seven and no one had cared. All she had known to do was cry.

Smithy climbed into the *Maria*. Dempsey, he saw, was coming toward him.

In his better days, Smithy thought, he would have gone against Dempsey. Maybe. Maybe not. He'd never know now.

Smithy started the motor and the *Maria* began to move from the pier. He waved to Dempsey, a silent gesture of respect.

He held the wheel steadily, and he was thinking of Cathy. She was dying, he felt, and he began to cry. It was the first time he remembered crying.

The dwarf had been lying on the bottom of the *Maria* when Smithy took off from the island.

Opening his eyes now the dwarf saw Smithy at the wheel. The moon was full; the night, clear.

The dwarf sat up, feeling his body. It was whole and without wounds. It was over, he knew. His journey of a thousand years and a thousand days was at an end.

He looked back to the island where Dempsey had remained.

He said to Smithy, "He forgave you, didn't he?"

Smithy did not respond, and the dwarf knew that Smithy was cognizant of what had to be.

Ahead of them a bank of fog began to appear.

"How much time do I have?" Smithy asked.

"The time is now," said the dwarf.

Smithy was silent again.

"I'm sorry it had to be you," said the dwarf.

The *Maria* became shrouded in mist.

"I didn't know it was to be you," the dwarf said to Smithy. "I thought . . ."

Smithy turned, asking, "Why me?"

The dwarf shrugged.

The *Maria* went further into the obscure mist.

"How will it end?" asked Smithy.

"As all things must—in God."

Smithy's face was covered with mist.

He turned again later and saw no one behind him.

The dwarf was gone, and gradually his memory of the dwarf receded, and in time all recollection of the dwarf passed from his mind.

Smithy was alone, and for him it was the first night of a long journey into belief.

> *". . . when I stand empty in God's will and of
> all his works and of God himself, then am I
> above all creatures and am neither God nor
> creature, but I am what I was and evermore
> shall be."*
> —MEISTER ECKHART

Dempsey was kneeling by Cathy, holding her hand; and he held on to her and to the life within her. He began to pray.

Once, as he looked up, he saw a meteor crossing the skies. It flared momentarily and descended, perishing in the heavens. And it was in him now as it had been meant to be; he was the son again, come to the Father.

And in the quiet of his spirit, he spoke, saying: *Thy will be done.*

When the men from the mainland came, Cathy was still alive, holding on to life.

Later, when the men went to look for the dwarf they found nothing. It was as if the dwarf had never existed.

Within a week after the disaster on the island off Veracruz, Colonel Dufar, chief of intelligence, was dead—a suicide, it was reported.

In the hills, where several battalions were moved up against the rebels, Ligny met with savage resistance. In time, elements of the Fifteenth Regiment, the nation's elite, had to be thrown into the scales.

Twenty-three days later, on a tour of inspection at a command post in the field, General Ligny, commander of the *armée*, was cut down by a sniper's bullet.

In the spring of that year, Barras, the iron soul of the nation, was felled by an assassin. Barras, and his dreams with him, were buried with great pomp and circumstance. Except for his family, few wept at his bier.

Not long afterward, Saint-Just, leader of the insurrection, rode down the main boulevard of Port-au-Grasse to the National Palace at the head of a triumphal column. Amid tumultuous acclaim, Saint-Just was installed as president of Caribe in the *Salle des Bustes*, and the nation was resanctified with the name *People's Republic*.

In time, under the supervision of a shadowy figure known as Svensk, arms and technicians began to flow in vast quantities into Caribe. The technicians were of the usual sort: agrarians, teachers, advisers and so on; and they came from the usual far-off places.

In time airports were expanded to accommodate supersonic jets. The army was augmented and missile sites established within the ranges from which flowed the turbulence of Massacre River.

For the peasants, now serving new masters and dogma, life

went on as before. As the saying went, there was change but nothing had changed. The peasants worked, sweated and died, and new ones were born to work, sweat and die.

Dempsey was with Cathy when she first became aware of movement in her legs. He was with her when she sat up alone, when she took her first step and, later, when she could walk across the room to him, crying and laughing at the same time. He was with her when her child was born. It was a girl, and Cathy took it in her arms, loving it with all the joy and love that were in her.

In time he had to take his leave from her, for he had his own way to go.

Before he left he kissed her; he kissed her face and her hands, her heart and her being. She was crying, and he remembered her that way, crying with tears of love; and he loved her too with the same tears.

A FABLE

Truth begins, and ends, in a fable.

In Caribe, a new dwarf suddenly appeared. It was thought at first he was the old Latour, but closer observers could note that the new dwarf did not have Latour's bulbous nose; rather the nose was beaky, like a hawk's perhaps; and his eyes were the eyes of the dead.

It soon became apparent that the new dwarf was quick and clever and gifted with languages; and in time he made himself useful, in one way or another, to the new masters of the island. Later, he took service as an assistant to one of the technicians, who by chance happened to be a specialist in submarine warfare.

One morning an incident occurred. At 0205 hours that morning, a Soviet submarine and its nuclear warheads exploded under mysterious circumstances in the warm waters outside Port-au-Grasse.

The dwarf managed to express shock and surprise when he heard of the incident; it was the same sly surprise he showed when Ligny was felled and Barras cut down.

By 0827 hours, in Caribe and in the nerve centers of the world, missiles bearing nuclear warheads became poised, readied for their awesome trajectories, prepared to obliterate in fiery holocaust man's flawed evolutionary course, to erase all memory of man in one last cry of violence on that killing ground, earth.

The dwarf was quite pleased with the mischief he had managed to bring about. His time on earth, he had calculated, would be cut short and he would be spared the burden of endless life.

As for the world, what did it matter? In truth, what was there worth saving? Were there ten beings alive for whom God would spare the world? If not ten, five? Or three? Perhaps one? Did even one such being exist? If so, let him come, the dwarf thought slyly. Let him come and reveal himself!

In the mountains Dempsey rose up from his time of fasting and meditation. A deep peace was in him, and he was what he was, as it had been meant to be, now and always. Alone, he began to descend into the abyss below, into the world of men where a dwarf waited for him—a dwarf with the eyes of the dead.

Catalog

If you are interested in a list of fine Paperback
books, covering a wide range of subjects
and interests, send your name and address,
requesting your free catalog, to: